MW00581879

HOLY TERROR

John R. Dougherty

First paperback edition August 2022
Book Cover & Design by Fiona Schneider
Edited by Melody Bussey

ISBN: 978-1-66786-108-1

contents

ACKNOWLEDGEMENTS

First of all, let me say that I am extremely honored and humbled that you, the reader, are taking the time to read my book. There are so many outstanding books available which you could spend your time enjoying, so I feel very blessed that you have selected this one for now. I hope you are entertained, inspired, or maybe some of both. If you are a student of God's Word, the Holy Bible, you may be interested to watch for all the hidden Bible "Easter Eggs" contained herein. And if you are not a Bible student, maybe something about this fictional story will move you to brush up on some Bible reading and find out about all such Bible connections contained in my book.

There are a host of individuals I need to acknowledge and personally thank, who played a part in supporting me through the journey of publishing this book. To my nephew, Wes, you referred me to Melody B. who helped you with the writing of your own book. She turned out to be a real gem in helping me with mine! Hence, next, Melody B., you have been an immeasurable help in getting my book published. Your writer coaching, your editing, your encouragement, your disagreements, they have all helped me arrive at this point of my journey—I will be forever in your debt! So, by the way, if you are reading this, and also an aspiring author, I know *someone* who can help you out. :)

Cheryl M.—years ago, you knew I was undertaking the writing of a book, and you kept hounding me all the time, that I needed to finish it, and let my voice be heard. Well it took a "few" years, but I got here—and I will always remember your encouragement to me!

Many people helped and supported me in a variety of ways, and I so much love & appreciate you: Jennifer S., Ed D., David L., Jerry H., Leigh G., and all my children!

God, the Holy Trinity: Father, Son, and Holy Spirit—everything I am, I owe to you. My greatest desire, despite how many times I still frequently fail at accomplishing that desire, is to give you all the honor and the glory in everything that I say and do (and write!). As the Apostle Paul wrote in 1 Corinthians 10:31, "...whatever you do, do everything for the glory of God."

FOREWORD

"Holy Terror" represents John R. Dougherty's initial foray into the world of novelists and is the first part of a planned trilogy of novels based on the interaction of the natural with the supernatural worlds. His work resembles the kind of allegorical approach to angels and demons found in the works of C.S. Lewis and Randy Alcorn. While perhaps of greater interest to Christians familiar with the Biblical accounts of these beings, the work would have a much wider appeal to a general audience, including the non-religious, given that interest in the supernatural is intrinsic to humanity. The appeal to that mysterious, other dimension is timeless, as many of us remember the television series "The Twilight Zone," and today "Stranger Things."

The transcendental issue that John addresses is the question of to what sense supernatural beings can influence the course of this life, and to what extent and from what source justice can be administered. John moves from scenes on earth to scenes in that other dimension, as he develops a plot that expands to several scenarios among different humans and angels, and then ties them together, at least partially, for he leaves the door open to a segue to his next installment. His work maintains the reader's attention and interest, and John does well in character development and delineation. One finishes the work anticipating hearing more about these supernatural beings, whom we have come to know, whom he carefully describes in terms of their rank and authority and their interactions with humans.

The book should appeal to people of all Christian denominations, to other religions, and to non-religious people. I mention these different groups simply to indicate that theological differences would make no difference in enjoying this book, because we all love a good story, and we are all curious and fascinated about that "other" world, that "other" dimension.

— DAVID LAWRENCE

Author of *Martin Bucer: Unsung Hero of the Reformation*
Scholar in-residence at Stephens Valley Church, Nashville, Tennessee

*"...in due time their foot will slip; their day
of disaster is near and their doom rushes upon them."*
— Moses, the book of Deuteronomy

CHAPTER I:

THE SHAPE OF THINGS TO COME

The early morning shards of sunlight were just beginning to streak across the wispy morning clouds in shades of pinks and oranges. The renowned Miami heat was already firing up, despite the early hour, quickly devouring the residual cool breeze of the overnight darkness. The street vendors had already begun preparing the day's wares, so the air was filled with the scents of a variety of tasty delicacies.

Ian Jelani ignored them all. The Miami detective stood at the crime scene, baffled over what was before him. In all his twelve years on Miami's Police Force he had witnessed a lot of crazy crime scenes, but this one might top them all. And that counted the crazy stuff during the race riots in St. Louis, when being a black policeman was a sure-fire way to get things thrown at you. Ian was a man of average height, athletically built, in good shape for a veteran cop. His clipper cut curly, dark hair was showing tinges of gray around his temples, a shade that extended to his goatee.

Ian exhaled slowly. He had investigated more than his fair share of gang violence and ruthlessness, yet he found himself dumbfounded today. His dark eyes darted about the area, then rubbing his hands over his face in disbelief, he turned and called out to his partner, "Hey Lane, you better come over and check this one out for yourself. You are not going to believe this, partner."

Ian watched his comrade, Detective Lane Madigan, begin to make his way over to the crime scene. He could see the questioning look in Lane's eyes. Lane was younger, a little taller, probably six feet four inches, and he looked like he could have played as a football defensive end once-upon-a-time. His dark brown hair was perfectly in place, and his green eyes widened as he approached.

Despite the grisly scene before them, Ian suddenly noticed the smell of fresh Cuban burritos wafting in the air, particularly noticeable because he was already hungry for some breakfast. The call to this crime scene had disrupted his normal morning ritual.

"After more than two years of working with you, bud, I know exactly what you're thinking," called out Lane. "I can smell them too. We definitely need to go get a couple."

"Well I hope you're still hungry after what you look at here," said Ian. "It's almost enough to kill my appetite...but only 'almost', because I'm starving," he said, watching his friend advance.

Still looking down at the implausible situation presented to him by this overnight homicide, Ian wagged his head in utter disbelief. *What kind of force did it take to actually nail someone's head into a concrete sidewalk?* With his bewilderment under control, his experience and training took over as he contemplated the crime scene. Aside from the obvious, he also noted a large rock lying on the ground near the dead man's body. Puzzled, he thought to himself that the sticky wet red stains on it would not clear up this mystery any sooner.

Ian, long-having refused to give into all the electronic gadgetry of the day, scribbled on his old-fashioned notepad. He glanced up from it to see Lane walk up beside him. "Not another one," Lane muttered quietly so only they could hear. Ian saw the younger detective looking for answers in his eyes. Ian was sure the only thing Lane saw there was the very same frustration and shock.

Ian maneuvered carefully around the victim's body to get a closer view of the head. He turned on his penlight to get a better view in the still dimly lit morning hour. He let out a slow whistle. *That is one big spike, driven right through this poor guy's temple. Could the perp have used that softball sized rock nearby to drive the spike in? Get a grip, Jelani, he told himself.* It was no wonder forensics had not yet been able to extract the spike. Not only would the extraction process further damage the victim's head, conventional human strength had simply failed to budge it. He leaned in a little closer to inspect below the head as it lay in a large pool of congealing blood on the sidewalk. The spike went at least several inches down into the concrete, best as could be seen.

Ian stood up from his crouched position over the body, making the sign of the cross. "Question is," he said, looking back over at Lane, "was the victim killed with the rock, then he was impaled, or was the perp hammering the spike into this dude's head *with* the rock?"

"Or maybe neither," retorted Lane. He was dressed in his wrinkled khakis and department issued T-shirt," noted Ian. That sort of ensemble only comes after having dressed hurriedly in response to an early morning call out. Lane continued, "It looks like there is *some* blood on that rock, but honestly not that much. I mean you would think it would be covered if it had been used either way. This is the second one of these bizarre crime scenes this week; the fourth this month. I just don't think I can take another one, not this early in the morning." He exhaled noticeably.

Lane was not a morning person, Ian remembered. Especially when his day started out like this. In fact, Ian was not sure he'd ever seen him eat breakfast before 10:00am in the two years they had been partners. Good thing, thought Ian. He quickly thought how thankful he was that he had not yet eaten any breakfast either, despite the pangs of hunger he felt.

"What does the Doc say about this one?" Ian asked to distract himself.

"A male, of Middle Eastern descent," Lane replied, as he abruptly broke off his response. Ian looked at Lane, as if to say "Well, duh!"

"I could have figured that much out myself, Captain Obvious," responded Ian "That's it? I sure hope Doc can find it in herself to dig up a little more information for us than that."

"Maybe you should spend a little more time with the good Doctor to move things along," Lane said with a smirk.

Ian shot Lane a look of slight disgust over that last comment. "Okay pal," he responded," you better watch your mouth." Ian knew that Lane was only trying to get a rise out of him over comments about Dr. Lauren Willis, and it was all in good fun. But still, he just did not tolerate any inappropriate suggestions about her, even from his best friend.

Lane grinned, clearly pleased with how it grated on Ian's nerves. He spread his arms wide, "But hey, why break the streak—we haven't had a decent lead on any of these 'Hamburger Homicides', so bring on yet another sickening, unsolvable crime."

"Oh I'm getting pretty disgusted with investigating these ridiculous crime scenes," Ian said, obviously irritated. "I've had it up to here with the meddling media and their 'Hamburger Homicides', as they like to call them. You and I have seen a lot of crazy stuff in our day, but I tell you what, nothing tops these crimes."

"I hear you," answered Lane. "But listen, no one out there is going to miss any of these nut jobs who are no longer wandering the streets. A repeat rapist, a street gang leader, a pedophile. Maybe their mamas miss them, but heck, probably not even them. I can't wait to hear about this latest dude. No doubt, he'll be right in that same category. Wanna make a bet on that one?"

Ian shook his head. "Nope, not touchin' a bet like that," he retorted. "But look, all life is sacred, man. It may be hard to hear it when it comes to guys like this," he motioned his hand toward the corpse before them, "but it's the honest-to-God truth."

Lane rolled his eyes a bit at Ian's commentary. "Okay, sure, whatever you say, Ian. That's not the first time you've tried to remind me of your thoughts on the subject."

As the photographer showed up to take several pictures of the crime scene, Detectives Madigan and Jelani started to head back to their squad car. Lane broke what had turned into a long silence. "Jelani, I've said it before, you know that I think all these scumbags got just exactly what was really coming to them."

Ian interrupted him. "Oh yes, you have not been quiet about that, buddy. But it's *our* job to put these whackos away, and the problem is that some gang has decided to take it upon themselves. They are not much better than these perps."

Lane inclined his head and screwed up his face, "Well that's where we have a little disagreement…in theory only I guess. I applaud getting these ruthless criminals off the streets any way it can happen, but don't get me wrong, I get it. We just cannot have people taking the law into their own hands, or else things get really crazy for us good guys." He paused to run a finger under his nose as he considered his words. " What are we supposed to do? No worthwhile evidence has yet to turn up. No traceable murder weapons, no fingerprints, no footprints, no tire tracks, no hair samples— nadda, nothing!" He gestured wildly with his right hand to make his point.

Both men stopped and looked at each other, with somber faces. Ian spoke first, "You thinkin' what I'm thinkin'?"

"Oh my God," responded Lane. " I don't want to even think about this being a serial killer. That will send this city into a panic, and put the media into a feeding frenzy. Don't mention this out loud yet, man."

"No one is going to hear it from me, that's for sure," said Ian grimacing. "I've been through one of those cases before. It's the worst. The media hype just gets in the way, and really screws up the investigation. Beyond that, these kinds of guys are freaking nuts. I mean the way they think, it's just plain scary."

"Only one way to deal with those guys," Lane insisted, with a fire in his eyes.

"Okay, buddy, calm down," Ian interrupted. "Just do your job, we'll figure this out. We do the investigation, make the arrest, and let the guys downstream take care of the next step. How many times do I have to remind you, we are not the judge, nor jury, nor executioner."

"I just don't see it as cut-and-dry as you do, my friend," Lane said with a sigh. "These kinds of morons don't deserve any mercy."

Ian muttered under his breath, as they both climbed into their squad car. "This boy has got a lot to learn. But, honestly, so do a lot of other people running around out there."

Both car doors slammed, as Lane threw the car into gear and the tandem sped back toward headquarters. Both men sat in silence as they mentally reviewed these recent homicides, including today's bizarre crime scene. They were anticipating results from the coroner's office, hoping that this time, some detail, some minor piece of evidence, would turn up to help them solve this case.

Lane and Ian turned into the police station, where Lane pulled into their normal parking spot. Both officers walked inside, not saying a word to each other, still pondering recent events. The typical smell of fresh coffee in months' dirty pots filled their nostrils, as both men headed toward their respective desks. At least two dozen officers, a mix of male and female, seasoned veterans, rookies, and everyone in-between, busily worked away at their desks. Any newcomer might find this place chaotic. A variety of phones rang, keyboard clicks rattled, multiple conversations happened, papers shuffled, filing drawers slamming. To these officers, and everyone else accustomed to working there day-in-day-out, it was business as usual. Lane and Ian sat down in their office chairs just across the aisle from each other, where they began filing appropriate reports and catching up on emails at their computers, their earlier hunger forgotten.

After a few moments, Lane spoke up. "Hey Ian, what do you think about all the painting and remodeling they've been doing in here?"

"I hate it," Ian said very matter-of-factly, without looking up from his computer screen.

"I don't know. I think I kinda like it, myself," continued Lane, almost as though having a conversation with himself.

Ian looked up finally, perplexed. With an alarmed tone, he said "What? Come on, this old building is a historic location. Some of the first real police officers of Miami roamed these halls. The powers-that-be should be paying tribute to their legacy by maintaining the old look and feel, but just keeping it in good repair. Instead, they listen to the shrinks—stuff about 'wall color affecting our mental and emotional state', or 'keeping the ladies happy with a more trendy look'. What a crock!"

"Good grief, man," Lane answered with a laugh. "I mean I guess I just don't have such strong feelings about it all. Obviously I have really struck a nerve here."

"Some of the new stuff just bothers me, it gets under my skin," Ian said. "If it ain't broke, don't fix it."

Lane laughed again, and said "Dude, you sound like my grandpa or something."

A couple of hours later, several of the usual doughnuts and cups of coffee now consumed, Lane's phone rang. "Detective Madigan here."

"Detective Madigan, this is Dr. Willis down at the coroner's office. We have managed to make a positive ID on that body found this morning. His name was Ramah Bin Shazid."

Lane knew exactly who this person was. "You're kidding—Shazid the Slayer? The military has been trying to nail this guy for years!" he blurted out. From the adjacent desk, Ian nearly spewed his coffee in reaction to the news. Lane caught a glimpse of Ian's reaction, and could see the great surprise in Ian's eyes.

Lane continued. "Ramah Bin Shazid is a known Syrian terrorist, who is strongly suspected of several bombings over the past three years, claiming the lives of several hundreds of people. My God, you're telling me he was right here in Miami? Do you have an estimated time of death, or cause of death?"

"It looks to have happened around 3:00am. I suppose by 'cause' you're looking for an answer more definitive than 'spike through the head'?" replied Dr. Willis sarcastically.

"I think that's fairly obvious, Doc. Yes, I want to know what happened to the guy: how did he end up the way we found him with the rock, the spike, the order of events, all that?" said Detective Madigan, as his voice began to grow loud and excited.

"We don't have an exact answer, as this is a new one on us. But I would speculate that to do what was done to him, we're either looking at someone stronger than anyone I have ever known, or the use of some mechanized assistance. The rock found near the crime scene definitely had the victim's blood on it, but it was not the cause of death. I would say the man's head was first struck by the rock, and then the spike was driven through his head, " answered Dr. Willis.

"Were there any signs of a struggle—skin under the fingernails, bruised fists...," continued a very excited Madigan.

"No, not at all," replied Dr. Willis. "Either the rock knocked him unconscious, or the perpetrator was able to hold him down on the sidewalk long enough to nail the spike right through him," she finished.

"Hold him down?" Who in the world is strong enough to hold some-one down, no doubt against a frantic struggle, and also drive a spike so far into the sidewalk that nobody else can pull it back out?" He paused for a minute considering something. He shook his head and said "The rock must have knocked him unconscious first."

Dr. Willis responded, "Well I really don't think so, Lane. The injury from the rock was quite mild, as it was virtually a simple breaking of the skin. It certainly did not hit the man hard enough to knock him out, unless he was just an absolute 'glass jaw.'"

"Amazing!" Detective Madigan says, with almost a sense of admiration. "So, can we conclude this case is related to the other recent 'Hamburger Homicides'?"

"Well, I would almost have to say…uh, DEFINITELY! Once again, no revealing physical evidence was retrieved at the scene of the crime. It was another what I would consider to be a beyond-imaginable method of killing, just like all the others. It is the 21st century, Detective. Some pretty crazy people are wandering the streets out there. Whoever is doing all this has a very unique imagination," concluded Dr. Willis.

Detective Madigan noticed Ian leaving his desk and coming to stand next to him, eager to hear the news.

"Well that's certainly a nicer way of putting it. Thanks for the info. Let me know if you guys come up with any other helpful hints. At this point, no detail is too small. Help me out here, Lauren. I'll talk to you later," Detective Madigan spoke with a tone of disgust in his voice, as he started to hang up the phone. He then paused for a moment, put the phone back to his ear, and spoke again. "Sorry Lauren, I don't mean to sound angry with you, I'm just disappointed in our lack of information here."

"No apologies necessary, Lane," said Dr. Willis. "I get it. It *is* frustrating."

Lane dropped the phone into its cradle.

All along with these recent murder cases, Lane thought that there was something familiar about the forms of execution taking place. He had a sense of it being on the tip of his tongue, but he just could not recall it. "A spike through the head?" he muttered to himself. "Where have I heard that before?" He shrugged off that feeling, and hung up the phone, a heaviness weighing on his shoulders. "Well, I guess it is official ", he said to Ian who was half leaning against the front of his desk.

"What's up? So come on, spit it out, what did they turn up?" He crossed his arms and looked expectantly.

"Your girl has done it again, Jelani. She really knows her stuff, you know," said Lane.

Ian smiled sheepishly, "Don't you know it, she's good!"

Lane continued without missing a beat. "Once again, there is no physical evidence to speak of. But ID'ing the victim is important. Dr. Willis believes that rock was only periphery to the event, and also once again, she has never seen anything quite like this. I suppose you had better go ahead with calling the press, Ian. Let the Feds know what we found too, as they can deal with the military inquiries, considering who is our dearly departed. Might as well get this over with," he replied disgustedly.

"Whatever you say Boss," Ian said with a nod. He knew what this meant. The media had been begging for a statement, especially once they had heard about the fifth body today. Miami PD hated to make this public, but this was not news that could be kept quiet any longer.

Ian picked up the phone, and dialed his local news contact. "Detective Jelani here. Miami PD has an official statement to make. It looks like we have a serial killer on our hands." Ian paused as whomever was on the other end of the call was obviously speaking, then he continued, "Yep, come on over I guess."

"Hey Chief," Ian called out, as he started walking toward the office of Julie Franklin, captain of the precinct. "The media is headed our way. You can be sure there will be a bunch of 'em too."

Later that afternoon, Lane decided to log the serial killings on the National Criminal Justice Reference Service. Every time he used it he was amazed at how the voluminous database could help to track and catalog crimes committed around the country. As he keyed in the information, he thought how he probably should have done this sooner, but had held off as long as possible. Miami already got enough attention, of the wrong sort, and this would just add to it.

By 5:00pm, Lane saw some responses coming from various parts of the country. "Hey Ian, come take a look at all this."

"At what?" answered Ian, but without acting as though he was going to heed Lane's request.

"Just come over here, man," Lane said in a bit of a hushed tone.

"Okay, okay, don't get your panties in a wad," said Ian. He walked over quickly to Lane's desk.

Lane looked up at Ian. "There are a few other police stations reporting eerily similar incidents, just like some of the crazy stuff we're seeing here."

"Seriously?" said Ian, more intrigued, crouching down to look at Lane's screen. "What are you talking about?"

"I mean like some of the same gruesome murders we are seeing," said Lane somberly. "Criminals of all sorts are falling. We're talking high profile offenders, local hoodlums, apparently even some other international criminals like Shazid the Slayer. This even sounds like some of this craziness is happening outside the good ol' US of A."

Ian started to get excited. "This is some news-breaking headline junk, my friend...we..."

"Look," Lane quickly interrupted. "We can't create some kind of nationwide firestorm here. I don't think anyone is cognizant of all this just yet. This is going to take some further investigation before I'm willing to take this anywhere."

A chill ran up Lane's spine, as he looked Ian squarely in the eyes. He said "What if this is some kind of nationwide crime spree, like some terrorist thing? Maybe some organized crime resurgence?"

"Maybe some kind of home-grown supremacy group, or some crazy crap like that," said Ian.

"Well none of these sound like great options," said Lane sarcastically. "And if there is some nationwide, or God-forbid, a worldwide connection in all of this, we are going to be in way over our heads real fast. We need some time to think about all this."

"It's getting late, and I'm starving and tired," said Ian.

"Sure is late," replied Lane. "And I'm glad you said it in that order, because I know for a fact it's the 'starving' part that comes first for you, then the 'tired' part." Lane chuckled.

"Yeah, yeah, you're a funny guy," Ian said dryly. "But you're absolutely right, you know me all too well."

"Well, I know my family is waiting on me, so I need to get home, for sure. We need time to sleep on all this anyway, take a fresh look in the morning," said Lane.

"Agreed" said Ian, "All right, I'll catch you in the morning, buddy. Enjoy your evening with the fam," and he shot out the door.

Lane left soon afterwards as well, and pondered this all as he drove home. "Maybe I'm just reading too much into all this," he thought to himself. "Maybe I'm just being too paranoid." He pulled into the driveway, and his thoughts turned to kissing his wife, hugging his daughter, eating a delicious home cooked meal, and then getting a good night's sleep. He was more than ready for this day to be done.

CHAPTER 2:

TERROR IN DETROIT, MI

Tommy and Michael had big plans for Henry Ford High School now that they were finally there. They knew as freshmen they were low on the food chain, but you have to start somewhere. The previous night, the boys had talked at great length with each other about which shirts they should wear on the first day of high school. They carefully talked through their options, made their final selections, then agreed that each of them had made the right decision. Tommy talked about some new hair gel his mother had bought for him, to keep his moppy blonde hair under control. Michael laughed about his dad trying to give him girl advice. Even though both boys were smaller in stature, they had big plans of playing high school basketball, and talked of trying to meet the coaches as soon as possible.

That first morning of school, they were engaging in their favorite pastime of trying to knuckle each other in the arm meat to see who would scream like a girl first. "You lose!" laughed Tommy, as he slammed his school locker shut and gave Michael a good natured shove. "C'mon, we don't wanna be late for Mr. K's class."

Their forward momentum was brought up short. Both boys' eyes were drawn to the width and breadth of Xavier Thomas, Senior. They knew Xavier was the star of the basketball team, but more intimidating were the rumors of his reputation as a member of one of the local gangs. Michael swallowed hard and glanced fearfully at Tommy, who said nervously, "Hey Xavier." All around them students continued to move down the hallway, moving around them as if they were rocks in a teenage stream.

Xavier glared down at them, his eyebrows furrowed. He reached down and flicked Tommy's shirt collar.

"What are those colors you two losers are wearing today? Don't you know those are not 'the right' colors 'round here?"

"What do you mean?," Michael blurted out. "We're just lowly freshmen, nothing...nobody. We don't know colors and we don't run colors."

Tommy quickly added, "Yeah, that's right, they don't mean nothin'. We just put on whatever clean clothes we had this morning." Tommy tried to smile, but it faded quickly as Dante Smithson joined Xavier. The boys also recognized Dante, the standout football player of Henry Ford High. He was sporting his highly decorated letterman jacket, despite the still-warm temperatures of August. The distinct skunky smell of weed filled their air, with Dante's appearance. Tommy and Michael glanced at each other more nervously, both having the same thought of the teachers busting them all because of their proximity to the weed-laden Dante.

Dante pointed a finger at them. "You don't give us no excuses, man!"

A third upperclassman, whose name Michael could never remember, came to stand behind Tommy and Michael. He leaned down and growled in Tommy's ear. Tommy felt like he was about to barf from the smell of alcohol on this third boy's breath. Towering over both the freshmen, with his sleeveless shirt revealing some muscular biceps, he said "How many times do we have to tell you punks, you'd better be checking in with us every morning when you come to school?" He punctuated his statement by shoulder checking Tommy, as he now walked past the boys to join Xavier and Dante, sending Tommy stumbling forward.

Tommy's eyes scanned the hallway for teachers, principals, even the janitor...some adult to help. There didn't seem to be anyone. All he could see was the formidable wall created by these three overgrown hoodlums. Michael held his hands up, palm forward trying to calm the situation. "Look, we hardly know you guys, we don't want any trouble, and we just need to get to class now."

"Yeah," said Tommy, taking Michael's lead, "we don't want to get in trouble with Mr. Kronowski. We really need to get to social studies, guys."

Both boys managed to weave their way around the gang members, and breathed a sigh of relief when they made it into their class. "Close call!" said Tommy, exhaling loudly as he slid into his chair.

"Those guys are bad news," said Michael sitting next to him. "We have to do better to avoid them from now on. They're gonna be looking for us else wise." Tommy nodded his agreement as Mr. K started the day's lesson.

Later that evening, at the Boys and Girls Club, Tommy and Michael crammed the last slices of pizza down their throats, closed their books and waved goodbye to Mrs. Jackson as they left the building. It was already getting dark, but as long as there were two of them, their parents had said it was okay to walk the few blocks home. They usually just cut down through the alley behind the Chinese restaurant. It was faster and you could chuck rocks at the rats.

"Did you guys really think we were going to let you off that easy?" said Xavier, stepping out of the shadows from the corner of a building. A sinister grin spread across his face, his teeth gleaming white in the dim light.

Michael and Tommy immediately turned to run, but Dante stepped into the alleyway. "Where you off to ya little rats?" Michael's heart throbbed in his chest and cold unmitigated fear clenched his stomach into a tight knot. Dante brandished an automatic rifle he pulled from behind his back.

The third member, whose name Michael finally remembered was Juan, said "I think these punks need to learn a little lesson." He emphasized the statement by twirling a small policeman's nightstick he was carrying.

Acting out of sheer terror, Michael shoved Juan making enough of an opening for him and Tommy to get out of the alley. Michael went right and Tommy went left to the opposite side of the street. Tommy whirled around to shout at Michael to follow him, but his cries were drowned out by a hail of gunfire aimed at his friend. He only had a few seconds to watch Michael crumple to the ground, then realizing he was next, Tommy turned and ran. He heard them following, taunting, jeering and laughing. The way they sounded, they had to be high on something, which meant they were twice as dangerous as they were normally. Michael ran as fast as he had ever run. Only one more block until he was home. He swung around Hessel Avenue, cutting across the road, aiming for the trees and bushes at O'Hair Park. His lungs were about to burst.

"Now we're gonna kill you too, you little asshole!" roared Xavier behind him.

Juan shouted, "Yeah, just like your little buddy back there in the ditch!"

Dante laughed his agreement shrilly.

Tommy pushed through the bushes and spied a large dumpster surrounded by trash cans. He squeezed himself into the shadows behind them, his breath coming in rasps. He was going to die. Just like Michael. For what? For what! The sheer hopelessness of it all brought tears to his eyes. He closed them tight and waited for the inevitable. He could hear the laughter getting closer. By his guess they were just past the bushes. They'd be on him soon enough. He waited and listened.

The laughing stopped. Suddenly. Abruptly. As if someone had hit the mute button. Slowly he peered out from behind the dumpster.

Another tall, dark figure now stood in the middle of the street facing Xavier and the rest. Maybe he was a cop? Tommy crept out a bit further. Would it be safe enough for him to run while these guys were focused on the newcomer? He risked it, then glanced at the tall figure again. The man's hair and eyes were glowing white...and he was very, very tall. Tommy had seen some tall basketball players, but this guy must be at least seven feet tall, with muscles bulging. The man was dressed like a biker, but with no motorcycle in view, Tommy was fairly certain this was no biker.

"Proceed no further!" shouted the stranger, the voice deep and resonant. The power of the man's voice made Tommy shudder, and he could tell that Xavier and his boys didn't know exactly how to deal with this unexpected visitor's arrival. They fell back on their usual M.O.: insults.

"Yeah, right" yelled Juan, "proceed this," and he held up his middle finger, with a sneering laugh.

Dante screamed, pointing his gun, "You just crossed the wrong street old man!"

Xavier chimed in "Nobody messes with us 'Lethal Weapons'. See? You're new, so we gotta teach you a lesson 'bout who owns this area." Tommy flattened himself back against the dumpster as gunfire erupted.

Tommy crouched down, covering his head and ears. He didn't want to watch the carnage. He was next. Why hadn't he run when he had the chance? The shooting seemed to go on forever, but finally it stopped, the smell of spent ammo and sulfur hanging in the air.

Hysterical laughter pierced the night air as Xavier and his group celebrated. The smoke that had filled the street slowly began to dissipate as the bright moonlight revealed an unbelievable site. Tommy slowly stood. Not because of any particular sound but because there was no sound. Zero. None at all. The laughing had stopped abruptly. There were no dogs barking, no stray cats meowing, no cars passing by—just dead silence.

Tommy saw all the Lethal Weapons members standing still, shocked, unsure. The stranger was standing there, now just a few feet away from the gunmen. He was *standing* there, not lying on the ground, just standing there, arms folded against his broad chest. Tommy felt himself walking slowly forward in disbelief. He knew he should turn and run away, but for some reason he just needed to understand.

In his thunderous voice, the stranger shouted "If thy right hand offends thee, cut it off!" And before Tommy could ponder the strange words and strange way the man was talking, the stranger was now suddenly holding a brilliant flaming sword. In an instant, the stranger effortlessly swung the sword, severing Xavier's right hand. In shock, Xavier stood there staring at his arm, where his hand used to be. Tommy could see the hand lying on the ground, thin wisps of smoke rising from it. Slowly, Tommy started to back away. Then Xavier screamed in fear and anger, which snapped the others out of their stupor. They started to round on the stranger. This was it, thought Tommy. Bulletproof vest or not...the man was outnumbered. Tommy started to move slowly back into the shadows, searching for the best way to leave unnoticed.

Tommy's backward movement was halted as he heard the tall man say "If thy foot offend thee, cut it off." The sword was a blur and then Juan fell to the ground, his severed foot lying at an odd angle beside him. Juan's breath was coming out in gasps as he writhed on the ground.

From behind the tall man, Dante roared and charged the stranger with a knife. The stranger shouted "And if thy right eye offends thee, pluck it out!" Tommy felt the bile rising in his throat as the stranger, with his longer reach, plunged the tip of his sword into Dante's right eye.

Tommy's knees were weak. He wasn't sure they would even carry him if he tried to run. Slowly, he leaned back against the side of the dumpster and slid to the ground, fighting back the nausea. He could hear Dante, Xavier and Juan crying out, begging the stranger to let them go. Tommy closed his eyes as he heard the stranger say, "Vengeance is mine!" Tommy didn't have to watch to know that all three boys had been killed, since now there was absolute quiet once again. Fighting back the despair and panic, Tommy slowly lifted his gaze, to accept what was next. All that met him was darkness. There was a faint light, coming from a flickering street lamp, popping with an occasional buzzing sound. Also, the flaming sword was gone, but now as his eyes began to adjust to the dim light, he spotted the decapitated bodies of the three young gang members. Tommy put his hands over his mouth, gasping in fear over the grotesque scene.

Out of the darkness Tommy heard a deep voice speaking calmly. "You must go home now, Tommy."

Using the dumpster to steady himself, shaking with relief, Tommy willed his legs to take him home. After walking a few steps he turned to thank the man. All that greeted him was a starry night, a warm breeze and the remains of his tormentors. Tommy didn't question it, and with new found energy tore out for home.

CHAPTER 3:

TERROR IN NEW YORK, NY

ohnny Whiteman, sitting in his high rise penthouse screamed into his phone. "Listen, Rick, either you find me some kids, or I'll find somebody who will!" Whiteman slammed it down in disgust, then ran his carefully manicured fingers through what was left of his thinning hair, easing back into his chair. Whiteman, dressed to the nines, pushed back away from his desk, trying to make room for his fat belly. Whiteman had no impressive looks, no charming personality, and certainly no physique that garnered him any female attention. He tried to make up for all of his "shortcomings" by dressing well, but even that did not help his "ugly short-man syndrome."

What was so hard about grabbing kids and teens, grooming them, and getting them to do what they were going to do anyway? Back in the day, he would have done it all himself. It is because they just did not make good assistants like they used to; people who were hungry to move up the food chain and would do anything without question. Now, it was all one excuse after another of why they could not do what they are told to do. *My porn is the best out there,* Whiteman thought to himself, *and I didn't make all this money by being a lazy ass like these idiots I'm surrounded by.*

He exhaled sharply as if to rid himself of his disgust. Assistants were as disposable as the rest of them. And the backlots and tosslots where he planted them once their usefulness ran out would testify to that point. Johnny rose and walked to the sideboard adjacent to a large bank of windows overlooking the nighttime city. He'd specifically chosen this area because it was right next to the docks, so close you could piss off the balcony and if you had good aim…hit the water. Laughing to himself, he poured a tall bourbon and turned to take in the lights of the city. It seemed oddly still to him rather than the usual bustling down below, to which he was accustomed.

Still feeling the aggravation from his disappointing phone call, Johnny picked up the phone once again. "Maybe this will make it all better," he said to himself, chuckling and beginning to dial. He waited for a moment, then told his assistant, "Bring her up here to my office." He avoided the pleasantries, and tossed his phone onto the desk.

A few moments later, Johnny's favorite bodyguard, Fred, entered the room dragging a half-naked young girl, as though she were a rag doll. Johnny loved the way Fred "handled" the girls every chance he got. He admired this gorilla-sized man with fists the size of hams. Not only did Fred know how to take care of these girls, he had saved Johnny's bacon on more than one occasion. He was a grade-A tough bodyguard.

Julia was dressed scantily. Remnants of mascara streaked down her face, and her hair was mussed. She was barely coherent from lack of proper nutrition and forced drug use. She held up her hand-cuffed hands toward Johnny, and spoke in a pleading voice. "Please Johnny, don't do this to me again, please! I just want to go home." She burst into tears.

"You are home, baby," Johnny quipped. "I own you." Eyeing her up-and-down with a glimmer in his eye, he cupped his hand under her chin, pulling

Julia up onto her knees. "And all the rest of your body too, you worthless nobody." He laughed and pushed her backward. With a thud, she collided into the couch, slid to the floor, and groaned in pain.

"Stay here with her until I get back," Johnny barked out to the bodyguard. "Then I'll make your dreams come true, baby," he said to Julia, as she now lay on the ground in a fetal position, whimpering. Looking back at the bodyguard, he said "You can take a turn with her first, if you want."

Johnny quickly tossed back the last of his bourbon, then took the private elevator up to the roof. He needed a smoke, and the roof was one of his favorite spots to relax and contemplate his next moves or to plot strategy. After staring out across the city from the rooftop's edge, he turned around to light his cigarette only to face a dark figure blocking his path.

Whiteman dropped his lighter and pointed at the figure, the unlit cigarette held between two fingers. "Who the hell are you, and how did you get up here? What happened to all my bodyguards?" Whiteman bent down to retrieve his lighter, paused to light his cigarette and said as he exhaled a puff of smoke, "Those idiots better start looking for a new job."

He fished inside his jacket's interior pocket for his cell phone, pulled it out, and began to dial security. He stopped short as a whirring sound began. Johnny was incredulous as a rope sailed through the air and before he could react, landed around his neck. Quickly he dropped his phone and tried to keep the rope from tightening. The stranger's grip was too strong and Johnny began to struggle to breathe. He tried to see who the person in the shadows was, who had dared to do this to him. He felt as if his eyes were going to pop out of his head.

Then the stranger spoke in a low, resonant voice, as if he were reciting Shakespeare. "It were better for him that a millstone be hanged about his neck, and that he were drowned in the depth of the sea." With horror and spots floating before his eyes, Johnny saw that the whirring sound had come from a large rock-like object swinging on the other end of the rope.

Johnny Whiteman flailed his arms wildly at the stranger as he realized where the other end of the rope was attached. But without warning, the stranger turned the object loose as its final revolution sent it toward the edge of the roof.

All Johnny could do was watch as the object cleared the roof's edge. Stumbling backwards, he grabbed the rope with both hands, feverishly trying to pull it off of his neck. Coil after coil of the rope continued to unfold. Johnny knew time was running out before the rope would be pulled tight, and he could feel his heart pounding, like it was going to explode out of his chest. He saw a metal pipe protruding from the roof, and he wrapped both arms around it. Just then, the rope stretched tight, and jerked him off his feet, breaking his grip around the pipe. The last thing he saw was the stranger's glowing eyes, staring coldly through him. He plunged off the roof headfirst.

Julia, still lying on the floor, a couple of stories below the roof, just happened to look out the window as Johnny zoomed past her view, screaming as he hurled headlong toward the ground. For the first time in a long time, a smile came over Julia's face.

The object hit the street with an explosive sound, shattering the nighttime quiet. A moment later, the sound of Whiteman's body smashing into the shallow waterway followed.

The shadowed figure squared his shoulders to the cityscape and declared, "Vengeance is mine!"

CHAPTER 4:

MEET ROBERTO VALENZUELA

DEA Special Agent Kim Hardesty opened one eye at the loud creaking of an opening door. The room spun around her, and she was aware of pain. All over, pain. Sunlight poured into the room where she was sitting tied to a chair, and in the open doorway she could make out the silhouette of a lean, well-dressed figure of a man.

Kim tried to inhale deeply, but the rush of air into her bruised lungs was painful. The copper taste of blood was on her lips, and the smell of ammonia and rotten eggs was overpowering. That distinctive smell was bad enough to turn her stomach, and she suddenly remembered out of her stupor where she was.

"Westwood," she whispered out loud, "I think he's here." Turning her head to her left, the side of her one good eye, she could now see Special Agent Tyler Westwood's head was tilted forward. He was tied into the chair next to her. "Tyler," she said in a louder, hushed tone.

A weak groan was the only sound Kim could hear coming from Tyler. Kim saw him trying to lift his shaking head, but he could not muster the strength, not even for that simple task.

"I'll figure something out," whispered Kim. "Hang in there, Tyler."

Next, Kim heard the telltale sound of leather heels, as they clicked across the concrete surface of the floor. The well-dressed man stopped beside her, but he was not looking at her, rather, he was staring down at Tyler.

"Is this one dead?" the man said disgustedly, grabbing Tyler's hair, pulling his head backward, then dropping it again like a limp noodle. "I told you I wanted them both alive *and* talking," the man said sharply, looking intently at the large bodyguard facing him.

Before the bodyguard could respond, the first man backhand slapped the bodyguard across the face.

"Apologies," said the bodyguard once he regained his composure. "We didn't mean to hit him so hard, Mr. Valenzuela. We had no idea he was so...", he paused, searching for a way to explain himself. "Weak and fragile," the bodyguard finished his sentence, casting a slight grin in Kim's direction.

"But he is not dead...yet," said the second bodyguard, also grinning at Kim.

"Even if he is not dead yet, he is no good to me if he cannot even speak," Valenzuela said with a shout.

"So it *is* you, eh, Roberto Valenzuela?" quipped Special Agent Hardesty, as she stared coldly back at the bodyguards. "Your idiotic goons don't know what they're doing, apparently," she said, as she spit a wad of blood out of her mouth. She was a good shot with her spittle, as it landed right on the first bodyguard's black shoes.

"Why you..." growled the bodyguard, as he lunged toward Hardesty.

Valenzuela held up his arm to block the bodyguard. "Relax, Julio," said Valenzuela. "You aren't letting this pretty little lady get under your skin, are you?" he said, directing a wicked smile at Kim. "Perhaps I should let my twin towers here, Julio and Jorge, have some *fun* with you," he said with a cat-call whistle through his teeth.

Julio let out an anticipative laugh, and licked his lips at Hardesty, with a gleam in his eyes. He glanced over at his twin brother Jorge, who was staring longingly at Kim.

Even though he was indoors, Roberto was wearing fashionable Oakley sunglasses. He was sporting some gold chains, as well as several gold rings on more than one of his fingers. He was in a light gray suit, and even though he was not nearly as tall as his extra large body guards, he imposed a formidable presence on everyone around him. He pulled a comb out of his pocket, and took a few strokes through his neatly slicked jet black hair.

"It won't be long before this place is going to be crawling with more DEA agents than vultures on a dead carcass, Valenzuela," Kim said, grimacing. "And who knows, if I'm lucky, maybe that dead carcass will be yours."

Valenzuela gave out a single, loudly sincere "Ha!". He started pacing back-and-forth in front of the two agents. "That's a good one, Agent Hardesty. I've heard you were tough...at least for a woman," said Valenzuela sarcastically. "But I do not think any help is on the way, my dear. Do you not think I know that you lowlifes from the DEA have been watching me, tracking me? How do you think I so easily captured you and dead-man-walking...er, I mean dead-man-sitting, over here," Valenzuela nodded his head toward Agent Westwood, and grinned again at Kim. "We knew you two were snooping around my building here, you were not as stealthy as you may have thought."

"Julio, this man is simply no good to me in his current state," said Valenzuela, clicking his tongue, wagging his head. He stopped right in front of Tyler.

Nonchalantly and without warning, Kim watched Valenzuela draw his nine millimeter pistol, firing multiple shots into Tyler's torso. "Nooooooooo," she screamed violently, shaking her body against the straps holding her in the chair. "No, stop, stop, stop," she kept screaming to no avail.

The echoes of the gunshots faded, and Valenzuela put his gun away. Kim stared at Tyler's dead body in disbelief. She looked back at Valenzuela, and cursed his name.

"Wow, what language for a pretty little lady," said Valenzuela, chuckling. "Jorge, the pliers, behind you."

Jorge handed Valenzuela a pair of pliers. "I always wanted to be a dentist," he said as strolled over to Kim.

She felt Valenzuela grab her head tightly, pulling it back locking it against his hip. He forced the pliers into her mouth, grabbed a tooth, and pulled with a groan. Kim screamed in pain as he ripped one of her teeth out.

"But unfortunately, I do not think I have the bedside manner for being a dentist," Valenzuela said, taking a couple of steps backward, laughing at his handiwork.

Kim's head flopped forward, as blood streamed from her mouth. She grunted, breathing heavily, trying to keep herself under control, despite the excruciating pain.

"Oh my, I think you must be pretty tough alright, Agent Hardesty, if that's all I get from you," said Valenzuela, nodding his head. "Don't you guys agree?" he said, looking over at the bodyguards, who said nothing.

"Now, I want you to tell me everything you know about my little operation here," continued Valenzuela. "How much have you heard about, how many other DEA dirtbags know about this, all the little details you can think of, hmmm?"

Kim continued breathing heavily, but only stared straight ahead, refusing to make eye contact with Valenzuela. She spit a wad of blood out onto the floor, as she cursed at them once again.

"Why are you making me do these things to you, Agent Hardesty?" said Valenzuela in a completely fake tone of sympathy. "This could go so much easier. Maybe I should let my boys have their way with you next, eh? They would love that, but I have a feeling you would not enjoy it very much," he said mockingly, shaking his finger back-and-forth at her.

Kim watched Valenzuela walking back toward her again, as he opened the pliers, letting her tooth fall to the ground. Once again, she felt him grab her head just as before, but from the other side. She felt the pliers being forced into her mouth again, and she could not help but start to scream this time. Now Valenzuela was grabbing another tooth from the opposite side of her mouth. He had to pull a couple of times, this time, and she felt another tooth coming out. More intense pain shot through her body, and she shrieked.

Valenzuela took a couple of steps backward again. "Whew, that was one tough little booger to get out, much harder than the first. Oh," he said as he looked down at the pliers. "That's why, I grabbed one of your eye teeth. Gosh, those suckers are in your head pretty good," he said with a laugh.

Kim felt more blood flowing out of her mouth, and felt her whole body pulsing in pain with every heartbeat. Her chin started to quiver now, and she could feel her tough exterior starting to slip away. She fought hard to keep the tears back.

Kim managed to let another swear fly at Valenzuela. "You are going to pay for what you've done here today, Valenzuela. You and your ugly goons," she said in a broken voice, throwing her head in the direction of Julio and Jorge. "Somehow, some way, what goes around comes around."

"Jorge, the machete please," said Valenzuela calmly, without missing a beat.

Kim watched Jorge place the machete into Valenzuela's hand, as Valenzuela stared coldly back into her eyes. She saw the gleam of the blade, and despite her best efforts to keep up her tough exterior, she knew fear was showing in her eyes. She started to shake her head slightly as she watched Valenzuela walking straight toward her.

He stopped right beside her and said "No," wagging his head. Horrified, Kim watched him swing the machete down with a surprisingly swift motion. She did not even have time to close her eyes before Valenzuela chopped her right arm in the middle of her forearm, and the machete blade lodged itself into the armrest of her chair.

"I will win, and that is that," said Valenzuela, without giving a thought to the gruesome act he just carried out.

For a moment, she could not even process what had just happened. Her hand, formerly tied to the armrest, was now still tied to the chair but severed from her arm. She looked up at Valenzuela in terror, and began to scream.

"Whoa, boss," exclaimed Julio. "That was wicked," then he and Jorge started laughing hysterically, turning in circles where they stood.

Julio shouted out excitedly again, pointing a finger toward Detective Hardesty. "Hey boss, look, she's starting to pass out."

Kim could feel her head swaying back and forth. Her head fell forward as she lost consciousness.

"Jorge, wake her up," commanded Valenzuela, clapping his hands together. "No, no, no, Detective, no time for passing out," he said, waving his finger in her face.

Jorge reached inside his jacket pocket, pulling out a slim zip up bag. He opened it, revealing a collection of tubes of various chemicals. He pulled one out containing some smelling salts, then waved it under Kim's nose.

Kim felt herself jolt out of her stupor and her head jerked backwards. But she was still woozy, and moaning.

"Yes, I want you awake, Detective Hardesty. And you know what?" said Valenzuela as he walked back over to the chair, grabbing the machete and pulling hard to get it dislodged from the chair. "Honestly, I don't really need any information from you, it's not important."

Kim, still moaning and disoriented, barely able to hold her head upright, watched Valenzuela walk behind her. He grabbed her hair, as he began to saw at her neck with the machete. Her eyes bulged, she shrieked. She could never have known that a moment later, Valenzuela would hold her decapitated head by the hair.

Valenzuela staggered backwards. He tossed the head aside, and dropped the machete into a large pool of blood. He looked at Julio and Jorge. Their laughter had stopped, and they stood staring in disbelief, their jaws hanging open.

Snapping his fingers, Valenzuela called out to Julio and Jorge. "Come here, both of you," he demanded. With zero remorse, Valenzuela continued, as the bodyguards walked toward him. "I remember a story from the Bible," he said, as he put a hand to his head, and started walking around in a circle. "It was in the Old Testament, in the book of Judges. A fascinating story, and what a fabulous idea. A man by the name of Micah, he cut up his concubine and sent her body parts to all the tribes of Israel. You will do that," Valenzuela said, as he stopped his circling, and looked at the bodyguards matter-of-factly.

"Uh, what did you just say, boss?" said Jorge

"Listen to me carefully, I do not want to repeat myself again," said Valenzuela firmly. He grabbed both of them by their ties, pulling them closer. "Box up her head, and mail it to the DEA office. Then, I don't know, cut up some other parts, and mail them to the police, the Feds, the Marshall. You know, put the fear of God...well, the fear of *me*, into them," he said with a sinister laugh. "Let them know I am king, I am in charge, they'd better not cross me."

He let go of their ties, shook his hands, and stepped back away from them. "Do it," he said sternly. "And if you can't, I'll just send you back to Nuevo Laredo to do grunt work in the fields. Then maybe I'll have *you* cut up."

Valenzuela started to walk away, toward the same door he entered. Julio and Jorge turned slowly, following Valenzuela's walk. He opened the door, looked both ways, and stepped outside. The door slammed behind him.

Jorge stared back at Julio. "Don't ask me, man, but I know this. I ain't goin' back to the fields, no way, no how," said Julio.

Jorge shrugged his shoulders, saying nothing, and they both set about the task of incredulously fulfilling their boss's request. But as tough as they were, the mess they were faced with was a sickening affair.

"Wait, go outside and grab a couple of the guys keeping watch out there," exclaimed Julio. "You and me can go outside and keep watch, while they come in here and deal with *this*," he said, waving his arms across the floor.

Jorge shrugged his shoulders again. "Okay, brother, whatever you say. Doesn't bother me that much, but sure, I can think of other things I'd rather do."

Jorge walked over to the door, and gave a shout toward a couple of other men who were waiting outside. Those two men stepped inside, and both were taken back by Valenzuela's handiwork.

"Here's a couple of bags," said Julio. "Boss wants to keep the, uh, loose pieces. Otherwise, get this cleaned up pronto, and get rid of the bodies."

CHAPTER 5:

TERROR IN MOBILE, AL

Howard Washington and his girlfriend Georgette Truman, walked out of downtown's Heroes Sports Bar and Grille, and stepped onto the sidewalk. There was a distinct smell of burgers and beer in the air. A nice cool evening breeze was a welcome relief as patrons exited the bar which had grown so hot from the shoulder-to-shoulder crowd inside. Compared to the normal bar crowd, they were both well-dressed and groomed in sharp attire. They had met in college, both coming from hard-working, blue collar families, and both were first-generation college graduates from each of their families. Their success and high-on-life personalities exuded from their faces.

"Whew, what a game, babe!" said Howard. "I mean 'Bama just keeps cruisin' right along. That Crimson Tide is lookin' good. We just beat second place Auburn 45-10." Howard skipped a couple of paces in obvious excitement. "Once again, the Iron Bowl goes to 'Bama. I'm tellin' you, I really think we're headed for another national championship this year. Yeah baby!" he exclaimed with a fist pump into the air.

"You say that every year, dear," answered Georgette, flashing her pearly white smile, pushing back her long, perfectly styled hair out of her face. "But you're probably right. Our Roll Tide is always in the runnin' for the championship."

"And winnin' a cool hundred bucks to boot," added Howard, "you can't beat that. I'm gonna treat you to one nice dinner tonight. Me and my beautiful lady, out on the town, now that is sweet!"

Georgette giggled, "Yeah, very nice sweetheart, but I sure wish you wouldn't mess around with Joey, honey." Her demeanor quickly changed, as she started talking about Joseph Bo Nickerson ("Joey" as he was known to the community). "He is one crazy man, and he sure doesn't like to lose. Besides losin' that money, you know that nobody around here is as hateful as he is. He has got one bad reputation, why, he is as rude and hateful as they come." Georgette scowled as she added "Did you see the look in his eye when he handed that hundred dollars over to you? He had been drinkin' more than any man ought to be able to drink."

"Well maybe one of these days he'll figure out his Auburn Tigers are just no match for us, Roll Tide, baby! And look, in today's world, there just ain't room for that kind of hatred anymore. People like him have just gotta stop all that nonsense," said Howard. "It is plain ridiculous!"

Inside the bar, the crowd noise was deafening. Joey glanced up at the wall behind the bar, and spotted a souvenir baseball bat displayed there. Grabbing the bat off the wall, he spoke to some of his barroom buddies. "I can't believe I just handed over that hundred dollars without a word."

"Joey, wait a sec," interjected the bartender. "You can't take my souvenir bat; that's an heirloom to me. That's worth a lot of money."

"You better shut your mouth, barkeep, or I'll shut it for ya!" yelled Joey. "Besides, I'll be done with it in a few minutes, and I'll put it right back where you like it. But I'm warnin' ya, it might be a little messy when I get done with it." He gave out a loud single "Ha," directed at the barkeep, who just turned away wagging his head.

Holding the bat in his right hand, he began slapping it into his left hand, as his blood began to boil. "I can't believe I lost my hard-earned money to one of them losers," he said, nodding in the direction of other patrons in the bar.

Joey slammed the bat down onto the bar, shaking all the glasses sitting nearby. "And they sure aren't getting away with it," he yelled. He grabbed his glass, threw back the last few swallows of his Wild Turkey, dropped the glass onto the floor, and stormed out the front door of the bar, ball bat in hand.

"Hey!" shouted an enraged Joey, stumbling out onto the sidewalk, barely able to walk. Howard and Georgette had gotten nearly a block down the sidewalk. "Ain't no home boy gonna steal my money and just walk outta here!" Joey slung drunken expletives in their direction, and lumbered after them determinedly.

"C'mon Howard, the car is right there. Let's just go. Forget about that crazy man!" Georgette tugged frantically at Howard's arm as he turned to face the enraged Joey.

Georgette was flung like a ragdoll sending her sprawling onto a nearby car, from Joey's rib-cracking kick. Howard cried out "Georgette, just get outta here!"

"Howard, look out!" shouted Georgette as she could see what Joey was about to do. But her warning was too late. All she could hear was the sound of Joey's bat cracking the back of Howard's head, splattering his blood across her face. She gasped, placing her arms in front of her defensively.

"You're gonna wish you never met me," screamed Joey. Completely dazed, Howard turned around only to suffer another blow to the front of his face. Howard's limp body fell to the pavement. Joey's rant of expletives continued to pour from his mouth as he pummeled Howard's now lifeless body.

As Joey raised his bat to deliver another unnecessary blow, he felt the bat ripped forcefully out of his hands. He whirled around, clenching his fists. "So you want some of this too?" he shouted, ready to fight someone else. All he could see was a large booted foot coming right toward him.

Joey felt himself go airborne, smashing into a tree on the other side of the sidewalk. He grunted in pain, "I think you just broke all my ribs!" He looked up to see a tall dark figure, standing between him and the woman, who was lying helplessly on the hood of the car, in a state of shock.

With one arm across his chest, Joey pushed himself up off the tree with his other arm, trying to walk back toward the hulking stranger. Barely able to speak, he muttered "You're gonna pay for this, you mother…"

But before Joey could finish his sentence, the stranger grabbed his face covering his mouth, so that he could not talk anymore. He felt himself lifted like a cheap toy in a crane game, where he was forced to view his victim's limp, lifeless body. Blood spread in a fan beneath the man's body. He could tell the man was dead, and he began to think he might be next. He tried to struggle, but it shot pain through his body. He was powerless against this stranger.

Georgette laid helplessly across the hood of the car, feeling the cool metal against her warm face. She stretched out her arms, trying to brace herself, and with great difficulty raised her head to try to see what was happening. She could now see some bright stars shining in the sky, with the glow of a full moon partially illuminating the area. As her gaze came back to the struggle between Joey and the stranger, she noticed the same burning white of the stars in the stranger's eyes.

Indeed the stranger's eyes burned white with fury, as the night's cool breeze blew the white strands of his hair away from his face. "An eye for an eye, and a tooth for a tooth," he said sternly. With both hands grasping Joey's head, he began to squeeze. His skull began to make small popping sounds. Tight gurgling sounds bubbled up through his open mouth, but his airwaves were closing off preventing him from screaming through the agonizing pain. He could feel his eyes now bulging, then abruptly his head smashed together like a pumpkin being thrown to the ground. Joey's body slumped to the ground. The stranger stood over the body and wailed "Vengeance is mine!"

Georgette managed to finally push herself up, where she could sit on the edge of the car. She looked down at the sidewalk, where she saw Joey's lifeless body next to her beloved Howard's body. Quivering with fear, she looked back up to see what the stranger would do next, uncertain of her own fate. But he was gone in a flash.

CHAPTER 6:

SEARCHING FOR JUSTIFICATION

Thumos, after his intense human encounters, paced frantically back and forth. He was alone in absolute silence. The area where he stood was a vastly large expanse, full of pure, unadulterated light. It was not a blinding light, but a light that seemed to emanate from all around, leaving no shadow. There was no single source from whence the light originated. Even though this area appeared a bit plain and unimpressive, there was an overwhelming sense of calm and serenity for the beings occupying this place, known to the angels as the Neutral Realm.

"I know what I am doing is right," Thumos reasoned with himself. "All those humans, the evil humans that they were, they got what they deserved. They would rather follow in the ways of Satan and his dark forces, than follow in the ways of the Trinity. In fact, they probably got off easy."

He stopped pacing for a moment, as if he had reached a eureka moment. "Yes, exactly, after all the despicable things they have done to the Father's Children, they have received their just recompense of reward."

Thumos smiled, very proud of himself, and resumed his determined pacing. "I just need to keep going. There will be more angels of the Agathon who will keep me informed of the evil, of the terrible things which more humans will no doubt carry out."

He slammed the tip of his staff-like weapon, his rhabdos, into the ground. "And when they do so, I shall be there to make them pay. Just like I have *always* done for the Father."

"Thumos, my brother!" shouted a voice suddenly.

Thumos stopped, looking up and around, startled out of his preoccupation. Floating above him, he looked to see a familiar face. It was the archangel, Raphael.

"Thumos, I have not seen you in a very long time," said Raphael kindly as he landed next to Thumos. They embraced as good friends, laughed, and stepped back from each other, with their hands still on each others' shoulders.

"It is truly good to see you, my friend," said Thumos cheerfully. "I am grateful to see a fellow angel of the light. How did you know I was here?"

"Your old compatriot, Tachu, is very fast and very stealthy. Thumos, we must reminisce together soon," continued a smiling Raphael. "We have so many great memories to share, hard-fought battles to recount." Raphael's demeanor grew more somber, and his arms fell to his side. "But Thumos, I believe you are in grave jeopardy."

"Me? In trouble?" questioned Thumos innocently, now crossing his arms across his chest. "Raphael, why would you say such a thing?" Thumos's smile of gladness was quickly replaced by a straight face, puzzled eyes.

"We, the archangels, are searching for you," answered Raphael. "And it is not for a friendly social call, from what I hear. Have you been on Earth, going rogue again or something?"

"Going rogue?" said Thumos, now sounding more irritated. "And 'again'? What do you mean by leveling these accusations against me,

Raphael? We are trusted friends, are we not?" Thumos said, slapping Raphael on his arm, while trying to resurrect a smile.

Raphael's serious look did not alter. "Of course we are friends. Close friends, in fact, do not doubt that," he said reassuringly. "I am not accusing you of anything. I felt it was important to contact you. Clear this all up. Talk angel-to-angel."

Raphael began to walk in a circle around Thumos. Thumos stood still, still with his arms crossed. Raphael continued speaking. "Everyone knows why the Father created you, Thumos. He bestowed great power and privilege on you. He has used you gloriously since your quickening."

Thumos allowed a slight grin to come over his face. He nodded in agreement.

"But it is no secret, Thumos," Raphael said, "that the Father has had fewer and fewer of those kinds of missions for you, for many centuries that has been the case now."

Thumos's slight grin gave way to a slight scowl now. His eyes began to squint.

"You have a ferocious temper, Thumos," Raphael pressed on. "With all that power the Father has bestowed upon you, comes that notorious temper."

"A temper?" Thumos retorted, still with his arms crossed. "I am Yahweh's right hand of justice. Nothing more, nothing less."

Raphael shook his head in exasperation, and continued his speech. "You are the last of Yahweh's angels whom He created, Thumos, the youngest of us all. I myself, as well as the other three archangels, were there to witness your glorious quickening." Raphael paused his pacing, looking back at Thumos, who was now sporting a slight grin of pride.

"I bear the flaming sword of vengeance against those who would carry out evil and hatred against Yahweh's righteous ones," said Thumos forcefully.

Raphael laughed in agreement. "Oh yes, you certainly do *that*. We still remember to this day what Yahweh revealed to us about His purposes for you. We had no idea what humankind was going to be. That was before He breathed His life into the first man and woman. But Yahweh specifically created you to protect His children, to be dispatched on His specific missions. That became more clear after Adam and Eve's great fall."

"I am not the only protector of the Children amongst the angelic host," said Thumos, finally relaxing a bit. He held up his hands, puzzled.

"Oh of course you are not, yet, Yahweh has always relied on you for that more heavily than any of His other angels," Raphael said.

"We archangels saw what the Father had to do to contain you during the Epikentro. By then, there were only three of us archangels left. You were so distraught over what the Romans were doing to Jesus the Christ. The three of us could not contain you, and Yahweh had to intervene. After that is when things began to change for you, is it not?"

"I remember the Epikentro, Raphael," replied Thumos, in a low growl. "Yahweh's missions for me grew more-and-more infrequent after that, for some reason. That often infuriated me," Thumos said, throwing his hands up in the air.

"'Peace, be still' is the answer I would hear frequently from the Trinity," Thumos said sadly. "But I was not created to be an instrument of peace," he said as his demeanor angered. "I could stand by no longer."

"So it was after that, when you have been known to, at times, take it upon yourself to, shall I say, 'fill in the gaps' you were seeing in Yahweh's plans," said Raphael as he stopped behind Thumos, unsure of what kind of response to expect.

"I have no idea of what you are referring to, Raphael," said Thumos dryly.

"Oh come on, Thumos," said Raphael in a mocking laugh. He resumed his circling pace. "You do not have to pretend with me. Maybe the other angels are unaware of this, but we archangels, we know. We are *archangels* after all, we know things, that's what we do, we have the inside track," Raphael winked.

"I am not pretending about anything, Raphael," Thumos answered, continuing his very stoic stance, looking straight ahead, refusing to make any eye contact with him.

"Do you want me to give you the list?" Raphael said sarcastically. "Even I probably do not even know of all such occasions, Thumos. Let's see…"

Raphael began to list out several historical events as he ticked them off on his fingers:

"You tried to stop the great persecution of the early church."

"I did *not* do that," Thumos said defensively.

"The onslaught of the Huns?"

"Ha, no."

"Church desecrations by the Vikings?"

"Never saw it."

"You appeared as a soldier of the Crusades?"

"I do not know what you are talking about."

"You wanted to stop the enslavements of humans."

"You are mistaken."

"The Holocaust? Remember when you killed those Nazis…"

"All right!" screamed Thumos, interrupting Raphael. Thumos threw his hands down to his side. "Enough, Raphael." Now he was staring intently into Raphael's eyes. "You speak of things you simply do not understand. I am the battle arm of Yahweh, I am His outstretched hand, meant to smite the evil of the enemy. I am the avenger of Yahweh!" Thumos roared.

"Oh you are definitely all those things, Thumos," Raphael said very calmly. "I was there at your very beginning. But when you take Yahweh's laws into your own hands, you are playing with fire, my friend. You are taking this vigilante thing to a whole new level." Raphael stopped his pacing, putting his hands on his hips, staring straight at Thumos. "Before, you carried out these acts of terror in stealth, or at least you *thought* you were. Now, you are being brazen about it. And I am not even sure I know just how many times you have struck lately, but I know assuredly it is more within the last few weeks than you carried out in all the centuries prior!"

Thumos huffed in disgust, turning away from Raphael. He began to walk away.

"Please Thumos, heed my words. Beware, Satan and sin are crouching at the door. Look around, look at all the other angels who have succumbed to his sinister, twisted logic, joining forces with him. You are a prime target for him, Thumos. Do not give place to the Devil. You, of all angels, know him. For the sake of all that is Godly and good, you worked closely with him once-upon-a-time. *I* know him all too well, as well as you do."

Thumos threw his hands upward, and spun around to face Raphael, who now was rising over him. "Raphael, you know me. You know that will never happen to me."

"Take heed, lest you fall, Thumos. I will beseech the Son, the Great Advocate, on your behalf," Raphael shouted back.

Thumos called out defiantly. "You can forget about telling the other archangels where I am, Raphael. I will be gone before you can return with them."

"I know that Thumos, I wanted to try to talk some sense into you first. But we *will* find you. May you stay strong in the Lord." With the sound of a sizzling lightning bolt, Raphael was gone.

"I am Satan's worst nightmare," Thumos said out loud to no one, with his teeth clenched together in anger. "Vengeance is mine, I will repay!" Thumos's voice reverberated. Another sound of a sizzling lightning bolt blasted out, then all was quiet once again in the Neutral Realm.

CHAPTER 7:

TERROR IN KANSAS CITY, MO

"It has been nearly a year of planning," said George Akram, older of the two Akram brothers, to his younger brother Peter. "And tonight is the night, " he said confidently, gently patting the top of their car, as he climbed into the driver's seat.

Peter pumped his clenched fist downward, as he slid into the front passenger seat, grinning from ear-to-ear. "Yes, brother, tonight *is* the night," said Peter Akram, to his older brother George, tousling his curly jet-black head of hair, looking out the window from the passenger side of their inconspicuous Honda Civic. He breathed in deeply, filling his lungs with the hot, humid air. "Finally, all these months of preparation are going to pay off for us. They will know who we are after this night." He grinned broadly, reveling in their accomplishments.

George pulled out of the driveway, and jetted down the street. Moments later, they arrived at a self-storage complex. He pulled carefully into the parking lot, and drove toward the back of the complex, to a place farthest from the street, and parked their car behind one of the larger of the storage units.

It was a hot, sunny day, as the brothers exited their vehicle. They opened the garage door of their storage unit, and were greeted with the unmistakable smell of carbon and metal. A plain white, windowless old panel van was parked sideways, right inside the garage door of their storage unit. It was clearly blocking the view of whatever was stashed in the back of the storage unit.

"The FSA is going to be so proud of us, and the world will see that we cannot be ignored any longer," Peter said, with great excitement in his voice. "Shazid will probably want to reward us," he added. "Especially if there are Jews and Christians among our victims."

"Calm down, Peter, and start loading the van with our gear," commanded George sharply, as he inclined his head toward the rear of their self-storage unit, giving his little brother Peter a stiff nudge. George pulled a large, long envelope sticking well out of his back pocket, and opened it. "Everything is here." "Passports, cash, two one-way airline tickets to Istanbul. Very good."

"Don't forget to grab the suitcases," George ordered. "We will need our clothes and things for the trip, as we will never again return to this country of arrogant fools."

They eventually finished the loading process, and stopped, facing the open rear doors of the van. Both of the brothers were drenched in sweat from the muggy heat and stale air of the storage unit.

"We have spent the last year amassing this great arsenal of weapons," said George, as he motioned with his hand over their large collection of guns and ammunition, knives, and explosives, now all packed into the van. "And no one has ever suspected that here, in this small suburb of Gladstone, we have been quietly developing our plot to punish the puny 'City of Fountains,'" he said, with a sarcastic inflection about Kansas City's nickname.

"I only wish mother and father could open their eyes, and support us," said Peter. "They moved us to this country of infidels when we were so young, and I don't remember anything about our homeland of Istanbul."

"Well brother," responded George, "your eyes will behold the beauty of Istanbul very soon, for we shall fly there after our work tonight is done."

"I can't wait for that," said Peter, with a gleam in his eye. "If only mother and father could go with us."

"Peter, you know that will never happen," said George sternly. "You know the plan. After we have finished Allah's work tonight, we shall return to our house, and ensure that mother and father never see another sunrise." George's tone began to grow more and more cold and disconnected.

"They must be punished for their betrayals," George continued. "They tried to hide us from the grace of Allah, and from our brothers-at-arms. They thought they could suppress our will, change us into weak *Americans*," he said disgustingly. "But they were wrong. We have been brought to the light, thanks to the Internet allowing us to reconnect with our heritage. Praise Allah, that our eyes were opened."

"Yes, praise Allah!" shouted Peter.

"Sssshhhh," retorted George, holding his hand up. "Not here, but later, you can say such things."

Peter, with a child-like giddiness, answered "This city will never know what hit them. Many men, women, and children will die tonight. America's Midwest is too distant from both coasts, and they will never expect nor be prepared for the likes of us."

George, continuing in his stoic tone, said "The Power & Light District is such an extravagant place. It is the perfect example of what is wrong with the people of this country. They are fat and lazy, and have far more than they could ever need, yet men, women, and children in so many other countries don't even have enough to eat. We will teach these stupid ingrates a lesson they won't forget. I can't wait to hear about it in the news afterwards!"

George and Peter finished packing up their van, and just before 10pm, pulled slowly out of the sleepy suburb of Gladstone to drive to downtown Kansas City. The city was abuzz with all kinds of night-time activity, as the Akram brothers drove down Main Street, passed by the popular downtown streetcar, and found a quiet street a few blocks away where they could park unnoticed. They climbed into the back of the van, put on their black stocking caps and skull half face masks, further adorning their all-black outfits with which they had clothed themselves. They proceeded to arm themselves to the teeth.

"Get two of the pistols, Peter, and your knife" ordered George. "You can slide the guns into your pants behind your back, and the knife on your side. And put some extra ammo in your pockets."

"I am not a child," answered an annoyed Peter, as he followed George's instructions. "I know what I need to do."

George grabbed a nine millimeter Uzi, which he slung over his shoulder. Peter followed suit. "And take this too," said George, as he placed a string of hand grenades over Peter's shoulder on the opposite side of the Uzi.

It was getting dark now, but despite the leftover heat of the day still hanging in the air, their final adornment was a black bomber jacket which concealed all their weaponry. They exited their van to begin walking toward the popular entertainment destination of downtown Kansas City, the Power & Light District.

George and Peter rounded a corner, near the intersection of 13th and Grand. They were walking westward, and could see the last rays of the setting sun, disappearing behind the tall skyscrapers of downtown. They could hear the music of a live band coming from ahead of them, where lots of partygoers were dancing at the bandstand of Power & Light.

Suddenly, George noticed a young woman walking toward them. She was quite tall, compared to the average female, and athletically built. Her long blonde, almost white hair was pulled back in a ponytail, and she was dressed as though ready for a workout at the gym. He glanced at his brother Peter, their dark brown eyes met, glimmering at each other in understanding.

"Our first victim" whispered George. Peter nodded.

With just a few feet left between the brothers and the young woman, George and Peter slowed down their pace to get a better look at the woman. George looked at Peter once again, tapping his finger to his own neck. In a hushed tone, he said "Do you see what I see?"

Peter nodded once again. "A cross necklace."

The woman stopped and stood a few steps away from the men, in between them. "Oh, are you admiring my cross necklace, gentlemen?" she asked, seemingly oblivious to the strange attire and equipment that these men were sporting. She reached up to cup it in her palm, glancing back and forth to the men on either side of her.

"I wouldn't say we were *admiring* it, lady," said George. "More like *despising* it." He began to slide a large hunting knife out of its sheath on his belt. He looked across at Peter, standing on the other side of the woman, and chuckled. He saw Peter following suit, drawing out his own similar knife.

George looked back at the woman. "Tonight, you will be the first of many to pay for America's tyranny," he said with an ominous tone. He fully expected to see terror in the woman's eyes. George tilted his head in a puzzled way, as he saw, not terror, but a smile. The woman was still just smiling back at them.

Angered by her lack of respectful fear, George lunged at the woman, dragging her several feet away from where they originally stood. He wrapped one arm around her waist, as he jumped behind her, spinning her around facing toward Peter. George quickly brought his knife up to her throat, walking the woman backwards. The woman instinctively reached up with both hands, trying to hold back George's arm as he drew the knife in close to her. Still, the woman uttered no sound.

Peter shouted excitedly, "We will spill her blood tonight!"

George's backward stepping stopped. No blood was spilling.

Peter yelled "What are you waiting for, George! You aren't getting cold feet now, are you?"

George retorted, "No, of course not." Peter could now tell George was exerting all the force he could muster, trying to slash the woman's throat, but was stuck. He raised his second hand, and now had a double grip on the knife, but still was unable to cut her. George continued, "I…can't…move…my…hands…," his voice straining. .

Peter ran toward them brandishing his knife, said "George, you are such a weakling, I will take care of this fool!" But just as Peter got within arm's reach, George's knife swung out under the control of the woman. George's knife sliced Peter's arm and ripped the fabric of his jacket. Peter shrieked in pain, and shouted "What the hell are you doing, George, you idiot?"

George yelled, "That wasn't me, she made me do it!" Both men stared at each other in disbelief for only a moment, just as the woman spun around swapping positions with George. She was able to overpower him, grabbing his knife away from him. Now the woman held George at knife point, in a complete role reversal. George could feel the blade starting to cut his throat, but was powerless to do anything.

Peter, now red hot in anger, shouted at the woman "Time for you to die!"

The amazingly calm woman finally spoke again. "I don't think so, Mr. Akram, I believe you've got that backwards." George felt his knife ripped from his hand, just as the woman spun him back around facing her.

George screamed, as he felt the woman land a massive head butt into his forehead. Dazed, he fell to the ground as he watched the woman run toward Peter.

George managed to shout, "Peter, get her!" He watched a startled Peter fumbling with his gun strap, desperately trying to find his weapon. Just as Peter swung his Uzi from under his jacket, the woman was standing right in front of him.

Wagging her finger at him, the woman said "I don't think so." Grabbing the gun and pulling it from his hands, she bent the weapon as though it were only a toy, and threw it to the ground, a smile still on her face.

George watched in shock as Peter grappled with this woman. Never in his life had he seen a woman so strong and able to defend herself. He rose to his feet just as the woman planted a roundhouse kick to Peter's head, which sent him crashing to the ground. The woman stood over Peter, picked him back up to his feet by the back of his shirt, and then landed an elbow punch to the other side of his face, sending him sprawling to the ground once again. Everything was happening so fast, and George felt like he was stuck in quicksand, unable to help. She again grabbed Peter back to his feet, and began punching his face like a boxer punching a speed bag. George could tell the woman's knuckles were covered in Peter's blood. How could she be doing this, he thought to himself, bewildered. As Peter slumped to the ground, his hat and mask now gone, George was horrified at all the blood covering his brother.

Anger welled up in George, as he finally felt the strength coming back into his legs. He screamed "I'm going to kill you!" He pulled out his 44 magnum handgun. He got off several rounds, but the woman stood there defiantly and unscathed. Infuriated, George rushed her, pistol leading the way until he held the gun point blank at her forehead. It did not even register with him that the woman just stood there unflinchingly waiting for him.

George yelled "You can go to hell!" and started to pull the trigger. Before the pistol's hammer could strike, the woman cuffed the barrel of the gun away from her face with such force that the pistol exploded into a cloud of fine gray dust. George did not have time to absorb this information before the woman's fist landed a crushing blow to his jaw. Staggering, he tried to ward off the other bone breaking blows as they eventually drove him to the pavement. George sprawled out on the sidewalk next to Peter, gasping for breath.

As if hearing her from the back of a cave, George heard the woman say "You just got your asses kicked by a woman, boys. Tell that to those male chauvinist pigs of the FSA."

He heard footsteps walking away, then that sound stopped abruptly. The woman seemed to remember something, and slowly turned to regard them. "Oh, but wait, I just remembered, you won't be able to tell them," she said in a sarcastic voice. "But I think the message is going to get through to them anyway." Through swollen eyes, George noted several curious bystanders who had gathered, some with their phones out recording the last few moments of action. The woman walked back over to him, her eyes narrowing tightly. She squatted down, her elbows on her knees.

"And by the way, there aren't any seventy virgins waiting for you boys where you're headed." She stood, and pointed her index fingers toward them. "May fire come down from heaven and consume you!" she shouted. Huge flames swooped down from above, and engulfed both men. She walked calmly away, to the shrieking and anguished screams of the brothers as they burned. Many of the bystanders screamed and ran away, while some people applauded and cheered. Through the smoke and haze they heard the woman say "Vengeance is mine!" And then she was gone.

CHAPTER 8:

A HAZY DREAM

The soft, faint glow of the sunrise was just beginning to stream through the Madigan master bedroom window. A gentle breeze through the open window lightly tossed the curtain sheer back and forth.

Despite the idyllic peaceful Miami morning, Lane's sleeping body writhed. Beads of sweat dotted his forehead, as his hands clenched tight over the sheets.

"What? No!" cried out a desperate sounding Lane, as he shot straight up in bed.

"Lane, honey, are you okay?" said Janie, as she in turn jumped out of bed, in her satin pajamas. She glanced around the room, half-expecting to see an intruder. When she realized no one else was there, she darted around to Lane's side of the bed and sat next to him. "What is it? Were you having a bad dream? Is something wrong?"

"Huh?" responded Lane, in a state of confusion. "What are you talking about?" he continued, wagging his head as he tried to shake himself out of this stupor.

"Something really startled you, babe. You just shot straight up in bed and called out 'What? No!' She drew in a breath and said, "You don't remember this?" Placing her hand over her heart she gave him a wry glance, "You just about gave me a heart attack!"

Lane looked back at the clock, now realizing where he was and who was speaking to him. "I don't know, dear, just some kind of weird, bad dream I guess. I don't remember any of it right now. But it's six a.m., so I need to get up and get with it anyway." He trailed his finger down the side of her face tenderly. "Sorry if I startled you, Janie-baby. That's pretty odd for me to wake up like that."

"Well that's quite the understatement," Janie answered, now grinning at Lane. "You never wake up that quickly, 'Mr. Snorehead'. Usually I'm the one practically jumping up and down on you trying to wake you up!"

"Hey, look here beautiful, you feel free to jump up and down on me any time you want," Lane said with a sparkle in his eye, a big grin sweeping across his face.

"Hmmm…now that sounds like you're trying to proposition me, Officer, " answered Janie in a seductive voice. Suddenly her tone changed. "But we're going to have to rain check that little fun, mister," as she leaned over and gave Lane a brief kiss.

Janie's shoulder length blonde hair bounced playfully, and her blue eyes glistened in the morning light. Lane loved how she took pride in keeping her tall willowy body trim, and imagined her in workout clothes getting ready for a run.

Lane grabbed her hand "Hey, wait a minute, what are you talking about? Don't leave me hanging here, you big tease," he said laughing.

"As usual, you don't hear as well as I do, buddy," Janie answered, just as their bedroom door flew open and in walked Elizabeth. Lane looked back at Janie, grinning sheepishly, as he contemplated the embarrassing situation they just avoided.

"Morning!" shouted Elizabeth, still wearing her Disney princess pajamas. She ran and jumped into her dad's arms, giggling. Janie dove down onto the bed, and began to tickle Elizabeth. The four year old youngster laughed with glee, as her dark curly hair jostled playfully.

"Dadda-dadda, mommy is tickling me. Make her stop!" Elizabeth said, barely able to get the words out through her laughter. Elizabeth's brown eyes pleaded with her mom, yet there was also a look of sheer joy, not really wanting the tickling to stop.

Lane said "You brought this on yourself by being so cute, little Lizzy. Your mama can't help it." And with that, he began to tickle both Janie and Elizabeth.

"That's not at all fair!" Janie called out, as she jumped out of the bed, laughing and out of breath. "Somebody around here has to get breakfast started for you two."

"Yay, breakfast" shouted Elizabeth. Her dad let her escape his tickling clutches, as she bounced out of bed and ran off toward the kitchen.

Lane rose out of bed, and slipped on a Miami police department t-shirt. He spoke loudly so Elizabeth could hear him, to preempt the inevitable request he knew was coming. "Dad is going to make his famous blueberry banana pancakes this morning."

"Yippee!" shouted an elated Elizabeth from down the hall. "I can't wait!"

Lane looked over at Janie as she was putting on her robe, and said "Why don't you grab yourself a cup of coffee, dear, check out what's happening on the news this morning, and I'll get breakfast covered? You've got a busy day ahead, so you should relax just a little longer."

Janie smiled lovingly at Lane, nodding her head in approval. Lane walked over to where she was standing, gave her a big hug and they kissed again. "Yeah, you hot mama, I'm hoping we can cash in that rain check tonight," Lane said with a wink.

"You better believe it, you hunka-hunka burnin' love," said Janie slyly. She slapped Lane's butt as he walked out of the bedroom.

Janie came out of the bedroom a moment later, to find Lane had already poured her a hot cup of coffee. "Dark roast with a splash of cream," Janie said. "Just the way I like it," she said as she cupped her hands around the mug and headed over to sit down on the couch. She turned on the TV as Elizabeth sat next to her intently coloring in her Disney coloring book.

Lane began mixing up the pancake batter and began to ponder that startling dream. He thought to himself that some faint memories of it were starting to come to him, but just not enough to have any strong recollection yet. His thoughts of wrestling with those memories were suddenly interrupted.

"Johnny Whiteman was found dead in a streetside waterway in front of his high-rise New York penthouse early this morning," reported the early morning newscaster on the TV.

"Whiteman?" Lane questioned out loud. "I know that name."

Janie answered "How would you know somebody all the way up in New York? Is he someone famous or something?"

Lane spoke again. "Wait, yes he is someone famous. Well, *in*famous, I should say. He is one nasty bad guy out there."

"Whiteman was an infamous, long-suspected, but never proven guilty, high-profile pornography ring leader," continued the reporter as if on cue.

"Well he sounds like an awful person," Janie said. "Can't say that the world is going to miss someone like that," she added.

"Definitely not," said Lane. "But he's probably got a long line of successors waiting to take over the reins. But maybe this will slow down his operation for a while. That guy is connected to crime syndicates all over the country, probably the world. We've seen some of his handiwork here in Miami, unfortunately."

"...is currently being reported as a suicide" continued the TV newscaster. "But a police spokesman has said foul play cannot yet be ruled out."

Lane focused back on his pancake batter, continuing to work on mixing everything up. Suddenly he dropped the spoon into the bowl. "Dammit, it can't be," he said out loud.

Janie glanced over at Elizabeth to see if the youngster noticed her dad's use of profanity. Elizabeth didn't miss a beat, and continued right on with her coloring project. "Watch the colorful metaphors, dear. *Someone* is with us," Janie said, pointing her finger in Elizabeth's direction. "So what is it? Something wrong with the pancakes?"

"No, no, nothing with the pancakes," Lane said in a distracted tone. "I'm just thinking about a case at work."

"Oh, okay, dear," Janie said without really hearing what Lane was saying. Her attention had turned back to the next news story.

Lane did experience a moment of regret for using a swear word like that in front of Elizabeth. He had grown up in a church-going family where the use of profanity was highly discouraged, and regarded as nearly the same as a cardinal sin. But over the years, working in his chosen career, he had realized some people speak in those terms without even thinking twice about it. It comes as naturally as breathing to people, and he had certainly relaxed his own opinions about it. He even had added some of it to his own repertoire of words, under some circumstances, anyway.

"Colorful metaphors," as Lane referred to such language, was maybe not such a great habit, but honestly, witnessing the kinds of terrible things people did against each other, now that was what was truly bad. "If there is a God, and He is supposed to be all-knowing, and all-powerful, and all that, why would he allow people to do the terrible things they did? How could He let people suffer like they suffered? He shifted on his feet, wondering how many times he had had this conversation with himself, about whether he really believed in God anymore. Sure, it was an ideal way to live your life, but how realistic was it, really, to live a holy and pure life? He shook his head as if to dismiss the notion. When he had seen the horrific things he had seen throughout his career, believing in a caring God became harder and harder each year on the job.

Lane thought to himself *Wow, I've seriously digressed here. Back to reality.*

Lane quietly said to himself, "Could there be some connection to the Shazid case? I mean these scumbags don't seem to have anything to do with each other, but a couple of high-profile lowlifes like these guys, dead within a few hours of each other, and yet far removed geographically."

Lane shook his head, and went back to thinking. *No, that's crazy, there's no connection here. But a couple of real bad guys off the streets—can't argue with that.* A smile came across his face, as he thought about the positives of neither of these guys walking the streets anymore, as he poured some batter into the skillet.

The unmistakable smell of pancakes began to fill the air, along with some freshly brewed coffee. Janie gripped her coffee with both hands, giving her cup a deep sniff. Taking a sip, she gave out a gentle sigh of satisfaction. She set her cup down, poured coffee into another mug, and walked over to Lane. She placed her hand gently on his shoulder, as she set the cup down in front of him.

"Thanks babe," Lane said. He leaned over and gave Janie a peck on the cheek, smiling at her. "That smells delicious, just what I needed while I'm slaving over the hot griddle."

Janie laughed at his exaggeration of effort.

A few minutes later, with several blueberry banana pancakes on a platter, Lane moved over to the breakfast table and said "Order up." Elizabeth did not need to be told twice, as she instantly broke out of her coloring intensity, much to Janie's surprise. Janie smiled and said "Well I guess that little squirt is really hungry," as she got up, turned off the TV, and walked over to join Lane and Elizabeth at the table.

Janie said "Okay guys, let's pray first."

All three of the Madigans prayed in unison "Bless us oh Lord, in these thy gifts which we are about to receive from thy bounty through Christ our Lord. Amen."

Lane smiled after the "amen," looked at Janie, and said "You know I love you, right?" He was remembering the thoughts he had just moments ago about his fading faith of not too long ago, and being pleased that his lovely wife had helped work toward restoring his faith.

"You know I love you *more*, right?" Janie said with a teasing smile on her face.

"What does 'dammit' mean, Daddy?" chimed in Elizabeth, with a big mouthful of pancake. "Is it something about beavers?" she added. "I think beavers are cute, and I want to have one as a pet."

Janie shot a look of "I told you so" at Lane. Lane, with a slightly guilty grin on his face, said "Yeah, Lizzy-baby, I was looking at some beavers when I said that. Maybe later I can show you some pictures of beavers and the dams that they can build."

Lane shot back a look at Janie as if to say "Yep, you were right, watch my mouth!" All three fell silent and went back to eating their breakfast. Sunrise had started to creep in several minutes ago, and beams of light danced across the kitchen floor. The smell of pancakes and maple syrup filled the air, as all three Madigans enjoyed their family breakfast together. This day was off to a great start.

The doorbell rang, and Janie made her way over to the front door with Elizabeth tagging along with her. Janie took a moment to peer through the peephole to find Detective Jelani waiting. She quickly opened the door.

"Well good day on this beautiful mornin' to two of the loveliest ladies around!" said Ian, throwing his arms wide to emphasize the sentiment..

"Come on in, Ian," said Janie. "Lane is just about ready to roll."

"Jelani!" shouted Elizabeth, as she wrapped her arms around Ian's legs, hugging him tightly. "Can I go with you today?" she said, a wayward curl falling over her face.

Ian flashed a big grin, and said "You know that would be a blast, little one."

Janie, knowing full well that Ian was not really serious about that, spoke up. "Elizabeth, Daddy and Mr. Jelani have to go to work, and they won't have time for you to be there today. Besides, we have lots of errands to run, and I really need your help."

"Okay," Elizabeth answered in a disappointed tone. "But I want to come to the police station soon," she said, directing her demand toward Ian, her hands on her hips.

"You better believe it, kiddo," responded Ian. "I can't wait for you to come back to the station. Everyone there is just crazy about you, and loves getting to see you."

Lane walked in and said "Now who invited you in here, man. I sure didn't give you permission to bring your ugly self into my home."

"I am here to drag *your* ugly self away from these beautiful ladies, and put you to work, my friend. Let's get with it," responded Ian winking at Janie.

Lane grabbed Janie, and gave her a big kiss. "I love you my dear," he said.

Janie put both hands on Lane's cheeks and said "I love you too!"

"Okay, enough of the PDA you two," said Ian. "I haven't had coffee yet." Clapping a friendly hand on Lane's shoulder he gave him a shake on his way out of the door. "Let's roll."

Lane leaned down and kissed Elizabeth on the top of her head, then stood upright again. He ran his fingers through her hair, as he turned to walk out the door, when Elizabeth grabbed his pant leg, and said "Daddy, I want a hug too!" He bent down on one knee, they hugged each other. "I love you too, you little munchkin," and he headed out the door behind Ian.

As the door shut, his thoughts quickly turned back to the Whiteman case he heard about on the news. Once again, he was flooded with questions of connections to any other cases.

"You look like you got somethin' on your mind, partner" said Ian.

"I do," answered Lane.

"Well I need some coffee before you make me start thinkin' too hard," responded Ian. "That is our next stop, then you can pour out your heart to me all you want."

The two detectives hopped into the squad car, and took off down the street.

CHAPTER 9:

A COPYCAT EMERGES

WICHITA, KS: FAIRMOUNT NEIGHBORHOOD

The clock radio blared as it struck 7am and turned on, screaming the day's headlines. "…dubbed 'The Holy Terror', because his attacks seem to be exclusively aimed at other criminals…" Jimmy Whitaker wouldn't hate his job at Wichita State University so much except that they expected him, as the grounds keeper, to arrive so horribly early. Like before the birds started singing. Bleary eyed, he slammed his hand down onto the alarm to shut it off. Climbing out of bed, yawning and stretching, shaking his head trying to wake himself up, he stumbled out of his bedroom, down the hall and over to the front door, opened it, and grabbed his daily-delivered copy of the Wichita Eagle.

One of Jimmy's morning routines included perusing the news, reading about the latest crimes taking place in Wichita, whether on the local news websites or on social media. This activity, he knew, only served to amp his anxiety disorder. But, like a wreck by the side of the road, he was hard pressed not to look. Worse yet, what could he really do about any of it? Lock his doors? Hope for the best?

Wagging his head in disgust, he tossed the paper down onto the living room couch, and headed over to the kitchen. He started brewing his normal morning pot of coffee, walked back out to the living room, grabbed the remote, and flipped on the TV. KSAS, Wichita's Fox affiliate network, came on. "So Chief Ramsay, what are your thoughts about this national story gaining a lot of traction everywhere, as everyone is talking about this mysterious figure known as 'The Holy Terror,'" said the Fox news anchor.

"Oh my, God," shouted Jimmy in frustration, although there was no one else there to hear him bemoan the one-topic television broadcast. His disgust grew in intensity as he turned off the TV and threw the remote back on the couch. "I'd rather just check my Facebook likes than to hear any more about that stupid 'Holy Terror' idiot."

He walked back into the kitchen, then made himself a bowl of cereal. As he poured some coffee, and sat down at the kitchen table, he whipped out his trusty cell phone. Surely there would be something there. As he opened up the Facebook app on his phone, it was littered with comments and stories all about "The Holy Terror." Jimmy was a slender, wiry man. His red hair was giving way to some balding, and so for a couple of years now, he just kept a crew cut of what hair was still there. His freckled face frowned with disappointment over what he found on Facebook, or that is, what he *did not* find on Facebook, not much of interest.

Jimmy swore under his breath and slammed his phone back down onto the table. He immediately realized what he had done, grabbed his phone quickly, and turned it over to make sure he had not shattered the phone face. Fortunately he had not, and this time, he gently placed the phone down onto the table. Jimmy sighed in relief. He did not have many friends, and was in-between girlfriends at the present. His cell phone was very important to him.

Then the wheels started to turn in Jimmy's head. He started pacing around his house; it helped him think, get his blood pumping. He had his best ideas when he was walking a hole into his carpets. Now he really began talking out loud to himself a lot.

"I could do all that," he said in a confident voice. "If this 'Holy Terror' quack can do this kind of stuff, I can do it better." Jimmy completed one loop around his small living room, and he paused his pacing momentarily. Then once again, he continued his pacing, at a slightly faster rate now.

"Yes, I can disguise myself," he continued speaking, his voice getting a little higher in excitement. "I can fix up and paint an old truck for driving around town. I can go to the gun show to buy some weapons that are harder to trace." He stopped pacing abruptly, and looked down as if surprised that his movement had stopped. He realized he had smashed his thigh into the recliner, momentarily forgetting where he was. He sidestepped, and continued walking determinedly.

"I've got a squeaky clean record, so no one would suspect me in a million years. I could run around after dark at night. If that 'Holy Terror' can get this much press, wait till the media sees what I can do. I'll show them—it's time to take this city back from the criminals!"

"Ow!" Jimmy screamed. He looked down to see that now he had stubbed his toe into the leg of the couch. He realized that the time was getting away from him. At that, he glanced at his watch.

"Nuts, I'm going to be late!" he exclaimed.

Jimmy dressed, ran out the door, and drove to work. But all day long, he had a really hard time concentrating. He just kept thinking about all his plans, and how he so desperately wanted to exact a little justice in his own town, vigilante style.

The very next weekend, Jimmy attended the local gun show. He showed up at the Century II Expo Hall, anxious to find some good weaponry. He walked confidently through the front door, like a movie cowboy shoving his way through the swinging doors of a saloon. The place was bustling. He could hear the dull roar of a sea of people carrying on many different conversations. Food vendors wandered the halls selling their wares. His nose detected an odd combination of smells. Maybe it was cleaning oils, gun powder, stale beer, and greasy food. All things being equal, he thought a corn dog and some root beer sounded like a great lunch idea. Wandering through various booths, he stopped at a promising one.

"Surely you have some good ARs here, don't you?" Jimmy asked of a woman standing behind the booth table.

"We sure do, sugar, we have some of the best assault rifles you can find around here, but stop calling me 'Shirley'," the woman replied matter-of-factly.

"Sorry, I wasn't trying to call you 'Shirley', I meant the word 'surely', as in 'certainly'," Jimmy answered apologetically.

"I'm just messin' with ya, hun," the woman answered with a laugh. "That's from an old movie, 'Airplane'," she said with a good natured shrug. "You're probably too young to get it."

Jimmy just stood there staring at her, as he definitely did not get the joke. Awkwardly he said, "Uh, no, guess not."

"Shoot, that's okay," said the woman. "But you know what's really funny? My name *really* is 'Shirley'," she said, thrusting her shoulder forward to emphasize the name tag she was wearing.

Jimmy chuckled slightly. "Oh yeah, that is pretty funny."

Shirley continued. "All righty, so what are you lookin' for, hun? Are you a hunter?"

Jimmy fumbled over his words, growing nervous over his first time of looking at guns, let alone, trying to *buy* a gun. "Uh, yeah, hunting, that's right."

"What's the matter, cat got your tongue?" said Shirley. "Have you ever fired a gun, like, before, sugar?" She grabbed an AR-15, an empty magazine, and walked around the table, to stand next to Jimmy.

"First, check the chamber to see if it's empty," she said, pulling back the bolt to show an empty chamber. "Next, pop the magazine in like this," she said as she inserted the magazine into the bottom of the gun, popping her hand on the bottom of it to ensure it was secure. "Now, you're ready to shoot." He held the gun up in a shooting position. "This automatic rifle is a semi-automatic. You know what that is, right, honey?"

Jimmy shook his head, still acting nervous. He shoved his hands into his pockets. This entire ordeal better be worth it.

Shirley smiled again. "You're a real greenie, ain't ya? Okay, a semi-automatic is a gun where you have to pull the trigger to fire each round. An automatic weapon is one where you just hold the trigger, and the gun keeps right on firin' till you empty that mag. Clear?"

Jimmy nodded, swallowed heavily and stood there staring at her.

"Okay, here, you try it. Now don't be nervous," Shirley said. She popped the magazine out, and handed that and the gun to Jimmy. "Now, what do you do first?" Jimmy noted that she'd adopted the same pitched voice as his teachers in Oakview High school had.

Jimmy pulled the bolt back, and looked inside the chamber, ensuring it was empty.

"Very good, sugar. Then what?" the woman said.

Jimmy inserted the magazine, and popped his hand on the bottom to make sure it was inserted all the way. He looked up at the woman, smiling as though very proud of himself. Then he lifted the gun up to shoulder, and took aim over the table.

"Well, you are a fast learner, honey," Shirley said, wiping a sweaty, hammy hand over her forehead.

"Can I get this assault rifle as an automatic?" Jimmy asked.

"Hold on there, rookie, this is not an 'assault rifle," Shirley corrected him. "AR, for this gun, stands for 'ArmaLite Rifle. It ain't no assault rifle, hun. One step at-a-time, sugar, I don't think you need any automatic weapons just yet. We can't have you goin' off half-cocked, and shootin' somebody by accident, now can we?" she said with a laugh, her wig sliding slightly askew. Huh, apparently Shirley was not really a blonde with fat old-woman curls.

A serious look came over Jimmy's face. "Oh, uh, no, no, definitely not. I was just wondering if it came that way."

"Sometime down the road, you could look at puttin' a bump stock on that sucker," Shirley said. "A 'bump stock' is another piece of equipment you can buy that turns a semi-automatic into an automatic. But those have gotten a lot of god-awful press over the years, and they're hard to come by these days. Why, I just don't think you need to worry your pretty little head with somethin' like that for now."

Jimmy set the AR back down on the table. "What about a pistol? What would you recommend?"

"For a beginner, you sure are diving in head first, aint' ya sweety?" Shirley answered. "Personally, I just prefer the nine mil. It's an easy gun to fire and maintain. The ammo is pretty easy to find." She walked back around the table, and grabbed another gun, then shuffled back over to Jimmy. "This Smith and Wesson nine millimeter is a classic." She ejected the magazine, popped it back in, and pulled the hammer, showing off her prowess with the gun. "I own one just like this," she said, handing it to Jimmy.

Jimmy mimicked her motions with that gun as well, then pointed it across the table at nothing, and pulled the trigger. He smiled, and set that gun down on the table. "I like it," he said with a grin.

"Well, sugar?" responded Shirley. " Which one?"

"All," Jimmy said in his best Arnold Schwarzenegger voice. He laughed out loud. "Now I'm quotin' movies at you. You know? 'The Terminator'?"

"Yeah, I got that, honey. Pretty doggone funny alright," Shirley said with a smile. "Lemme have your credit card, hun."

"Oh, no Shirley, I've got cash. Here you go," Jimmy said, as he shoved several hundred dollar bills into her face.

"Well look at you, ya big spender. We love cash here," Shirley said with an eager smile, as she took the money. "Lemme get you some change."

"Nah, it's not worth messin' with that, Shirley," said Jimmy. "You've been a big help to me, and I appreciate that."

Shirley smiled once again. "Well that's awfully nice of you, sweetie. Thanks a bunch. If you want even more help, get on over to Range 54, over on Kellogg. Those boys over there will help you out a bunch. They can have you shootin' like a pro in no time."

"Thanks again Shirley," Jimmy said as he picked up both guns. "Don't I have to fill out some papers or something?"

"You're a pussy cat, sugar, you just go on and I'll deal with that myself, later," Shirley said.

Jimmy's green eyes squinted a bit with a big grin that swept over his face. He winked at her, and walked away.

Shirley laughed under her breath as she watched him swagger down the hallway, and wagged her head. "That boy is probably gonna shoot off his own hand or foot. Lord have mercy." But she noted how confident Jimmy was looking now, as he strutted out of the expo center, looking very proud of himself. She felt good knowing she had helped boost his confidence a bit. Shirley turned to the next customer. "Hey, sugar, what can I do you for?"

CHAPTER 10:

OUTSIDE THE BOUNDARIES OF TIME

Five of the Agathon, the angels of light, congregated together in the Neutral Realm. One of the angels, a tall, slender one known as Phluaros, broke the silence. Speaking in a hushed tone, he tried not to void the setting of serenity and tranquility.

"The Neutral Realm is such a great place of comfort and rest. I always find refuge here," said Phluaros in a very relaxed tone.

"Affirmative," said Krino, another of the angels assembled. He rose to his feet from a sitting position, his thickly muscled body seeming to dwarf Phuluaros. "This demilitarized zone provides us with a much needed respite from time-to-time. Even though it is not the same as actually being in the presence of Yahweh, you can still feel His presence all around you."

Phlularos responded. "I have even seen some of the Makria here, but not very often."

"Yes, but they have to be in a desperate situation to seek refuge *here*." said Krino. "All of Yahweh's created angels can come here, but the Makria generally do not relish the idea of being here, as we Agathon do."

"What do you know about Thumos?" asked Krino, speaking in strident tones.

"Well I heard he has become some sort of vigilante on Earth." exclaimed Phluaros, in a disgusted tone. "I have heard rumors that Thumos has done this kind of thing a few times over the centuries, but nothing compared to what he is doing now."

Krino looked around in several directions, taking note of who was listening. Furrowing his brow, Krino replied quietly. "What? Why? I mean, why is he *that* concerned with the Children? They all die eventually anyway. One way or another, they all end up in our realm whether they like it or not."

Phlularos shifted his weight, leaning more toward Krino. "I really cannot comprehend Thumos," he said. "I suppose you have to serve in the ministry division to have some inkling of what he is trying to accomplish."

"Many of us *are* ministering spirits, sent to help the Father's children," said Eleos, another of the Agathon. He was also a tall and slender looking angel, much like Phluaros. "But Thumos has always apparently had a very unique role in that way. That is for certain."

He joined the conversation so abruptly, that Phluaros and Krino were both startled slightly. "Those angels are very sympathetic regarding the variety of plights in which the children find themselves," said Eleos.

Kategoreo, a large and lumbering angel, now spoke up as he walked toward the group. "But typically the Children put themselves in those plights. They have every opportunity. Created in the image of the Father, innumerable blessings from the Father, and a beautiful place to live. What more could they ask for?"

"But the original two ruined it for everyone!" Eleos chimed in again, throwing his hands up in disgust. "Earth may be beautiful, and the Children have many great blessings, but it is a fallen world, and a fallen race. Do you not understand, that is why the Father's Son had to live there, as one of them, for a short time?"

After listening to everyone else's commentary, Krino finally jumped back into the discussion. Stepping into the middle of the group, waving an accusational finger at no one in particular, he said "Now do not get me started on that one! That is one situation I will *never* understand."

"It is not something which has been revealed to us angels," answered Eleos, patting his chest with both his hands. "Even so, I so wish I could understand it all. I long to figure all that out."

Periago, who had been listening intently to the rest of the conversation, now began to speak. "But as fallen as the Children are, you have to admit, some of them are actually very talented. They have some singers that are amazing. Some love to sing almost as much as we do! " He swept his arms around the circle. "Why, there are some pretty impressive Children serving right now in the presence of the Father, those who have left the earthly realm and become part of ours. For humans, I have to say, some of them are surprisingly impressive. Then some are still living on Earth, whom I cannot wait to see what they will do here in the heavenly realm." He stared off into the distance, as though imagining something.

"You mean *if* they are here in the heavenly realm," said Krino, in a reprimanding tone. "The Father has made it crystal clear that only He truly knows the destiny of all humankind. No one else is capable of knowing that. None of us has seen the *alternative* place, and we all want to keep it that way," he said with a wry smile.

Flashing a look around, as if to see if the coast was clear, Periago continued in a quieter tone. "So who are some of your *favorite* Children?" he asked the others, as he shifted his weight, leaning toward the center of the group.

Something that sounded like a clap of thunder rolled in the distance. At the same time, that pure light of the Neutral Realm seemed to flash off-and-on a few times, as if someone were flickering a light switch.

All the other angels scowled back at Periago. They all threw their hands, palms facing outward to Periago, giving him a silent look that said "What were you thinking?"

"You know that the Father does not like for us to have favorites amongst His Children," said Krino, yet again in a quietly harsh and reprimanding tone.

"Okay, okay, I know that," said Periago. He looked sheepishly at all the surprised faces staring back at him. "Of course they are all equal in the Father's eyes, but that does not stop *me* from having some favorites myself," he said, holding his hand up to his mouth, as if trying to hide his words. "It is too difficult to avoid considering how much more talented some are than others."

A bit louder clap of thunder sounded, as if the source of the sound was a little closer this time. That startled all of them. Periago said "That was a little shocking. We all jumped, and we never startle easily."

"Would you just stop?" said Kategoreo, very exasperated with Periago. "We love *all* of the Father's children equally, of course." He spoke intentionally loudly, as if trying to make amends for Periago's mishap. "What you meant was there are some whose light shines greater than others, that is impossible to ignore."

All the angels looked at each other. One by one they all nodded their heads, spoke loudly in agreement, affirming Kategoreo's statement. There were a few awkward moments as throats cleared, feet shuffled, and eyes looked downward in embarrassment.

Suddenly, Michael the Archangel appeared. All chatter ceased, as they stood at attention.

Michael spoke in a very commanding, authoritative voice. "My angelic friends, it is time for all frivolity to cease and desist. We have a job to do. The Master has summoned you for a journey." Michael started to leave, then quickly turned back around. Everyone else stopped abruptly, as they had begun to file in behind him. "And of course, bring your rhabdoses!" With that, Michael quickly swirled around, and began to march away from them emphatically.

"Uh-oh," said Phluaros in a hushed tone.

The cavalier looks on all their faces turned into something of a more determined look. Taking rhabdoses on any journey was a sure sign of impending battle. They now all knew unquestionably who was awaiting them at the end of this impending journey. An electrical sizzling sound culminated with a thunderous pop, and they all vanished from the Neutral Zone.

Thumos stood at-the-ready, like a sentinel standing guard. He could sense something familiar was approaching. His eyes darted around, as he could see the misty, London-fog-like cover hid whatever surface there was here. It was a much darker area, far less light than the Neutral Realm, but certainly not utter darkness, like in the Banished Realm. It seemed like what you would find at dusk on Earth.

His vigilant gaze rose upward slowly where he could see the sky-like setting, dotted with points of light. Many, many more points of light than that of a star-filled sky on Earth. But these points of light were not stars, they were simply light. It was a much different feeling than the serenity of the far-away Neutral Zone, yet it was clear the presence of Yahweh actually was here also. This was the Twilight Realm, the primary habitat of all angels, both the Agathon, and the Makria (the angels of darkness).

Thumos suddenly heard the sound of a sonic boom come from behind him. He knew instantly who had arrived, and he slowly turned around. His eyes met with two archangels, Raphael and Gabriel. Thumos noted how they both appeared in a fighting stance. He could see the distinguishing marks of the sunburst tattoos on each shoulder of them both. No other angels sported those marks.

"Thumos, how can you justify your actions?" questioned Raphael, who pointed his finger vehemently toward Thumos.

"You have been wreaking havoc on Earth, Thumos, and it is time for us to put a stop to it," demanded Gabriel, as he slammed the tip of his rhabdos down onto the ground, generating an ominous sound which reverberated around them.

Raphael looked at Gabriel, and gave a single nod of his head in agreement. He then looked back at Thumos angrily.

"Why seek justification for dealing out justice?" Thumos roared back, immediately taking a defensive tone. He shook his fist, and said "Those with whom I interact are simply receiving a 'just recompense of reward.'"

"But you are putting yourself in the place of Yahweh," retorted Gabriel, taking a deliberate step toward Thumos.

"I am simply an instrument of Yahweh, acting as I always have acted, in His service," answered Thumos, now settling into a calmer, more reserved tone. He stood upright, folding his muscular arms across his broad chest.

"Do you honestly believe the Father is pleased with you, Thumos, after all you have done, lifting yourself up as judge, jury, and executioner of these poor souls?" replied Raphael. His white eyes squinted, and began to glow more intensely.

"What?!" thundered Thumos, immediately being set off once again. In an enraged voice, he continued. "Poor souls? Are you serious, 'poor souls'? How can you possibly use that phrase to describe those whom I have dispatched? What about the Children who suffered unthinkably painful deaths at the hands of the Romans? What about the atrocities of the Nazis, who crushed and robbed so many of their humanity and dignity? What of the freedom-seekers whose blood was spilt on Tiananmen Square? What of the innocent youngsters slaughtered on city streets, or the mothers mourning the loss of their sons and daughters killed on the senseless battlefields of mankind? What of the unborn, destroyed all over the world, without a voice to be heard? And what of the victims of those who suffered at the hands of these few guilty wretches I have eliminated? What about all of these people? They are the 'poor souls', not my victims!"

Just then another sonic boom sounded, and Michael also arrived on the scene, with a group of angels, all armed with rhabdoses.

"We have been commanded to put a stop to this outrageous behavior of yours, Thumos," spoke Michael in his very imposing voice. He walked up from behind Raphael and Gabriel, both of whom stepped aside perfectly orchestrated, without a backward glance, making room for Michael in between them.

"Peaceably is our preference," Raphael added, in a notably calmer voice.

"But by force, if necessary," said Gabriel, as he scowled harshly at Thumos.

Thumos looked at the angels accompanying Michael. He could see puzzled and shocked looks on some of their faces, while others looked away, refusing to meet his gaze. Thumos knew they had no idea that they had come to face off with *him*.

"What is going on?" exclaimed Eleos quietly, looking back to the group of angels with whom he had arrived. He saw the same bewildered look on everyone's faces. "We are here to do battle with Thumos? I assumed it would be the Makria once again."

"Thumos is the fiercest and most devoted of all the angels," Periago spoke nervously. "Why would we be expected to fight *him*?"

"He was created specifically by the Father for the explicit purpose of war and battle," Kategoreo said. "Michael conveniently neglected to mention *he* would be our foe."

"Silence, all of you," commanded Krino, as he tried to sound unwavering. But he fooled no one. They all could hear the apprehension in his voice, too.

"I do not have time for this, nor do I intend to battle with any of you, my brothers," said Thumos. "I am on a very important mission, and I will not be stopped!" exclaimed Thumos. "My work is not yet complete, and has nothing to do with any of you!" And upon that statement, he simply turned to attempt an exit.

All three archangels swiftly moved into his path, to block him. All the other angels formed a line behind him.

With a loud cry, Thumos charged the archangels, but without his rhabdos.

"I will not take up arms against any of you," shouted Thumos. "I wish you no harm."

Thumos watched Michael step into the lead, charging forward with his rhabdos extended. Thumos spun, easily dodging Michael's attempt, and planted a hard kick right into Michael's back sending him sprawling.

"Stay down, Michael," Thumos commanded, pointing his finger at Michael.

Thumos looked away from Michael, to see that Gabriel and Raphael now were both charging at him simultaneously. He ran toward them in answer. They each swung their rhabdoses together, but Thumos performed the perfect limbo move, causing them to miss completely.

"Stand down!" Thumos demanded. He now appeared behind them, grabbed their heads, knocking them into each other. Grabbing one in each hand, he tossed them effortlessly. Michael, who had risen quickly to his feet, spun around just in time for the flying bodies of Gabriel and Raphael to send him crashing back down again.

Whirling around, Thumos found himself surrounded by the other five angels now. They enclosed him in a circle. Each one quickly attempted to land a hit on Thumos with their rhabdoses, but no one touched him as he fluidly avoided each angel's attack, sending them all sprawling into the pile of archangels.

Thumos, standing over them, huffed. "I told you, you will not stop me." He disappeared in a flash of light.

All the archangels and angels slowly rose to their feet, heads hung low. Gabriel spoke first. "Thumos is truly amazing," he said with a tone of admiration.

"Visions of grandeur. He's been watching Chuck Norris or Jackie Chan re-runs," Raphael said chuckling. Gabriel and the other angels all cracked up over that statement.

Michael, in his typical somber voice, spoke. "Enough of your insolent levity. We have failed the Father. I pray for Thumos's safety." It grew still as each contemplated the gravity of his words. If Michael was worried, what must become of Thumos?

CHAPTER 11:

ENCOUNTERING EVIL

Thumos materialized in an empty area of the Twilight Realm and pondered his next move. He intently waited for any word from any angel who would share with him some impending event on Earth requiring his intervention. While roaming Earth, he of course could find such events on his own, but while in the angelic realm, he was more dependent on angelic word-of-mouth. Some angels he knew were only too willing to share such intel with him, while others avoided the situation entirely. He sensed the burden he placed on each, as his brethren must make a choice.

Thumos's mind reverted to his acts of vengeance carried out most recently back on Earth. He grappled with so many diverse thoughts, and he was filled with a veritable flood of emotions.

"Every last one of those wretches absolutely got what they deserved," he reasoned with himself. "How could Yahweh allow people like that to continue to roam free?" He felt an anger welling up inside. "Centuries ago,

Yahweh commissioned me specifically to dispatch such characters. I am only continuing to carry out that mission."

But with every emotion of fury which Thumos felt, he quickly countered himself with doubts. "But why has He stopped sending me on such missions? Should I be acting on my own in these ways, without specific orders?" he questioned himself.

Thoughts of watching the Son of God being tortured and eventually crucified appeared in his head. "I could have stopped all of that from happening. Single-handedly. Decisively. I could have crushed every last Roman soldier in an instant," he thought to himself. "And after that, for centuries, so many other of Yahweh's faithful suffered at the hands of the filthy Roman empire, puppets of the Evil One. All Yahweh would do is command me to stand by and watch, doing nothing," Thumos thought indignantly. Once again, he could feel the anger coursing through his body. "I refused to stand by any longer and do *nothing*."

Thumos continued the emotional roller coaster in his head. "But why has Yahweh not spoken to me recently; why has He not summoned me? If He was displeased with what I have been doing, He surely would have called out to me. He always gave me my orders directly, but for some reason, that stopped when Jesus Christ set foot on Earth." Now, Thumos felt those sensations of doubt once again. "I was even there to protect His blessed one. She had no idea of what Satan and his minion had in store for her. Yet I remained steadfast, and delivered her," he thought to himself, feeling a great sense of pride coming over him. "Something changed after the Christ was born to her, though."

Suddenly, Thumos's sense of smell was befouled by a noxious fume. There was only one source that produced such a stench, and he turned around ready to strike, as his rhabdos mystically appeared in his hands.

"The valiant Thumos. What a delight to see you!" said Satan enthusiastically entering the area with his hands raised, palms out in surrender.

Dressed in his typical blacker-than-night flowing robe, he approached Thumos with a knowing smile on his face. He extended his hand to Thumos. "Why, what are you doing here, my dear Thumos? Did I catch you daydreaming?" he said with an evil smirk. "Are you on your way to wreak your special brand of havoc on some unsuspecting Children?" His smile broadened as his outstretched hand went unacknowledged. Slowly he lowered it to his side, seemingly annoyed by Thumos refusing to reciprocate.

It was then that Thumos noticed several shapes coalescing behind Satan, the Old Red Dragon. They were the Makria. Many of whom he had once cherished and loved, and some he did not know as well, but now they are all lost forever. Thumos took note of a very large member of the Makria behind Satan. Goliath was unmistakable.

Thumos turned away, not intending to engage in a conversation with Satan.

"No one turns his back to the King when he speaks!" shrieked someone. It had been centuries since Thumos had heard him speak, but there was no mistaking Kakos' voice. Kakos lunged for Thumos, attempting to grab his elbow to spin him around, but he was halted at a word from Satan.

"Calm yourself, Kakos. Thumos regards no one as his King. Do you Thumos? You have your own agenda these days, do you not?"

Thumos had refused to turn around even when he had sensed Kakos' attempt to assault him. He continued to speak over his shoulder. "Yahweh is my master, you accursed fool," said Thumos as he began to step away. Head bent low, his voice restrained, Thumos continued. "I only answer to Him," he said as he clenched his fists and began to walk away.

"My lord," hissed Kakos again. "Let me punish him for his insolence!" The other Makria growled in agreement.

The Old Red Dragon followed Thumos, closing the distance in an instant. Waving a dismissive hand at Kakos, he barely acknowledged his evil lieutenant.

"Come now, Thumos," Satan said, placating. "Surely you cannot continue to claim allegiance to the Father."

"The Father! How dare you refer to Him as 'Father,'" said Thumos vehemently as he spun around to face Satan. "You and all the rest of these low-lifes," said Thumos waving his hand toward Satan's entourage. "You are all betrayers of the Father, and betrayers of us all. You know what the destination of the Father's betrayers is!" he said defiantly.

Satan continued unfazed. "Thumos, you have been on this personal crusade of yours for decades now, in fact centuries. But lately you have been striking even more frequently than ever before. Are you growing desperate? Maybe you are uncertain of what you are doing? You surely know how displeased the Father is with you, Thumos. Even I already know about the incident from which you just fled—your encounter with my old friends, the Father's 'Yes-Men.'"

"The archangels would never consider you as a 'friend', you father of lies. They know you better than any of the rest of us angels," Thumos chided.

Satan attempted to put his arm around Thumos' shoulder, but at the first hint of Satan's move, Thumos slapped away the grotesque appendage, once again stepping away in disgust. To his surprise, Thumos wondered to himself why he had not stricken Satan down immediately. In the past he would have. What was the matter with him? The shock of it must have registered on his face as Satan grinned again.

"Now Thumos, you know me almost as well as the Father's Yes-Men do. And guess what, I know exactly how you feel," Satan said sympathetically. He took a breath to continue but was cut off by Thumos' heated remark.

"You have no idea how I feel!" Thumos fists were clenched tightly at this side. He stepped forward to challenge the Fallen One and was immediately aware that the Makria had closed ranks again.

"Oh, but I do," Satan said, as he shook his head and moved closer. "I can see the conflict within you," he said with a slight grin.

As Thumos hesitated, Satan continued. "You are finally coming to grips with what I have known about the Father for eons. He makes a great pretense about His 'love for His children', yet when it comes right down to it, He really only cares about Himself. Ultimately, only He matters. He allows these *supposed* Children of His to suffer, and to struggle, and to destroy each other. It's quite pitiful, actually." He placed a gentle hand on Thumos's shoulder. "Tell me I'm wrong."

Thumos's discomfort was palpable. Why did he not rebuke this creature and leave?

Satan removed his hand and leaned in to whisper into Thumos's ear. "And what's even worse, is that He actually *prefers* them over His superior creation…Us." Satan motioned toward Thumos and his Makria. "We should be the ones who are the Father's favorites. We should be the ones who rule His beautiful creations, such as Earth and other places."

Satan continued his verbal assault. "Everyone knows, Thumos, as the 'Angel of the Lord', you are virtually the only angelic being left now whom the Father has allowed to engage in direct physical contact with humans, other than those ridiculous Yes-men. Sure, I have done that on occasion, but only when *He* allowed it. Then there are those dreadful archangels, but they don't count. However, you, you my special friend, have an elite commission. If you were working with *me*, why, the results could be spectacular. Do you not remember how we *used* to work together, so very long ago, Thumos? It could be just like old times, and now, it would be even better."

Thumos remained facing away from Satan. He closed his eyes, clenched his fists tighter, but felt his rage boiling. The same rage that sent him on his crusades was rising to the surface once again.

Thumos could feel his face growing angrier, and realized that Satan could no doubt sense that anger rising within him, and could taste it like a fine wine.

Satan continued. "The Father sits back like a bored couch potato, watching the world go by, without lifting a finger." He chuckled dryly. I'm convinced He actually enjoys watching His Children languish and suffer, and gets some kind of sick thrill out of watching His perfect creation dissent and battle each other, all in the name of His so-called cause. It's all just a big game to Him."

Thumos clapped his hands to his ears. "No! No! No! That is not right! That is blasphemous!" However, in the deepest recesses of his thoughts, he acknowledged the same thoughts he had entertained. Then he considered the source and knew it all truly was profane. He would not house such thoughts of betrayal. It enraged him and he shouted, "You and I cannot possibly think alike!" As soon as it was out of his mouth Thumos realized his error. That was something he should never have allowed Satan to hear.

Satan shoved his hands in his pockets confidently. "You are such a passionate angel, Thumos. You try to portray yourself as an angel of light, but maybe you really are not. In fact, you remind me so much of myself, back near my quickening."

"Impossible! Leave me! " shouted Thumos, falling to his knees, hands still clasped to his ears. No matter how hard he pressed, he could not shut out this Old Red Dragon's words.

Satan knelt beside him, motioning the others to step away to give them some space. "I desperately want to help you with your quest." You know the Children's old saying 'you scratch my back, I'll scratch yours'? I can help you." He reached up to pull away Thumos's hands from his head, saying , "We can help each other. If we just joined forces, we could accomplish far more than you ever imagined. We could just put *all* the Children out of their misery, not just the bad ones. We would be unstoppable!" Satan's voice rose in excitement as he punctuated his last statement with a clenched fist.

Thumos rose slowly to his feet, regaining his composure. Satan had overplayed his hand and Thumos was able to think clearly. Satan only wanted what he had always wanted: to destroy all of humankind. Thumos stepped toward Satan, his head bowed. Satan stood, hands on hips, very proud of himself.

Thumos slowly lifted his gaze, with a renewed look of clarity in his eyes. He shot his hand outward, connecting with Satan's chest, catching him completely off guard. The impact resounded like a cannon shot and sent the fallen angel careening backwards into the throng of his Makria.

Thumos pointed at them all and began to speak. "Get thee behind me, Satan, for it is written…"

Satan held up his hand, palm outward and said in exasperation. "Do not go there, you fool. You are no 'Son of God', so do not quote Him to me. Do not even mention *Him* to me. *His* coming to Earth in the flesh is what ruined all of my wonderful works. You shall not do the same now."

This was an adversary he knew, and Thumos was enjoying the discomfiture of the devil.

"Do you not understand what I am offering you?" Satan said, standing and brushing off his robe. "Don't you see what you could truly accomplish by fighting alongside me? I would immediately give you command of one of my legions," he said as he swept the space with his arm. "My side grows stronger, while His side faints. My loyal subjects are all over the Earth—you could learn of virtually all the tragic events about to take place there, and do something about them!" He paused for effect, then continued. "Once you have proven yourself to me, I would grant you the opportunity to pursue the same quest on other of the Father's worlds. Now, surely, all that has some appeal to you, does it not?"

Now Thumos could see in Satan's eyes that he was becoming less certain of his position with Thumos. "Wouldn't you prefer that over the Banished Realm, Thumos?" Satan said, trying to alter his tactics.

Thumos looked at Satan, in irritation. "Are you trying to threaten me, now? Don't worry, I know about the Banished Realm. The Son's apostle

John wrote of it in his book, Revelation. He called it 'The Abyss'. Actually, I believe *you* are the one with a reservation there!"

Satan waved his hands disgustingly. "Okay, okay, I don't need a lecture. I was there when *the Son…*" he said sarcastically, shaking his head, "cast some of my best demons, Legion, into a bunch of squallering swine. Those traitors begged for their very existence, like weak little cowards. They traded the Banished Realm for drowning pigs."

Satan glanced back at Kakos and the other Makria, then putting his hand to his mouth, said quietly, "Maybe not such a bad trade."

Thumos could see the subject made Satan uncomfortable, so he continued. "Only the Father can destroy an angel, cause him to cease to exist. No other created being can do that to an angel. Still, even that would be a fate better than the Banished Realm. It is reserved for defeated angels, and rebellious angels, like all of you," Thumos motioned toward Satan and the crowd of Makria. "I've heard it's more terrifying than anything else anyone has ever encountered—enough to make even the strongest of angels melt in fear."

Thumos, now fully back in his right mind, did think for a moment that he could certainly exploit this situation. He would really be able to accomplish more than he could by himself. While there was no way he would ever submit to this hated enemy, leveraging Satan's tools and resources to exact punishment on the guilty was a tempting thought. But it was only a thought, and it was very brief. Inhaling, he dismissed the thought.

"I don't think so," said Thumos calmly. "You can take that offer to join you and your lackeys, and, as they say on Earth, shove it!"

"Very well," said Satan dryly. "Kakos, tell Thumos about the error of his ways, and what happens to those who reject my generous offers." Satan fluffed out his robe and was suddenly gone.

Kakos's rhabdos swept across Thumos's head, sending him reeling into the mist. "By your command!" shrieked Kakos, now standing over Thumos where he had fallen.

"Makria, let us banish this ingrate!" shouted Kakos.

In an instant, all the angels in Satan's company armed themselves, and stood poised, ready to attack.

"I've been waiting for centuries for this very moment!" Kakos railed at Thumos. "Prepare to say 'goodbye' to your Maker!" he said laughingly.

Thumos leapt to his feet, and in the blink of an eye, there in his hand appeared his rhabdos. He spun the rhabdos to his left, behind his back, to his right side. Then with two powerful swipes, left and right, he stood at the ready. "You are a weak, pathetic creature, Kakos," Thumos said with authority. "You are nothing but a sniveling idiot who takes orders from the Father's worst mistake of all eternity!"

Kakos screamed in fury and charged at Thumos. As if in slow motion though, Thumos parried, and easily landed two rhabdos strikes on Kakos— first in the face, then on the back of the head. Kakos flew, flailing into the mist.

Thumos whirled around to see half a dozen other Makria swarming after him. To him, they appeared to be moving in slow motion. He scanned the area, calculating his next move. Thumos broke into a sprint, running straight toward them. He slid to his back, right in the middle of the group, with his rhabdos held crossways to his body, taking out the entire group like a bowling ball crashing through pins.

Jumping to his feet, Thumos spun his rhabdos like a pinwheel, giving off a whirring sound. The Makria scrambled back onto their feet. "You guys would be better off if you just stayed down," shouted Thumos. Again, he ran toward the group, with a leaping dropkick into the first of the Makria, sending him skidding into the ground. "One," Thumos said. He landed on his feet in between two others, quickly hammering both with his rhabdos. "Two…three…" he continued counting.

Sidestepping the riposte of another Makria's rhabdos, Thumos leveraged that angel's forward motion, kicking him in the backside sending him flying. "Four!" he shouted in a more elevated tone. Without missing a beat he yelled "Five" as he smashed one end of his rhabdos into the face of another Makria. "And six!" he said matter-of-factly, ducking down to one knee while spinning around as he swung his rhabdos like a baseball bat taking out the legs of the last standing Makria.

Thumos stood up slowly, when from behind, he heard a recovered Kakos shout "I will destroy you!" Thumos whirled around to meet him, but turned straight into the behemoth body of Goliath, who had been standing aside waiting for the right moment to attack.

"I have you now," said Goliath in his deep voice, as he grabbed Thumos by the head. He squeezed intensely, and was able to slap Thumos' rhabdos from his hands. Thumos felt like his head was in a vice grip. He grimaced in pain, as he reached up with both hands trying to loosen Goliath's grasp.

Goliath held the dangling body out in front of his own face, giving a dull laugh. "You don't look so tough anymore, puny angel," Goliath said, as he tossed Thumos aside like a rag doll.

Before Thumos even hit the ground, he felt sharp stabbing pains in his back. He groaned, realizing Kakos was jamming his rhabdos into him, with one foot smashing down on his neck.

Kakos laughed, enjoying the turned tables. "Well done, Goliath," he called out, as he took a golf-like swing, connecting with Thumos's head.

Thumos lay there dazed, not knowing up from down. He could smell his own angelic flesh sizzling from Kakos' rhabdos imprints. With his face down in the ground, he could feel a rumbling beneath him.

Goliath, in no hurry whatsoever, lumbered toward him. Thumos could hear Kakos maniacally laughing over him.

"Yes, Goliath, send this weakling Thumos to the Banished Realm!" Kakos shrieked gleefully.

Kakos shouted out. "Finish him now, Goliath!"

Goliath's hulking figure straddled Thumos' dazed, limp body. He pressed his weapon into Thumos' back, laughing in his dull, deep voice.

"You will pay for this!" Thumos groaned, barely able to get out the words due to the excruciating pain. Dark streaks like a window shattering started emanating across his back, coming from the place where Goliath's rhabdos touched him.

"You'll never get the chance, Thumos!" Kakos said as he laughed, walking over to Thumos's now pinned body, and kneeling down, he spoke loudly into Thumos's ears. "You'll never see us again after this day." He touched another spot on Thumos with his own rhabdos.

Thumos let out another scream, as all the Makria began to laugh at him. Then Goliath kicked him a few times to make the point.

CHAPTER 12:

THE WARRIORS COME OUT TO PLAY

Kakos paused his assault on Thumos, walking over to stand before Satan. "You see, my lord, we have no need for Thumos. Look at him over there; he is defeated. Why are you so interested in winning him over to our side? Whatever you need, I can do," Kakos said with an air of superiority.

"Kakos," replied Satan, obviously irritated with him. "You are such a fool. Think of what we could do with Thumos on our side," Satan said with a gleam in his eyes. "Do you not see it? He has the ability to interact with Yahweh's idiotic flesh-bags, just like those three brown-nosing Yes-men. We do not have free reign to do so, like we once did—like *I* especially once did. We can exert *some* influence over them, but not like in the good old days."

Satan paused, looking around as if wondering if anyone else was listening. "But our time is coming once again."

"Well, when is that?" Kakos asked, startled by Satan's statement.

"Only Yahweh knows that, probably the Son too. But we will be released for a short time," Satan said slyly. "Until then, we need Thumos."

Satan looked back over at Thumos with great anticipation, clapping his hands together. "Yes, so much we could do with his capabilities," he said with a menacing laugh.

A sound from off in the distance reached everyone's ears, silencing the laughter of the Makria. Kakos and Satan both abruptly stopped their conversation, their facial expressions instantly became somber. Goliath withdrew his attention from the attack, leaving Thumos slumped on the ground. His head turned slowly toward the sound, as Satan and Kakos stepped up next to him. All three of them took small, tentative steps toward the sound coming toward them. The others shifted uneasily around them. In hushed tones, Goliath asked, "Does human music reach into the Twilight Realm?" It was clear the sound that advanced toward them was music in nature, and it was growing louder.

One of the Makria began to back away and nearly stumbled backwards over Thumos's prone figure. The gnarled and angry angel held his hands over his ears as the music, reminiscent of a heavy metal band on Earth, began to fill the area with sound. All the Makria began covering their ears, and some began to stagger. Thumos rolled to his side, half of his face covered in black streaks. He also heard the music, but knew what it was. Involuntarily he started to grin, but the pain that coursed through him held his joy in check. Slowly, he struggled to his feet as the Makria continued to retreat, some now shouting in agony.

Another group of angels began to come into view, as a voice could be heard singing some lyrics to this song that was creating so much discomfort for the Makria. His head finally clear enough, Thumos was able to recognize the song. His memory flashed back to Earth year 1986.

ORANGE COUNTY, CA—JANUARY 1986

"Mike, it feels like you're stuck, man. Got any ideas for our next big hit?" said Robert Sweet, to his brother Michael. "'Stryper' is becoming more of a household name, little brother, after how successful Soldiers under Command was. We've set the bar high!"

"Sure, sure, I'll come up with something. Don't pressure me," said Michael.

A plainly dressed man slipped into the back corner in one of the rooms of the Casbah Recording Studio, where the band members were brainstorming together.

"Hey guys, love your music!" called out the stranger. "It's really inspiring to me, a great example to people today."

"Hey man, thanks for telling us that," said Michael, a little bit perturbed at the interruption. "Uh, who let you in here anyway?"

Robert piped up, calling out to the station manager. "Tommy, can we get some privacy here, pal?"

"Sorry, I didn't mean to be a bother. I'll get out of your way," said the very tall stranger. "I'll be excited to hear what you guys put together next. Revelation—what a great book of the Bible, huh? You gotta love it, 'to hell with the devil', right? Peace out guys!"

The stranger lowered his sunglasses slightly, and gave a wink at Michael. His eerily, practically completely white eyes, were a real shock to Michael. Quickly, the stranger was out the door.

"Dudes, did you see that guy's eyes?" said Michael. "That was really weird! But did you hear what he said? That part about 'to hell with the devil'? I mean, I love that. It's perfect! We could use that. Wait, I feel a song coming on…"

Thumos collected his thoughts, shaking his head back to the moment at hand. "Hey Armada, I love that song, my friend," he shouted loudly, as a drum riff closed out the song. "Have I ever told you the story about how that song came about?"

"I do not recall you ever telling me that tale, Thumos," Armada answered loudly. "Sounds like you owe me a story."

All of Satan's Makria looked around dumbfounded, as they stood there looking at each other in amazement at this seemingly casual conversation now happening between Thumos and Armada.

"You got it," said Thumos. "And by the way, it is good to see you and the rest of The Warriors. Your timing is impeccable."

"It looks like you need a little pick-me-up," Armada retorted. "You never know when we are going to show up and crash the party. We are a real enigma."

Thumos let out a big laugh. "Agreed!"

Armada shouted loudly, his tone less congenial. "Hey Kakos, you can shut up now. That laugh of yours is more irritating than anything else in the entire universe." All the Warriors began to laugh.

Armada spoke again. "I do not think the Makria know what to think of us Warriors, do they Thumos? You ran with us long ago, Thumos. You understand us."

"Well, most of the time, I think I do," Thumos answered, grimacing, still in pain.

Armada looked at the Makria standing around, now directing his speech toward them. "Makria, we are 'The Warriors'. This day, you will get to know us very well, if you do not already." He winked at Kakos, with a grin, and continued. "All of us are not like the rest of you angels, whether Makria or Agathon."

"Why do other angels fear The Warriors, Armada?" Thumos interrupted, teeing up a response from Armada.

"Many of The Warriors used to be human, or any number of other species of the Father's creation," answered Armada. Angels understand angels, but angels frequently do not really understand the Father's corporeal creation. A handful of the greatest of warriors from the Father's created worlds are allowed to join the angelic ranks from time-to-time. Over there is 'Kokkino'," Armada motioned to one of The Warriors.

"Yeah!" screamed Kokkino, sporting a long-flowing bright red beard, holding his rhabdos high over his head

"Kokkino was a ferocious Norse hero, from Earth, many centuries ago," Armada said. "And over there is 'Choros', a mighty martial artist from China, also of Earth."

Choros spun around, in a dazzle of acrobatic moves, then landed on his feet with a great shout.

"Like I said, we are quite a motley crew," Armada said laughingly. "Their human-like habits start to rub off on even us original angels, where you cannot tell us apart anymore." All The Warriors shouted, shaking their rhabdoses.

"And Lu-cif-er…" Armada continued, drawing the name out, in a mocking tone. "He hates it when you call him by that name. Reminds him of the good ol' days, before he became the has-been that he is now." The Warriors roared even louder in laughter.

"I know you are close by and can hear me," continued Armada. "Michael and the other Archangels may not be willing to revile you, but me, I love reviling you. You are one big lo-ser," he said defiantly forming an L shape with his fingers to his forehead.

"REVELATION!" Armada shouted out even louder. And all the Warriors belly laughed about that. Armada continued. "*Everyone* knows what John's letter tells about your fiery demise."

The Warriors were not conventional angels. To the Archangels, they were seen as questionable, with loyalty to Yahweh as unclear. To the Makria, they were seen as unpredictable, and probably loyal to Yahweh, but unclear. One thing was clear about them: they were angelic wild cards.

"Goliath, you lumbering cow, why don't you pick on somebody your own size?" Armada said.

"Like me," shouted another angel. Samson, another member of the Warriors, stepped out of the crowd, with footsteps thudding loudly. He looked as formidable and large as Goliath of the Makria.

"Let's get ready to rummmm...bbbbb...lllle!" shouted Tachu, another Warriors angel, in his best imitation of prize fight announcer Michael Buffer.

Samson started the melee, lowering his shoulder as he ran toward Goliath. Quickly the fallen angel assumed a similar stance and began to run, shoulders squared and braced, toward Samson. The two collided with a thunderous boom, the shock of the force blasting them back, dazed, a few steps. Each recovered quickly, then moved to confront one another face-to-face. Rhabdoes flared and cut wide swaths through the air as they came together with such force they were ripped from the angels' hands.

"You could not best me a millenia ago, and you cannot best me now, little one," screamed Goliath as he lunged for Samson. Locked together they grappled, each looking for a weakness in the other. A grin spread across Samson's face which caused Goliath to lose his grip. Samson knocked Goliath's hands away, and he landed two quick punches to Goliath's face. Goliath shook his head, then quickly grabbed Samson around the waist, threw him over his own head, and pile drived him into the ground. Samson glanced over his shoulder to see Tachu and Gamma were also engaged in a deadly struggle.

Tachu, using his tremendous speed, shot like a lightning bolt toward the Gamma of the Makria. In an instant, Tachu was standing right in front of Gamma, as he swung his rhabdos like a baseball bat, sending Gamma flying backwards into the mist. Tachu moved swiftly, off to assist others of the Agathon. He caught a glimpse of his ally, Exousia, fending off Phobos.

Makrian angel Phobos charged after Exousia of The Warriors, and with a flying leap, kicked Exousia to the ground. Phobos tried to push his rhabdos down onto Exousia's throat like a barbell to choke him. Exousia managed to grab the dark rhabdos, as his hands began to sizzle from grasping it. Phobos, having the advantage of being on top of Exousia, pressed down hard with his weight, touching the dark rhabdos onto Exousia's throat. He screamed as his throat began to sizzle now.

Suddenly, Phobos was flying off Exousia. He rose to his feet to see it was Tachu who had come to his aid. Tachu had struck Phobos with another lightning bolt maneuver. They gave each other the sign of peace, and Exousia chased off after Phobos. As Tachu turned away from Exousia, now he could see Agrios facing off with Machi, and just beyond them was Choros attacking Skliros.

Another of the Makria, Machi, squared off with Agrios of The Warriors. They both immediately attacked each other, with their rhabdoses blazing. They were striking so hard that what looked like flashes of lightning came off the collisions of their weapons.

Next to them, Choros, of The Warriors, jumped high, coming down on top of Skliros of the Makria, who blocked the leaping attempt. Preferring hand-to-hand combat, each angel tossed aside his rhabdos. Both were experts in the angelic martial arts, and they squared off in a flurry of kicks and punches.

A loud gurgling, coughing sound caught Tachu's attention, and his eyes began to dart about, trying to ascertain the source of the strange sounds.

Samson now found himself in a choke hold by Goliath, and his feet dangling off the ground. As big as Samson was, he was still not quite as behemoth as Goliath. But suddenly he felt his feet back on the ground, and Goliath's grip loosening. Tachu was standing behind Goliath, having hit the back of Goliath's knees with his rhabdos, weakening him a bit. They flashed the sign of peace at each other, and Samson grinned, as he grabbed Goliath's body, hoisting it up over his head, then body slammed him down onto the ground. Goliath let out a deafening groan, as his huge body crashed onto the ground.

Tachu surveyed the chaos of activity surrounding him, looking for any other allies needing extra assistance, when his eyes landed on the center of this epic clash of titans. He began to slowly move toward the leaders of these two angelic squads, anticipating their ensuing conflict.

Amidst so many pairs of fighting angels, there were now only two left standing in the center of the battle zone. Armada, leader of The Warriors, and Kakos, Satan's general, began circling around each other, as bodies flew about them from all the other fights. They both grinned, each other relishing the thought of their impending fight.

"I am looking forward to extinguishing you this day, Armada," said Kakos menacingly.

Armada replied unphased. "You'd better get some help, if you want to have a chance at that."

Kakos screamed angrily, running toward Armada. He swung his rhabdos at Aramada's head, but Armada looked like he was at a limbo contest as he avoided Kakos' attack by bending backwards.

"Whiff!" Armada shouted, as he spun around upright, flinging his rhabdos at Kakos' back. The rhabdos spun like a pinwheel as it hit Kakos several times before it circled like a boomerang back into Aramda's hand.

Kakos finally turned back around facing Armada once again, grimacing in pain. He screamed once again, racing toward Armada. At that,

Armada flung his rhabdos in the same way as before, but this time the spinning rhabdos pummeled Kakos in the face several times before zooming back to his hand again.

Now it was Armada's turn to run straight at his opponent. He swung his rhabdos at Kakos' legs, but this time Kakos avoided the strike by doing a hands-free cartwheel.

"Now who's whiffing?" Kakos shouted, as he landed on his feet. He tomahawk chopped his rhabdos right toward Armada's head, but Armada quickly spun around holding up his rhabdos with two hands to block Kakos' strike.

Armada somersaulted across the ground, vaulting straight up in front of Kakos, landing the blunt end of his rhabdos right under Kakos' chin. Kakos shot several feet up off the ground, landing squarely on his back.

"Had enough yet?" quipped Armada. "Maybe you better just stay down there!"

Armada glanced around, to check the status of everyone else. He could see Tachu had made quick work of Gamma and was assisting the other Warriors. For the moment, it was obvious Goliath was a non-factor, so he shouted at Samson, motioning toward Thumos. "Samson, get him out of here!" he commanded. "Take him to the Archangels."

"I'm on it!" Samson shouted, dashing off toward Thumos. He scooped up Thumos into his arms, and shot off like a bolt of lightning to find the Archangels, Thumos in-tow.

Thumos, still in a weakened state, mumbled "The Warriors need my help. I need to stay and fight with them. Let me go!" he tried to demand.

"Armada has the situation well in-hand, Thumos. You do not need to worry about him," responded Samson confidently.

"I do not need this interruption of my work," Thumos grumbled.

CHAPTER 13:

THE COPYCAT GETS HIS WHEELS

Jimmy Whitaker got to the end of another work week. Two weeks ago, he purchased some guns, then bought an excess number of ammunition boxes for his new guns.

"Next, time to find a truck," Jimmy said to himself Saturday morning. He opened the curtains in the front room, the sun pouring in on him. The gentle warmth felt good on his fair-skinned, freckled face. He closed his brown eyes, and smiled, crooked teeth and all.

Jimmy walked across the room, back to his computer desk. He pressed the power button on his computer, and plopped down into the chair. "I'm going to make this city a better place. I can't wait to get started." He opened up the Internet browser, and leaned forward in anticipation of a good find.

"Night after night this week I've combed the Craigslist ads searching for the perfect truck," he said to himself out loud. "This is the one," he pointed to one on his computer screen. "This should do it. It's just a few blocks away. I can just walk over there."

Jimmy jumped out of his chair excitedly, and went to his bedroom to get dressed. He pulled on some denim jeans, and slid his feet into his favorite cowboy boots. Grabbing a flannel shirt out of the closet, he pulled it on over a brown t-shirt he was already wearing. Jimmy left the flannel shirt unbuttoned and untucked. "Can't forget that," he said with a grin, grabbing a Kansas City Chiefs football cap from the top shelf of his closet. "Ho, oh-oh-oh, ho, oh-oh-oh," he sang out, with a tomahawk chop motion as he walked out of the bedroom, mimicking being at Arrowhead Stadium for a Chiefs game. "I hope they can win again tomorrow."

Next, Jimmy anxiously exited his house, and headed down the street. He was surrounded by a bright blue sky, as his thoughts were permeated with a great sense of purpose and motivation. He let out a big sigh of contentment. The smell of freshly mowed grass was all around him. After all the groundskeeping work he had done over the years at the university, he had come to appreciate that smell. Being outdoors was his favorite place to be, and he found himself with a little bit of a skip in his step as he strolled down the sidewalk.

Jimmy arrived at the address in the Craigslist ad, and found the two-toned red and white 1990 Dodge Ram truck sitting in the driveway. "Chiefs red even. I love it," Jimmy said under his breath. He smiled admiringly, and walked eagerly to the front door. After ringing the bell, and waiting a few seconds, an elderly gentleman opened the front door. He left the storm door closed, and angrily said "Whaddya want?"

Jimmy, startled by the old man's grumpiness, said "Hi, uh, I'm interested in your Dodge Ram out here." He pointed over toward the truck.

"That old piece of junk?" the old man said. "What in the world does a youngster like you want with that ol' tin can?"

"The ad says it runs great," Jimmy answered.

"Well a course it runs great. I wouldn't be tryin' to sell it if it didn't run, ya idiot," the old man said, sounding even more aggravated.

"And it's got a V8 hemi in it, right? Pretty new tires too, automatic transmission?" Jimmy said timidly.

"I fixed it up myself over twenty five years ago," the old man said, sounding a little friendlier finally. "I've been treatin' it like my own child ever since. That engine ain't the standard engine. I made a bunch of modifications myself. Added the hood scoop too. That baby will give you a good case of whiplash, boy. Just punch the accelerator and you'll see."

"Well that sounds really great, sir," Jimmy tried to speak politely. "The ad says you want fifteen hundred dollars. Would you take a thousand instead?"

"Don't you wanna drive it around first?" said the old man.

"No, I trust you, sir," said Jimmy. "That's the perfect truck for me."

The look in the old man's face softened, as he finally noted the Chiefs hat Jimmy was wearing. "Well, you look like a nice young man, plus you're a Chiefs fan, I see," he said, pointing up at Jimmy's hat. "How 'bout them *Chiefs*! But I ain't givin' it away for a grand. I'll take twelve hundred and fifty for it."

"Deal," said Jimmy. "*That's just what I was hoping for,*" he thought to himself.

The paperwork was completed, and Jimmy jumped into the truck. He fired up the engine, and it sounded awesome. He pulled into the street, and decided to take the old man up on his statement. He punched the accelerator, and the truck shot down the street, throwing Jimmy back into the driver's seat.

"Woo-hoo!" he shouted with the windows down, tossing his cap over onto the passenger seat. He headed for Interstate 135, and spent the next hour zooming up and down the interstate. The wind blew his hair wildly since he kept the windows down. The radio blared to the tunes of classic rock on KXFJ, FM 104.5, "The Fox", as everyone in Wichita knows it. To Jimmy, all was right with the world right now, and he felt not a care in the world.

Suddenly Jimmy came back to reality, and he recalled what he felt was his new mission in life. He got off the highway, and drove to the self-storage unit which he had procured a few days ago, and pulled the truck inside. He looked over at the corner, and smiled at his gun cabinet, where he had stashed all his weapons and ammo.

Jimmy already had some painting supplies and spray guns ready to go, so he got started. The truck was going to be painted black, and he had bought a glass tinting kit. The truck was going to get a makeover. The day was getting late now, though, so he shut the storage unit door, locked it tight, and walked back home just as the last rays of sunlight disappeared over the western sky.

Jimmy woke up early Sunday morning, and wanted to get started right away on his truck painting project. He made himself some coffee, then fixed some biscuits and gravy. He hurriedly cleaned up the kitchen, and bolted out the front door to head to his self-storage unit. He threw open the door of the unit, and stood for a few moments admiring his "new" truck.

"This is going to be so awesome," Jimmy said to himself. He looked around to see if anyone was in visual range, and once he determined the coast was clear, he slowly closed the door and locked it from the inside. He had strategically selected a unit with a rear door, so he could keep that propped open while he painted, so as to avoid passing out from the fumes. Hours later, after toiling all day long, he had finished. It wasn't a perfect paint job by any means, but he was satisfied. It was dark now, and after locking everything up, he started his walk home.

Jimmy whistled, and looked up into the moonlit night sky. He saw some stars twinkling, and felt very satisfied, yet very tired. It was almost time for him to start his new mission: crime fighter by night. That had a cool ring to it! But first, he was exhausted, and he needed to get to bed. Tomorrow, it was back to the regular grind of his groundskeeping job at the university. Crime fighting would have to wait for a few days.

CHAPTER 14:

LIFE-CHANGING EVENTS

A ringing phone broke the silence at Detective Lane Madigan's desk.

"Yeah, what is it?" snapped Lane, as he answered it. He was sure the phone call would be yet someone else interrupting his day with a trivial problem or complaint.

"Well hello Grumpy—where are the other six dwarfs?" said Janie, Lane's wife. She giggled and continued. "No, I have no complaints to lodge Officer Madigan. I only wanted to make sure we're still on for lunch."

Relieved, Lane hesitated for just the slightest moment, realizing he had forgotten about their lunch plans. "Uh, yes…" he said, as though speaking in slow motion, with a grin slipping across his face. "Janie, I just love you like crazy, do you know that? You have the innate ability to lift my spirits with your goofy humor, and I just love that about you!" Lane said playfully, trying his best to recover from his forgetfulness.

Janie laughed again. "Oh my dear, you're very sweet. But you forgot about lunch, didn't you?"

Lane answered, feigning confidence. "Oh, no, of course not. Mind like a steel trap. I never forget anything." He continued in a more relaxed tone. "Okay, you got me, but we are definitely still on, babe. I am really ready for a break and I can't wait to see you and Elizabeth."

"Well that's good news, because Elizabeth is all dressed and ready to go," Janie responded. "She has been driving me nuts all morning, asking 'is it time to meet Daddy for lunch yet?' And I'm ready to see you too, of course!"

"I wouldn't dream of disappointing the two most important people in my life," Lane answered anxiously. "But I do need to meet a little bit later. How does 1:30 sound, as that gives me about three hours?"

"Oh sure, that's no problem," Janie said. "Maybe we'll run a couple of errands we were saving for later, then we can meet you at 1:30. Don't be late!"

"When will we tell Daddy, Mama?" Elizabeth asked excitedly.

"Tell me what?" asked Lane.

"Oh, she has been wanting to tell you something all morning, and I told her she could tell you at lunch today," responded Janie.

"Oh, okay, sounds good. Well, I promise, I won't be late," Lane answered quickly. "The usual spot? McDonald's, with the PlayPlace?" he asked.

"Playplace, playplace, playplace," Elizabeth chanted gleefully in the background.

"As you can tell, that is exactly what Elizabeth is expecting," chuckled Janie. "We'll see you there at 1:30 dear. I really do love you, you know that, right?"

"I love you too, Janie," answered Lane, in a most sincere and passionate tone. "And tell my little Lizzy-Poo that Daddy loves her, and that he is really excited about going down the slide with her."

"I just wuv you Daddy!" exclaimed Elizabeth. Using his great detecting skills he determined that Janie had put the phone on speaker, since he could hear both of them clearly. He knew to anyone passing by his office door right now he was grinning like a complete loon. "Well," he thought to himself, "let them think I'm off my rocker, who cares?"

That's odd, thought Lane to himself, as he hung up the phone. Right at that moment, a wave of déjà vu swept over him, as this all seemed very familiar to him. He paused for a moment, unable to shake the feeling.

"Hey Jelani!" shouted Lane across the room. "Get your ass over here and help me finish up some of this paperwork. I've got an important lunch date to keep today."

"All right, cool your jets," said Ian, as he strolled across the room toward Lane's desk. "I can tell from that goofy grin who you were talking to about lunch. There is only one person in the world who can do that to you. Definitely one appointment you don't want to miss, my friend."

At the Mandarin Oriental Miami hotel, Roberto Valenzuela barked out orders to a wary bartender. "Yo, babe, get your fine behind over here with another drink," demanded the overserved Valenzuela.

The gentle sound of ocean waves gliding onto shore could be heard through the open doors of the bar. Sunlight glistening off the ocean poured into the bar, lighting up everything there. Crystal glasses, neatly folded linen napkins, and sterling silverware were on every table, but as early in the afternoon as it was, there were few patrons.

"But Mr. Valenzuela, you've already had five of those," replied the smiling bartender, a blonde woman with streaks of orange at the tips. At forty-five years of age, it'd been her act of defiance against a life that hadn't quite panned out. "It's only one o'clock in the afternoon, and I'm not sure you need another one. The Mandarin Oriental Miami doesn't want to be responsible for whatever you might do next." She smiled again, but was actually trying to be serious.

"Five? Really? Ah hell, who's counting, just pour me another one," Roberto said. "And get one for all these lovely ladies here, too."

Three women surrounded Valenzuela, all vying for his attention. A tall woman sporting nearly waist- length blond hair, wearing a tight mermaid style black dress stood behind him, with her diamond clad fingers caressing his shoulders. A shorter, athletically built redheaded woman stood to his left, running her fingers through his hair, while constantly leaning over kissing his ear and cheek. A very curvy brunette stood to his right, facing opposite him, resting her elbows on the bar, making her best effort to show off her cleavage thanks to the deep V-cut spaghetti strapped red Valentino dress she was wearing.

The bartender complied, wagging her head, pouring out drinks for Roberto and his lady friends. How could she refuse Mr. Roberto Valenzuela, and hope to keep her job?

"Ladies, I love the smell of the ocean breeze in here, and your stunning beauty." All three women flashed big smiles at him. Valenzuela continued, "This has been one great party, but it's time for me to blow this place," he said. "I've got important things to do, you know. I can't just sit around partying all day."

"But why not, Roberto?" questioned the one blonde.

"Yeah, come on, stay a little while longer," said the sultry redhead, tugging at his Armani sport coat.

The brunette spoke up. "We'll make it worth your while, Bobby, just come on up to our room."

"You ladies are very tempting, but hold that thought, and I'll be back in a few hours," said Valenzuela. "Then we can pick up where we left off."

Roberto walked out the front door of the hotel lobby, and a parking attendant was right there with his key fob, having pulled his Maserati up to the door. "Your car, sir," said the attendant.

"Thanks kid," replied Valenzuela. "Hey now, you keep your hands off my ladies in there. I'll chop 'em off if you don't," laughed Valenzuela.

The parking attendant swallowed hard, knowing full well Mr. Valenzuela probably meant it, even though he was laughing. "Of course not, sir, I would never dream of it."

"Don't gimme that, kid, you'd be crazy to not be dreaming about them hot babes!" shouted Valenzuela from behind the steering wheel. And with that, he punched the accelerator, screaming out of the driveway into a busy street.

Totally oblivious to the traffic around him, he accelerated to over seventy miles per hour, down the four lane, forty-five mile-per-hour speed limit expressway. The reflection of the "Golden Arches" splashed across his Ray Bans.

"London bridge is falling down, falling down, falling down…," sang Elizabeth, from her car seat. Janie started to pull out onto busy Bricknell Street, trying to get over to the nearby McDonalds.

"Oh boy, we're on fumes," Janie said out loud as she glanced down at the gas gauge. "We're going to need to get some gas right after lunch, Lizzy."

"You've got gas, Mommy!" said Elizabeth, letting out a burst of laughter.

Janie laughed too. "You've been listening to your father too much, you little squirt," she said.

Janie never saw it coming. In less time than it took her to smile lovingly at her daughter, or think about how much she loved her husband, a wildly swerving red Maserati ran a red light, careening into the Madigan's Jeep

Cherokee. The Jeep flipped into the air, instantly exploding, ignited by a fumes-filled nearly empty gas tank, torn open by the low-riding Maserati that had sheared right under the Jeep.

"Wooooo, what a ride!" exclaimed an amazingly unharmed Valenzuela as he jumped out of his car, after it came to rest from slamming into the guard rails. "Let's do that again, baby!"

Several bystanders ran over to Valenzuela, seeing his drunken state, and grabbed hold of him. "Can't you see what you've just done, you freaking idiot?" screamed one of them.

"Hmmm…did I do all that?" Valenzuela mused, as he waved his hand toward the Jeep now flipped over upside down, burning out of control.

"You just killed some innocent people, you bastard!" shouted another bystander.

"Who gives a rat's ass!" yelled Valenzuela. "Those dumbasses should've stayed out of my way!" he stammered.

"Ridin' the storm out…" sang Lane Madigan, along with the REO Speedwagon song he was blaring on his radio. He was driving his car a few blocks from his lunch destination of McDonalds when suddenly he was surrounded by sirens. He noticed a pillar of smoke billowing into the air in the nearby distance, coming from the direction he was headed.

That overwhelming sense of deja vu once again hit Lane. His mind went back to the nightmare which had rudely awakened him a few nights ago. Visions of a burning car, charred human remains, caskets, it all began to flood his memory. The waves of terror and anxiety that night had startled him awake with now seized his body. Lane's heart rate skyrocketed, his breathing became labored like an elephant was sitting on his chest, and his vision was blurring. *What if,* his mind kept screaming…*what if…* He tried to calm himself as he increased his speed. It's just this case that has me on edge, he thought. Everything's fine.

He quickly slapped a magnetic emergency light on top of his car, to join the foray of emergency vehicles zooming towards the smoke. Despite his best attempts, panic overcame him, as he pushed the car's accelerator as far as he could.

Lane's car came to a screeching halt, as he arrived at the crash site. Leaping out of his car, he saw the burning vehicle, and despite it being charred beyond recognition, he knew exactly who was in that car.

"Oh my dear God!" Lane shouted, as his voice broke. "No! No! No! Janie…Elizabeth…" Lane screamed, as he lunged toward the fiery, crumpled mass.

Two firemen grabbed him, shouting "You can't do anything, man. It's too late."

Lane's knees buckled, waves of nausea went through his stomach, and the ground felt like it was spinning beneath him. He fell to his knees, crying, screaming hysterically. "No, no, no, it can't be. God, no, this can't be happening!"

Ian ran over to Lane, and lifting him up by his arms, tried consoling him. "Lane, come on, get up buddy. Come over here with me," Ian spoke gently.

Lane came back to his senses, and lashed out. "What happened? Who did this? How did this happen?"

Lane began to look around frantically, when he spotted someone being handcuffed. Without a second thought, he knew immediately what was happening. The handcuffed person was a drunk driver, and he was responsible for murdering Janie and Elizabeth. He bolted out of Ian's grip, and headed straight for the perpetrator.

Ian tore off after him, knowing his best friend's thoughts. "Lane, stop! Don't do it!" he shouted.

Lane crashed into the arresting officers, knocking them away from Valenzuela. Lane uttered a loud guttural scream, and grabbing the man by the head of his hair, smashed his face into the hood of the patrol car, bloodying his nose. The man in custody shrieked in pain, and slumped off the hood down to the ground. Lane pulled him violently back to his feet, and spun him around face-to-face. Lane elbow-punched the man across his right cheek, then landed a hard left upper cut into his gut. His right hand came straight up under the man's jaw. Before he could inflict any more damage, several officers tackled Lane.

"Lane!" Ian shouted harshly, running over to the scene, trying to calm himself down, as well as Lane. As sympathetic as he was toward Lane, feeling like he could do the same thing, he continued in a more calm voice. "You can't do this, Lane."

Ian grabbed Lane by the arm, as he escorted Lane away from the area. "Listen," Ian said. "This is Roberto Valenzuela, buddy. Vice has been after this loser for years, and now we got him. I mean, we got him good—lots of witnesses, clearly DWI. He is SOL. Don't worry, this dirtbag is going to pay for what he's done. There is no way outta this one this time."

"But Ian," sobbed Lane, now becoming more docile. "This is *my* family, man, not some stranger's family like we deal with in other cases." He waved his hand toward the burning Jeep. " This is *my* Janie, *my* Elizabeth, how can I possibly survive this?"

Lane slumped to the ground, the sound of his own blood pounding in his ears. "It's my fault, my fault, all my fault. If I had just met them earlier, they would have never been here at this time. It's my fault, my fault, all on me."

Ian slid to the ground next to his partner. "Lane, listen, it is not your fault, not one bit." "You cannot predict the future, my friend. This is Valenzuela's fault, not yours," he said, jabbing an angry finger in the air. "Don't you ever forget that."

Ian continued. "Janie and Elizabeth never knew what hit them. They didn't suffer at all. The smoke eaters think her gas tank was probably nearly empty, full of fumes. And you know they are absolutely in a better place."

Lane had tried to listen to Ian's comments, but right now, none of that made any difference to him, nor did anything make sense to him. He was ready to explode.

"I don't care, Ian, I don't care where you think they are now. I want them here with me, right next to me, right here, right now. But you know what? That's not going to happen. Not now, not ever, they are gone, and I am coming unglued. I hear what you're saying, but honestly I cannot think about that right now. It's all just…just…just a big crock."

Lane's shoulders sank as he turned to walk away from the scene, drifting past the squad car where Roberto Valenzuela sat.

A wounded, drunk Valenzuela peered out the window from the backseat of his temporary prison. Despite his stupor though, he got a very good look at Lane Madigan. He threw an evil grin at Lane, as Lane walked right past the door, with his nose pressed right up against the window. As Lane walked by the patrol car, trying to ignore Valenzuela, he smashed his fist on the glass of the window. The vibration was enough to give Valenzuela a shock, restarting the excruciating pain in his broken nose.

Ian stood back watching everything unfold, and uttered a quick prayer under his breath, his heart breaking. *Dear God in heaven, I don't even know what to pray for. Father, please help us all!*

Lane, unable to bear the thought of going home, made his way back to the station. It was a flurry of noise and activity, as usual, but the moment Lane walked through the door, an immediate hush fell over the entire precinct. By now, everyone had heard what happened. Several people acted as though they were about to speak as Lane walked by, but no one knew what to say. Even if anyone had found any words, Lane was oblivious to the looks of sympathy, sadness and solidarity.

Lane walked into a conference room, and slammed the door. He then slumped down into one of the chairs, buried his face in his hands, and wept profusely. Through the tears began to burn a rage of fury, unlike any emotion he had experienced before. The muffled sounds of his rage filled the station.

CHAPTER 15:

A TURN FOR THE WORSE

Just as Thumos was whisked away, the Evil One, reappeared to the raging battle between Armada's Warriors and Satan's Dark Legion. Satan stepped forward to take matters into his own hands.

"Armada!" Satan cried out. "You really must learn to quit while you're ahead," Satan continued, musingly.

Armada spun around, and seeing Satan, lunged toward him. "I have been waiting for this chance for a long time, you worthless piece of..." Armada shouted.

But Armada's words were cut short as Satan swung his rhabdos, slicing Armada's rhabdos in half. Armada held the pieces, as its energy faded to nothing. He gasped in disbelief.

Satan grinned like a feral dog, as all the angels, both Warriors and Makria, gathered around to see what was happening. Satan struck Armada relentlessly, his rhabdos a blur of dark intensity. Each blow landed and each left Armada's body more and more streaked in black. Armada had long since fallen to the ground, but the Evil One continued the onslaught. In a place of stark silence the sound of rhabdos steel on angel flesh was an obscene symphony.

Suddenly Satan stopped, standing over the angel, his hand on his hip, his head tilted to the side as if he were examining an insect. "Now what was that you called me?" He stooped down to grab a handful of Armada's hair, lifting the angel's swollen and beaten head enough so they could meet one another's gaze. Satan snorted and continued. " Oh yes, I believe the term was 'Loser', was it not? Well now who appears to be the loser, my dear Armada?"

Still holding Armada by his hair, Satan stood, pulling him to his feet. Armada flailed blindly, his energy gone. Satan drew him close and whispered in his ear, "Say 'hello' to some of my old friends in the Banished Realm."

"Go to hell," said Armada with a grimace. Satan laughed, thoroughly amused. "Maybe later," he said. "But not right now. How about you go first?" Without preamble he plunged his weapon into the staggering angel's chest, his grin widening into a smile as the dying angel shrieked in pain. From the wound, a spiderweb of black veins began to spread throughout Armada's body. Soon he began to shake violently and Satan let him fall to the ground. Wiping his hands on his robe, Satan backed away from the crystalizing form of the angel. As it hardened, like sleek obsidian, it began to crack like glass under pressure. In one final heave there rose an anguished wail from Armada as the black crystal cracked and the once noble angel was gone.

All the Warriors, seeing the unexpected fate of their leader, stood in shock. They all looked at each other in disbelief and confusion.

Tachu raised a pointing finger at Satan, and exclaimed "He has dispatched Armada to the Banished Realm."

Exousia, in a hushed tone, said "No angel has ever returned from there. It is a horrific place, completely devoid of Yahweh's presence. How can this be?"

The rest of The Warriors froze at the realization that their leader was gone for good.

Tachu retorted, "I will find Samson and Thumos. The rest of you must leave this place...now!"

Tachu disappeared with a sizzling lightning bolt sound. The rest of The Warriors scattered in different directions.

Satan turned to Kakos, flipping his rhabdos over to his general. "You see Kakos, you simply need to be a little more assertive. Now then, I'm off once again. I have a lot of prowling about, seeking whom I can devour", Satan said with an evil grin and a wink at Kakos.

Even all the Makrian angels were standing silently, in fear and in awe of the events that had just unfolded before their eyes. With a smile playing around his lips, Satan turned and walked casually away, disappearing into darkness. Kakos and the other Makria followed after him, in utter silence.

Thumos was returning to his senses, and realized once again he was in the arms of the giant angel, Samson, on their way to the archangels as instructed by Armada. Thumos looked behind them, and saw Tachu zooming toward them at an overtaking pace.

"Samson," Thumos said weakly, "It's Tachu, coming up behind us."

Samson stopped his flight, and immediately Tachu had caught them.

Pausing in front of them, shaking with emotion, Tachu said in hushed tones, "Armada is gone."

"What?" answered Samson. "What do you mean *gone*?"

"Satan has destroyed him!" Tachu said, shaking his head in disbelief.

"That is impossible," interjected Thumos, as he shook off the grasp of Samson's large hands.

Tachu did not look at Thumos, but spoke to Samson instead. "I saw it with my own eyes. None of us could believe it. Satan returned to the battle after you took Thumos away. He scourged Armada, then plunged his rhabdos straight into Armada's chest. Armada fell to his knees, screaming in agony, then suddenly he was gone." Tachu cast his gaze down. "Retreat seemed to be our only option , so we left the area. All the Warriors escaped, save Armada," Tachu said exasperatedly. "And I told them I would find you two."

"He has been sent to the Banished Realm," Thumos said solemnly. "He is forever doomed." Thumos hung his head. "And this is all my fault; I am completely responsible for this."

"Yes, brother, you are," said Tachu, meeting his eyes, accusation and anger apparent.

Samson spoke, holding his palm up to quiet them. "Thumos, stop talking that way. This is not your fault. Armada and the Warriors chose to come to your aid. And Satan is the one who has disgraced Armada." He paced between them, his hands laced behind him as he spoke. " I hated Satan before, and now my hatred is burning hot within me!"

Thumos continued. "Armada is gone because of me, and I take full responsibility. I also will take vengeance upon Satan, myself." At that he raised his downcast eyes to view them all, a white light emanating from his eyes. The fires of righteousness rekindled.

"Samson!" Thumos's voice resounded. "I have no time to see the Archangels now. I must continue my quest, and now Satan has fueled righteous fire within me. Those on Earth who follow him, those in our realm who do also, and Satan himself, will feel the wrath of my vengeance." Thumos looked upward and outward, screaming "Satan, you have called down the thunder! I am coming for you, and hell is coming with me!" Thumos's voice reverberated, and the ground shook with his intensity.

Samson and Tachu looked at each other, as they had not seen anything like this before. Taken back as he was, Samson still answered "I have my orders, Thumos." He grabbed Thumos's arms. "I am taking you to see the Archangels right now. That was Armada's last order for me, and I do not intend to fail him."

"Not today!" shouted Thumos, and he thrust his foot into Samson's chest, launching him backward. Samson could not hang on to Thumos, due to the incredible force Thumos used. In the blink of an eye, Thumos disappeared.

Moments later, the Archangels appeared where Samson and Tachu now stood, empty-handed. Samson was speechless. He simply looked at the Archangels sheepishly.

Gabriel spoke first. "Let me guess. He got away from you, right?"

"I hate it when he does that!" said Raphael.

Michael, ignoring the sarcasm and attempted wit of the other two, said "Samson, Tachu, go find your comrades, the Warriors. They need you."

Samson nodded, still unable to muster the courage to speak. He and Tachu disappeared quickly.

CHAPTER 16:

ELIZABETH'S SURPRISE REVEALED

Lane sat alone on a couch in his empty house, staring blankly, pondering his situation.

Chief Franklin forced me to take a few days off. I really don't want to sit here alone. I tried to explain that to her. Just let me keep working, I said, that's what would be best.

He stood up, and started roaming through the house. He entered the kitchen, and grabbed a beer from the refrigerator. He took a few sips, while staring out the window into the backyard. There was Elizabeth's swingset that he had put together himself a couple of years ago. But no one was playing on it today.

Lane walked into his bedroom. He stopped in the doorway, looking forlornly at the emptiness of the room. Janie's makeup was sitting on the bathroom counter, exactly in the same place it was after she had used it that day she died. He had left everything intact.

He sipped his beer, and turned around in a zombie-like state, walking into Elizabeth's bedroom. Again, stopping in the doorway, his eyes darted around the room. He saw her bed all made up, with her favorite teddy bear sitting on the pillows. There were her dolls and dollhouse over in the corner. A few clothes were thrown over in another corner. Tears welled up in his eyes, as he turned to leave.

Lane's shoulders slumped, as he finished off his bottle of beer. The empty bottle simply slid out of his hand, falling onto the floor. He did not care. There were several empty bottles strewn around the house, just where the others had been dropped.

He collapsed onto the couch once again, lying down, staring up at the ceiling in silence.

Lane's quiet was abruptly interrupted by the loud ringing of the telephone. He first let it ring several times, and thought there was no way he was answering a call. But after a few rings, he rolled off the couch, and picked up the phone.

"Yeah?" Lane said dryly.

"Lane Madigan?" a voice questioned on the other end of the call.

"Speaking," he barked.

"Oh, sorry to bother you Mr. Madigan," the voice continued. "This is Doctor Rose Cartright, Janie's obgyn…"

Lane interrupted her. "Well Doctor Cartright, why are you calling me?" he said angrily. "Janie is gone, she is dead. Oh, and so is my little girl, Elizabeth, if you wanted to know."

He was about to slam the phone down, when the doctor quickly interjected.

"I am so very sorry, Mr. Madigan. I heard about the tragic accident," she said sympathetically. "I was Janie's doctor for a very long time, I delivered Elizabeth, as you know. I don't mean to bother you, I simply wanted to express my condolences to you personally. Losing three family members, I cannot even imagine your pain…".

Lane interrupted her again. "Three people? Doc, are you drunk or something, can you not count?"

There was a long silence on the other end of the phone line. "You there, Doc?" Lane said.

"Uh, Lane," Dr. Cartwright finally spoke. "You didn't know Janie was pregnant? Oh my God, I am so sorry, I mean, she had just found out earlier in the week, and I just thought she had told you…".

Lane threw his phone across the room, and it smashed into the fireplace. He let out a blood curdling scream at the top of his lungs. He grabbed a lamp and smashed it into the floor. He kicked the coffee table into pieces. He began punching the couch, as he began to sob uncontrollably.

"I am going to tear Roberto Valenzuela limb from limb," Lane screamed out loud, through his sobbing. He finally collapsed onto the floor, face down, pounding his fists onto the floor as he continued chanting "I'm going to kill him, I'm going to kill him…"

CHAPTER 17:

TIME TO SAY GOODBYE

Lane ran a hand through his hair and looked up at the doors in the back of the Corpus Christi Catholic Church. Had it really only been four days since the crash? He'd lost track of time. Nothing seemed real to him right now. He knew he was on autopilot, and even the words intended to comfort him did nothing.

"Give them, O Lord, Your peace and let Your eternal light shine upon them," said Father Mike Robinson. Crossing himself, he said "In the name of the Father, and the Son, and the Holy Spirit." Most of the other attendees followed suit, crossing themselves as well. The funeral mass had concluded, and next it would be time to go to the burial site.

Lane stood over three caskets at the cemetery. He recalled in his memory, the conversation with the funeral home over using three caskets instead of two. He remembered getting so angry with the funeral director, who had suggested he save money by using only two caskets instead of three. "You can save some money, Mr. Madigan, by only using two caskets. After all, there is no body for the unborn child," the funeral director had said. Lane knew the man was only trying to help, but still, he also remembered how red-in-the face angry he became over that suggestion. *That 'unborn child' was very much a human being, still my child, the son I would never get to meet, thanks to that monster, Roberto Valenzuela. I don't care if I never got to see that little baby, I will nonetheless dignify him as a person, as my child. How dare this man suggest otherwise?* Now he felt his stomach going into knots, as he relived that conversation in his mind.

Lane's attention focused back to the ceremony at-hand, and his anger began to dissipate as his roller coaster of emotions changed course. He now began to fight back the tears while Father Robinson spoke additional words there at the graveside. It was all gibberish in Lane's ears. He could not, or maybe would not, make out what the priest was saying. Slowly all those in attendance passed by him, shaking his hand, trying to say words of encouragement to him. He was oblivious to anything anyone said.

He recalled the last day he had with Janie and Elizabeth. It was the morning of the car crash. He had hugged and kissed them goodbye; had told them how much he loved them. It was a morning just like every other morning. He had said nothing unusual , just that he loved them. And yet now, none of that seemed sufficient. If only he had known that was to truly be his final goodbye to them, what would he have said or done differently? Now, he would not see them again, at least not on this earth.

Who am I kidding? Lane thought to himself as he stood by his family's graves. *Do I really believe I will ever see them again anyway? Where is God in all of this? If there really is a God, and He is who He says He is, how could this have happened?* He shoved his hands in his pockets angrily. *How could someone, like Roberto Valenzuela, be walking around scott-free, and my beautiful wife and baby girl are lying dead in coffins? Where is the justice? Where is the equity? How am I supposed to continue living?* He was feeling overwhelmed with emotion, and finding it excruciatingly difficult to maintain any semblance of composure. He felt his knees weaken and begin to buckle.

From behind him Ian grabbed his arm, helping him remain upright. Ian motioned to a couple of other officers from their precinct to come over to help. "Hey guys, stand here with Lane, and give him an arm up. I want to speak to the group that attended here today."

Ian turned to the crowd who milled about the graveside. Holding up his hands to draw everyone's attention away from Lane, he said "Family and friends, you all know Janie, and many of us here have known her for a long time now. Those of us who know her best, realize that if she could speak to us right now, she would be asking us not to weep for her, nor for Elizabeth, nor for their unborn child. She would tell us that although for those left behind on this Earth," he paused to nod toward Lane's direction, "death is a sorrowful goodbye. Yet for those who die in the Lord, it is just the beginning. It is the beginning of a new chapter in their existence. It is the culmination of a victorious life lived in service to Jesus Christ. And Janie lived a victorious life for her Lord and Savior, Jesus Christ." Many in the crowd nodded and spoke up in agreement. Ian continued "We will miss her here, and we will terribly miss that sweet little Elizabeth. But if I know Elizabeth, she is right now singing her favorite songs with the angels." A smile came over everyone's faces at the mention of Elizabeth singing, as they had all heard her do just that: singing at the top of her lungs.

"Janie would want us to know that although she will miss us who are left behind, and especially that man right over there," Ian said, pointing in Lane's direction. "She is joyously and anxiously waiting for the day when she can see us again, face-to-face, and she is going to be praying before the Father, petitioning Him on Lane's behalf most of all. But also for all of us. Make no mistake, those two still live on, and are more alive today than they have ever been before."

Ian continued his benediction. "Some of my favorite Bible verses are found in Saint Paul's letter to the church in Rome. In chapter eight, at verse twenty-eight, he wrote 'And we know that all things work together for good for those who love God, to those who are called according to His purpose. For who He foreknew, He also predestined to be conformed to the image of His Son, that He might be the firstborn among many brethren. Moreover, whom He predestined, these He also called; whom He called, these He also justified; and who He justified, these He also glorified.'"

Many in the crowd were nodding in agreement now, as Ian finished. "God chose Janie. He called her, he justified her, she served Him faithfully, and now He has glorified her, as well as Elizabeth too. Honor Janie and Elizabeth as we remember them today, and lay their bodies to rest here. All of you, please comfort Lane, and help him remember that God is watching over him also."

Lane gently placed a dozen roses on each of the caskets. He turned and shook hands with Ian, giving him a slight smile, and spoke a quiet "Thanks my friend" to him. But in his mind, Lane was really saying "Okay Ian, what a crock. That is all just a big crock." Lane turned away, to start walking back to the hearse, escorted by Ian and several other of his colleagues.

A small group of men, all clad in dark suits and sunglasses, approached Lane, intercepting his path. Unknown to anyone at the graveside, Roberto Valenzuela and some of his thugs had been at the graveside service also.

"I just wanted to express my deepest condolences to you in person, Detective Madigan" said Valenzuela dryly, flicking a single black rose onto Lane's chest. With a subtle grin, as though he were fighting back laughter, he continued. "You must know I know that I wasn't myself that day. I can't tell you how utterly terrible I feel," Valenzuela said in a most sarcastic and insincere tone.

Lane lunged toward Valenzuela. Ian and the other officers grabbed Lane, holding him back. Valenzuela's men reached for weapons, as some of the other officers rushed toward Valenzuela.

Ian flung himself into the center of the volatile situation. "Wait a second," snapped Ian. "Guys" he said, motioning toward Lane, get him out of here. Take him back to the car."

The others shuffled Lane off to the hearse, then Ian turned toward Valenzuela, gently forcing the man toward his own car. Valenzuela's guards moved in closely, until Valenzuela motioned to them to stand down.

"You must be Jelani, Ian Jelani. You're that Bible-thumping, Jesus-freak of the Miami police force. My parents also raised me in the Catholic Church, but all that is just hocus-pocus, meaningless rhetoric that is for children. But I will give it to you, that was quite the rousing speech you gave back there. Bravo—worthless rubbish of course, but very impressive" said Valenzuela. "I even remember you from back in your days on the St. Louis police force, Jelani. You and your friend Detective Madigan have a little something in common, no?" Valenzuela's face smirked with a big grin.

Ian, without showing his genuine surprise at Valenzuela's information about himself, spoke in a calm, reserved tone. Snatching the sunglasses off Valenzuela's face, he said drawing closer.

"Don't let my calm demeanor fool you, *Ricky*," Ian said condescendingly. "I may appear very serene on the outside, but inside, I'm a raging inferno. You had better hope you don't have to see that inferno come out all up in your face. I know your type—cocky, above-the-law, 'I can pay off anyone' attitude. I know you've hired the best scumbag lawyers your dirty money can buy."

Now Ian's tone was beginning to grow more intense, as he began to think about his days in St. Louis, a time he had tried to forget about. His thoughts quickly came back to the now, to Lane and his family, and the pain he knew they were feeling. The pain with which he *could* identify.

"You deserve to be fried in the electric chair for what you've done to Detective Madigan's family, and to the countless other families you've victimized in this country. But know this—that no matter what happens, you *will* suffer at the hands of justice."

Valenzuela gave an evil laugh, as he replied. "And whose hand will that justice come from, Jelani? You? I'll be back to the cemetery to spit on your grave before long!"

Ian continued undaunted. "You may escape the judgment of human courts, but you will not escape the judgment of Almighty God. And who knows, maybe God will give me the ultimate pleasure of dealing out some justice on *you*," Ian said as he poked his finger into Valenzuela's chest.

Valenzuela exploded in laughter. "Are you kidding me, Jelani? Are you still spewing out Bible rhetoric? Your so-called 'god' cannot touch me unless I give him permission, and guess what, I won't be giving anyone any such permission."

At that, Valenzuela snapped his fingers to summon his guards over to him. As the two hulking men started to advance on Ian, a tall dark figure unseen by anyone until now, suddenly collided with the two men, causing them to smack their heads together. The two henchmen fell down into a pile, dazed too much to get back up.

In all the commotion, Valenzuela and Jelani both spun around to see the tall dark figure shrugging innocently. "I guess your friends must have tripped and fallen. I've heard it said 'the bigger they are, the harder they fall.'" The stranger quickly headed off in another direction.

Neither of the men got a clear look at the stranger's face, but Ian did recall now that he had seen this person in the audience at the graveside, yet he didn't know who it was.

The stranger called out as he walked away, "Oh, and Jelani, loved what you said about 'justice.'"

"Now there is a man I must have working for me," muttered Valenzuela quietly.

"Hell would have to freeze over before that would happen, Ricky," shouted out the stranger, from a distance no one would expect he could have possibly heard Valenzuela.

Both men were standing there quite startled at what had just happened. So much so, that they had forgotten about their own conflict. Ian reacted first, following the trail of the stranger. A few minutes later he returned, shaking his head.

Ian headed back to Lane's car. He climbed in, puzzled and silent. "Everything okay?" questioned Lane.

"Oh yeah, everything is fine" Ian answered. "I got Valenzuela straightened out back there," he said with a grin. "Then this guy showed up, set his *employees* straight by slam dunking them onto the ground. That was awesome. When I went to thank him, he was just gone. I think I like this guy!," Ian said, grinning.

Lane still was so numb to everything, he barely heard anything anyone had said. But this story Ian told of the stranger showing up, did pique his interest. "Hmmm...very interesting," Lane said quietly.

The car pulled away, just as a bagpipe version of "Amazing Grace" started to play on the car stereo.

CHAPTER 18:

THE COPYCAT STRIKES

Six weeks after his initial brainstorm, Jimmy decided he was ready to see what he could do. He walked over to the self-storage unit after dark, slowly drove his tag-less truck out of the unit, and sped off toward downtown Wichita. He was nervous, but he was also excited. This was crazy—he had never done anything like this before, and in fact, never even imagined trying to do something like this.

Jimmy did not have to cruise around very long at all before he encountered a group of loud, obnoxious teenagers, carousing in their own pickup truck. He followed them at a safe distance for a while, witnessing all their mischief.

One teen leaned out the window, pitching a rock through a car window they passed by. They sped off as the car alarm sounded. Another teen leaning out of the other side of the truck pitched a rock through the window of a darkened street front store. All the boys laughed as they sped away from that scene.

They pulled up next to a car with a couple of girls in the front seat. The boys quickly began to taunt and jeer at the girls, yelling all kinds of obscenities at them. Eventually they turned down a more remote street.

Jimmy suddenly sped, easily passing them with his souped-up truck. He spun out in the front of the teens' truck, forcing them to stop.

The teen driver, Carl, jumped out of the truck and started walking toward Jimmy's truck. A couple of other boys jumped out to escort Carl, while two other boys stayed behind in their truck. "What do you think you're doing, you damned idiot?" yelled Carl.

Jimmy kicked open his truck door, and stepped out on the street. He was wearing a ski mask, and all black clothing, pointing a nine millimeter Uzi at the boys. As soon as the unarmed boys saw the gun, they turned around screaming, to get back into the car.

It was too late. Running toward the teenagers' truck, Jimmy opened fire, taking down the three boys who had come to challenge him. He continued firing through the windshield of the teenagers' truck, killing the other two boys in the backseat.

Jimmy ran back to his truck, jumped in, and quickly sped away. He pulled off his ski mask, his pulse racing, and adrenaline flowing through his body.

"Woo-hoo, I did it," shouted Jimmy at the top of his lungs. "I actually did something about those thugs. Those punks will never bother anyone else ever again," he continued. He got his truck put away in the storage unit where he also changed clothes. He locked everything up, and ran back over to his house, quickly shutting himself inside. "Holy smokes, what a rush!," he yelled in triumph from the privacy of his house. "No one is going to miss those losers, that's for sure!" Jimmy passed out quickly in bed, feeling very high on himself.

Wichita police arrived on the scene of the teenage massacre. Their truck now ablaze, had drawn a great crowd of attention. Much to their chagrin, the police could find no witnesses. A quick survey of the street revealed an older business district with no video surveillance cameras mounted outside.

Police officers later visited five different homes that night, delivering some tragic news to five different families. Five weeping mothers were indeed bereft over losing their sons in a tragic death.

Jimmy bounced out of bed. He ran outside, grabbed the morning newspaper, and anxiously opened it across his kitchen table. "Awesome!" he shouted out loud, immediately noticing a picture of a burning pickup truck displayed on the front page. His giddy demeanor quickly changed as he read on.

"Did the 'Holy Terror' Visit Wichita Last Night?" showed as the title of the article.

"The 'Holy Terror'?" Jimmy said in a shocked voice. "No way! That was me, not some idiotic 'Holy Terror'," he continued.

In a disgusted huff, he threw the newspaper to the floor, continued his morning routine, and headed out the door for work.

Several days passed before Jimmy had thoughts of returning to the streets. The excitement from his first adventure had died down, and the whole city had grown quiet about the previous incident. It was a Friday night, and as soon as the 10pm hour had passed, Jimmy sneaked over to his storage unit, ensured all his weapons were loaded, and quietly pulled his truck out onto the street. After driving around looking for some "action," Jimmy encountered what he was looking for just after midnight.

A woman ran out of the Mort's Martini Bar in downtown Wichita. Two men came running out after her, laughing and yelling in their drunken stupors.

"Come on, Beth, slow down!" called out the first man, Tom. The second man, Andy, caught up to Beth, grabbing her from behind. Both men dragged her into an alley, where they thought they would be out of sight. Jimmy watched intently.

Tom began to rip Beth's shirt off of her. "No, stop!" Beth screamed out loud. Andy put his hand over her mouth, and held a knife up to her throat. "You can just shut your mouth, girl," Andy said. "We just want you to share what you've got with us," he said laughingly.

Tom grinned. "That's right, babe" he said. "This won't take long" continued Tom, as he began to unzip her pants.

Andy pressed the knife harder to her neck, still with his hand over her mouth. She nodded quickly, with a look of terror in her eyes, realizing she had no other choice at this point.

Jimmy finally decided he had watched long enough. With his sawed-off shotgun, he casually stepped out of his truck and walked toward the men, hiding his gun behind his back. Andy finally noticed him, and pointed his knife toward Jimmy. "This is none of your business, pinhead, so beat it!" Andy Snarled.

Without saying a word, Jimmy pulled his shotgun from behind his back and fired. Andy's shredded body flew backward into the wall of a building.

Tom jumped up, pulling at his pants, stumbling as he tried to make a run for it. Jimmy fired again, hitting Tom in the legs.

Tom tried to drag himself down the street. Jimmy could hear the grinding sound of the man's useless legs against the loose gravel on the street and he grinned. "Please mister, don't do this," Tom cried as he tried to shield himself with his hands. "Don't kill me, man," he pleaded for his life.

Jimmy fired again, then turned and walked away.

Beth had remained huddled in the corner the whole time, uncertain of her own fate. But now she called out, "You saved my life, mister, thank you!"

Jimmy stopped, without turning around, pulled his mask below his chin, and said "You idiot, you were probably just getting what you asked for." The darkness of the night kept his face hidden from the young woman. He got into his truck and drove away.

"Wichita Has Its Own Vigilante!" Jimmy said, as he read the newspaper headline out loud. A big smile slipped across his face.

"Finally!" Jimmy continued. "With a witness left behind this time, my existence will be acknowledged." He was feeling quite pleased with himself.

The newspaper article reported there were no leads. The young female witness who saw what had happened could not give anything except very general descriptions. She could provide no specifics regarding the man who saved her, his truck, or any other pertinent details.

Now feeling more emboldened, Jimmy waited only a couple of nights before deciding he was ready to strike again. He got dressed in his dark clothes and face mask, then opened the back door to sneak over to the self-storage facility to get his truck.

As he drew his keys from his pocket and turned the corner, his body was slammed backward through the door. So hard that it knocked the breath from him. As he gasped for air, a massive, dark figure stepped through the doorway blotting out the light. The farther into the house he came, the farther back Jimmy's body was driven. It was like magnets repelling each other.

The stranger began to speak. "Look not at the speck in thy brother's eye, when there is a log in thine own."

Suddenly in the stranger's grip, Jimmy could see a long, thick wooden stick, with a sharpened end facing toward him. The stranger moved toward

Jimmy, but Jimmy's body was frozen against a wall of his kitchen. He began to wail.

"Vengeance is mine, not yours!" the stranger shouted, as he plunged this "log" straight into Jimmy's eye, but of course the wooden object was so large, it completely smashed in Jimmy's face. His lifeless body was now suspended by this piece of wood, as it penetrated through the wall.

A moment later, there was complete silence, and the stranger was gone as mysteriously as he had appeared.

"This 'Jimmy Whitaker' kid was our vigilante," said Officer Archie Waltz of the Wichita Police Department. A couple of other officers were standing next to Officer Waltz, inside the kitchen of Jimmy's house. A police photographer was snapping pictures all around them.

"Yeah, we had zero leads on this vigilante character. Then Jimmy's parents had come over looking for him, after not hearing from him for a couple of days. Poor people, they came into the kitchen to find his body pinned to that wall right over there," Officer Waltz explained, pointing a finger to one of the kitchen walls. "He had this huge wooden stake shoved right through his face. It went right through the wall, and there was his dead body, just hanging there. Ungodly sight. Never seen anything like it in my thirty years behind this badge."

Officer Waltz continued. "They called 911 right away, and I was the first one on the scene. At first, we figured this kid had been hit by our local vigilante for some reason." He wiped beads of sweat off his face, breathed heavily, and continued. "Then we started investigating the house, found a few clues, which easily led us to figure out *this very kid* was the vigilante we'd been looking for." Waltz paused, shaking his head, looking upward.

He composed himself, and looked back at the other officers. "Anyway, he had a self-storage unit just down the street. We found his unmarked pickup in there, and a whole slew of weapons. Quite a shocker. No one would have ever guessed it was this mild-mannered kid. Sheesh, can't imagine being his parents."

One of the officers finally spoke. "So who did this to Whitaker? I mean that sounds totally bizarre."

"Ha, now that's the question of the year," blurted out Officer Waltz. "We have no idea. No other trace of anything other than Jimmy's own fingerprints, DNA, shoe prints, nadda. It's as if that big ass stake came flying in here when he opened that back door over there—which was standing wide open when his folks found him. We got nothin' else."

CHAPTER 19:

SHARING OLD WOUNDS

Lane sat alone on his back patio. The sun having gone down over an hour ago, the heat of the day now dissipating, he started up his fire pit. Sitting back in his chair, he grabbed a Corona from the cooler sitting next to him, popped the cap, and began sipping. He gave out a sigh, and stared blankly into the night. A slight breeze jostled his hair, and the soft glow of the fire warmed his face, as if trying to comfort his sense of loneliness.

But there was no comfort to be found.

He glanced around, as if expecting to see his wife come strolling through the sliding glass patio door.

But she was not there.

He looked over at the princess playhouse sitting out in the yard, as though he expected Elizabeth to be giggling and playing there. But she was not there either. His eyes began to tear, but he sniffed, brushed his eyes with the back of his hand, and polished off the Corona. Just as he grabbed another bottle from the cooler, a familiar voice broke the painfully silent night.

"Lane, you out here?" said Ian, appearing from around the corner of the house.

"Yep, right here, buddy," Lane said, from behind the flickering flames of the fire pit.

"I rang the doorbell, but you didn't answer," Ian explained. "That's when I thought you might just be back here. Looks like I was right. How are you holding up?" Ian said, as he sat down in a chair next to Lane.

Lane stared at the fire. "Don't ask," he said, without looking at Ian. "I'm about to open another Corona. You want one?"

"Sure, I'd love one," said Ian.

Lane grabbed a bottle out of the cooler, twisted the cap off, and handed it to Ian.

"Now that's a pretty good grip you've got there," said Ian. "Those Coronas are usually tough to twist off," he said chuckling. Ian looked over at Lane's left hand, which was resting face up on his knee. "Uh, looks to me like your hand would prefer you use a bottle opener."

Lane looked down at his hand, to notice the blood welling up on his hand. The palm of his hand was slightly torn from the sharp edges of the bottle caps. "Hmmm. Didn't even notice that. I don't feel it. I don't feel anything right now. He sniffed as if to dismiss the discomfort. "So what brings you out this night?" He tipped the bottle to his mouth, and continued staring blankly across the backyard.

"Well I would think that's pretty obvious, my friend," said Ian. "I just wanted to check on you; see how you're doin'...".

Lane cut him off. "I don't need anyone's sympathy. I don't need anyone checkin' on me. I just need everyone to leave me be, he said gesturing with his beer bottle. There's nothing I wanna talk about; nothin' to say at all."

"Trust me, I get that," replied Ian. "I totally get where you're comin' from."

Lane turned red rimmed eyes toward Ian. "Oh yeah? What do you mean you 'get where I'm coming from?'" Lane said, sarcastically quoting Ian. "How could you *possibly* understand what I'm going through, what I'm feeling?"

"Look bud, you don't know everything about me," Ian replied calmly. "I'm what, ten, twelve years older than you? Some things happened to me long before I came to Miami. There's plenty you don't know about me." He stopped to take a drink.

"Okay, well shoot, tell me something I don't know about you," quipped Lane. "Explain to me how you *think* you get me," he said with a sneer.

"That's exactly why I came here tonight, Lane," said Ian very solemnly. "I have a story to tell you. I've never told you this before, heck, I don't think I've told *anyone* this story since I got to Miami. I don't like to think about it, and I have tried to forget it. Mind you I said I've *tried* to forget it, but that's never gonna happen."

Lane finally showed a glimmer of interest in having his friend with him there. "Well you've certainly piqued my interest, Ian, so lay it on me." He finished off the bottle, and grabbed a new one to take its place.

"Eve Bennett. Damn, it's tough to even say that name out loud," Ian said, exhaling sharply and wagging his head. "I think about her every day, but I don't remember the last time I said her name out loud." He paused to look skyward where the first nighttime stars glimmered above.

"Who is she?" asked Lane, sitting forward, acting more interested.

"Hang on, I'm gettin' there friend, just hang on," said Ian with a deep sigh. He sat his beer down on the ground, and gripped the arm rests of his chair. He looked somberly into Lane's face, and said "Eve was my wife."

Lane shot up out of his chair like he had springs on his feet. "What?" he shouted, dropping his beer bottle. Surprisingly, the bottle did not break, but the beer spilled out all over the patio. He stooped down quickly to pick it back up, and stared back into Ian's face. "Are you kidding me? Your *wife*? You've never told me about a wife before. I assumed you were a lifelong bachelor. I can't believe you've never told me about her before." He flopped back into his chair, as if exhausted. "You just blew my mind," he said, staring solemnly at the ground. "Didn't think that was possible, actually. Congrats."

"It's painful to talk about, Lane," replied Ian with a grimace in his face. "It brings back too many haunting memories, and until now, I had no reason to open up those old wounds again. But watching you go through what you're going through, I decided it was past time I shared this part of my life with you, despite how much it hurts me to relive the memories." Ian stood up, and began to pace around the patio as he continued talking.

Ian paused his pacing, looking back at Lane. "This is for your ears only, my friend, I mean it," he said pointing his finger at Lane. "I have not spoken of this since I got to Miami ten years ago." He resumed his pacing.

Looking forlornly back at Ian, he said, "Of course, Ian, you have my word. This goes nowhere else."

"Twenty years ago, actually a little more than that, hard to believe," Ian said, rolling his eyes. "I was a kid, about twenty-four years old, I guess, and had just graduated from the police academy. Boy, I was one cocky kid," Ian said with a reminiscing grin. "Whole world in front of me," he said, sweeping his arms outward. "Thought I was going to change the world, ya know, clean up the city single-handedly or some such nonsense." He chuckled, pausing again, looking back at Lane.

"I know the feeling," said Lane, with a slight grin. "I had that exact same ambition out of the academy."

"It's good to see some kind of a smile on your face again, man. Been awhile," Ian said in a gentle tone.

Lane, realizing he was letting down his guard a bit, quickly erased any evidence of a smile from his face. "Well, what next?" he said briskly.

Ian shoved his hands into his pockets, continuing to pace in a circle around the fire pit. "A friend on the force invited me to his Christmas party, bunch 'a people there. Most I didn't know. I went, to be polite, but I wasn't really into parties. You know me. Then *she* walked in through the front door," Ian slowed his pace, and a gleam came over his face. He stopped, looked back at Lane, and said "I was bedazzled. Woman was gorgeous. I felt like such a fool. Seemed like my jaw hit the ground as I stood there staring at her for what seemed like minutes. I'm sure it was just a few seconds."

"So this was Eve, huh?" said Lane, as he scooted forward in his chair, anticipating the rest of the story.

Ian nodded his head slowly, still almost like he was in a trance. He rubbed his chin, and resumed pacing, putting his hands back into pockets. "Yep, that was Eve. She caught my eyes, and smiled at me from across the room. Despite the noisiness and bustling of all kinds of folks running around, it felt like it was just her and me in the room for a moment. My friend came up from behind me, grabbed my arm, and escorted me over toward her."

I'll never forget what he said. "Ian, meet my wife's friend Eve Bennett. Eve, meet Officer Ian Jelani. He just graduated from the academy."

"Eve and I shook hands," continued Ian, "and that's how it all started."

Lane sat back in his chair again, and laughed. "That's it? I thought you were going to remember some profound, inspiring quote. 'Ian, meet Eve, Eve meet Ian', that's all you got?"

Ian, stopping again, looked at Lane with an irritated scowl on his face, then he quickly relaxed. "Okay, I know, it wasn't so much the quote I remember. Her name," he said dreamily. "I mean that name sounded like music to my ears as I looked at the most beautiful woman I had ever seen."

"So you dropped down on one knee and proposed right then and there?" Lane said dryly.

Ian laughed out loud, and slapped his leg. "Well the thought *did* cross my mind, but no, of course not," he said. But by Valentine's Day I had proposed to her, she accepted, and we were married that summer."

Lane whistled, and said, "That's impressive though, still a whirlwind of a romance even if you *didn't* propose that first time you ever saw her."

Ian finally stopped his pacing, as he was getting more comfortable with telling the story. He sat back down in the chair next to Lane, and picked up his beer. He took a few sips, and continued, as the fire light flickered off his glowing face.

Ian breathed deeply, and continued his story. "The first two years were amazing. We were the perfect couple, loved all the same things, loved going everywhere together, truly glorious. She was a God-fearing woman, and rekindled my faith which had fallen by the wayside I must admit, despite my parents' best efforts to raise me in the Catholic Church. Eve had me back in the pews, at the oldest Catholic church west of the Mississippi. Basilica of St. Louis. Wow, that was—is, I mean—a beautiful place. I really felt at home there, and felt the Spirit of God, that's for sure."

Ian looked at Lane, just as Lane rolled his eyes a bit, slightly scoffing at Ian's momentary spiritual diversion.

"Yeah, that's another story. We won't go there tonight, buddy," said Ian smiling.

"Thank you," said Lane, "I'm definitely not in the mood for Ian Jelani to put on his preacher hat."

Ian leaned back in his chair, continuing to relax. "She was a social worker, really wanted to help people. So there we were, both had ideals of 'saving the world', just going about it in our different ways. We were both dedicated to our jobs, both working some long hours, probably longer than we should have but still, everything was going smoothly."

"I am sensing a change of direction for this story," Lane said. "So what happened? Where is Eve now?"

Ian's demeanor changed drastically, as he crossed his arms across his chest. He sat straight up in his chair, and paused for a couple of seconds, his breathing becoming more labored. "She is not *here*," he said, as he uncrossed his arms momentarily, waving his hands across the ground. "She is *here*," he said, pointing a finger to his own heart, "but she is not *here* on earth," he said with his hands held upward slightly.

"Oh my God," said Lane in a hushed tone. "So you mean she's...dead, Ian?" Now Lane's demeanor changed significantly as well.

Ian looked coldly back into Lane's face, nodding his head silently.

"Her physical body is not here anymore, but I firmly believe she is still with me, still watching out for me," Ian said, his voice now starting to crack slightly.

Lane placed his left hand on Ian's shoulder gently. "Geez, Ian, I had no idea, I am so sorry. No wonder you haven't talked about this before. It obviously is too painful."

Ian wiped some of the small tears welling up in his eyes, and he stood up once again. He resumed a fast pace around the fire pit now. He stopped on the opposite side of the fire pit from Lane, and looked up. "Well here is why you needed to hear this story tonight, my friend," Ian said somberly, regaining his composure. "You have got to hear me out," he said, with a more demanding tone.

Lane squinted at Ian, puzzled by this quick change of emotions he could see in his fellow detective. "Okay," Lane said, rising slowly to his feet. "What is it?" he said with an almost callous look on his face.

"Eve didn't just die, Lane," said Ian. "She was murdered."

Lane's face loosened as he heard the words. He looked back at Ian, stunned and silent.

Ian could see Lane's face was starting to show more empathy. "During my third year on the force, I had busted several drug pushers. I was good at it. There was this little penny-annie crook who was dealing drugs. I don't know his real name, but everyone called him 'Hellboy', something about that cartoon character, he was some kind of a fanatic about it. I wouldn't care to ever hear that name again anyway."

Lane crossed his arms now, and said "Well go on, what happened?"

Ian now began to pace back-and-forth staying on the opposite side of the fire pit from Lane. His hands now started to shake, and move up-and-down forcefully as he continued recounting his story.

"I had pinched him, he was in jail, thought I had him nailed," Ian said. "That little weasel got out, crooked attorneys, you know that story which happens all too often. After he got out, he went to one of the shelters where Eve was working." His voice was now starting to escalate, and Lane could note a look of rage coming into Ian's eyes.

"There she was, just trying to help people," Ian said through a broken voice. "They were the people who *really* needed help, and she was doing her job." Ian looked up with fire in his eyes. "*He* waited for her to come out at the end of the day. That bastard shot her. Shot her twice."

Ian now was having a hard time getting the words out. Lane still stood there with his arms crossed, not reacting in any particular way to Ian's story.

"The shelter called 911. The ambulance got there within minutes, and I was close behind," said Ian through the tears streaming down his face. "I got to hold that beautiful woman, as she lay there, dying on the sidewalk, shot down like some old worthless dog," he said, as an angered voice took over the weeping voice.

"I thank God in heaven I got there in time, before she died," said Ian. "We both got to say 'I love you' to each other. And do you want to know what her last words were, Lane?" Ian stopped pacing, stopped, and stared back into Lane's eyes.

"What?" Lane said coldly.

"Vengeance is mine, I will repay, saith the Lord," Ian said in a completely, calm tone. "'Don't you go after him, my love' she said," Ian quoted Eve. "She said 'he will face justice either here on Earth by the law, or in judgment, by God', but you can't go after him, Ian.' That's what she said."

"So *she* is why you say that all the time, isn't it?" asked Lane

"Eve said that to me almost every day of our married life, man," replied Ian. "She knew the temptation we cops have every day we put the badge on. When our job is *'to serve and to protect'*, we are going to deal with people, sometimes some truly bad people, practically every day who tempt us to take matters into our own hands."

Both men stood still for several minutes, not staring at each other, but just in different directions.

"Did you ever get the guy?" Lane finally spoke, breaking the awkward silence.

"I was obsessed with finding the guy, and I had every intention of killing him myself," Ian said with almost a look of fear in his eyes. "He was all I could think about for practically a year. Practically lost my job on the force over it."

"So you felt that way despite what Eve said to you?" asked Lane. "Then you *do* know how I feel. Are you going to answer my other question, did you ever get the guy?"

Ian put his hands in his pockets, and looked at the ground. "Yeah. I got the guy."

Ian resumed his pacing, still with his hands in his pockets. "My Captain's ultimatum finally got through to me—give up trying to find this Hellboy guy, or I'm off the force. So I moved on, got focused on doin' the job." Ian glanced at Lane, to see if he was still paying attention. "The call came in one day, officer down, they needed backup. It was this Hellboy dude, with some other low-lifes, in a shootout with some of our men. Long story short, I got there, several officers were dead or wounded, and all of Hellboy's Scumbags were dead...but not him," Ian said, pausing again, looking up and seeing Lane's eyes fixed on him.

"No he wasn't dead, not yet anyway," Ian continued. "He was all shot up, probably as good as dead. But when I saw him lying there on the ground, coughing up blood, I walked over to him, and pointed my gun at his head. He actually laughed weakly, and said 'I remember you, you tried to get me before, and I made your wife pay for your mistakes, didn't I?'"

Lane walked over closer to Ian, and asked "Did you say something back to him about Eve?"

Ian shook his head. "Nah, I put a bullet in his shoulder. When he stopped screaming from that, I put a bullet in his head. He was finally done talkin' after that."

They both stood silently, looking at each other.

"They gave me the Medal of Valor, had a big ceremony, made a big to-do over me," said Ian. "Called me a hero. But I was no hero. I was a coward. I did exactly what Eve asked me not to do, what God Himself asks me not to do. And they both saw what I did that day."

Ian walked back over to his chair and plopped down into it, leaving Lane standing up. "It's been over twenty years, and I can't shake that thought. I can't forget how I let *them* down, let myself down." He looked up at Lane. "And I'm trying to keep you from going down that same path. Living in pain and agony day-in-day-out, throwing away your career, giving Valenzuela that kind of power over you. If you don't change your trajectory, I fear what this is going to do to you."

Lane looked away from Ian, out into the black night of his backyard. "Look, Ian, I appreciate you coming to tell me all this. My heart goes out for you, and I am really sorry for everything you've suffered." He looked back at Ian, and continued. "But my situation is all different, you can't compare our two stories."

Ian shot back up out of his chair, throwing his hands up in the air. "What do you mean? Have you not been listening to *anything* I said?"

Lane walked angrily over and stood face-to-face with Ian. "At least you got to tell your wife goodbye. I lost both my wife *and* my little girl." Lane's eyes began to well up with tears. "You've had twenty years to get over this, this just happened to me, you can't expect me to just forget it all," Lane shouted.

"I know our stories are different, I *never* tried to say otherwise," Ian said, sticking an accusatory finger into Lane's face. "The reason I came over here tonight is not to tell you how my story is the same as yours. I came over here tonight to turn you back from the edge you're about to walk over. Our stories have some things in common, but the one thing that is identical, is how we both reacted to it all."

Ian turned away from Lane, took a couple of steps away, then turned back to face him. "I love you my friend," with a couple of tears starting to roll down his face. "And I don't want you to spend the next twenty years dealing with the same toll I have been payin' that whole time."

Lane turned away, looking back into the darkness once again. "I think it's time for you to go, Ian." He continued to feel more tears rolling down his cheeks. "You've made your point. I need you to just leave me alone now."

"Can't I pray with you before I go?" pleaded Ian.

"No, I'm not having any of that," replied Lane, still unable to look Ian in the eye. "Just go home, and get some sleep. That's what I'm going to do."

"Okay Lane," said Ian. "I'll go. But I am always there for you, and I am going to keep right on praying for you. Will you please remember that?"

Lane's shoulders bounced up and down from his quiet sobbing. He composed himself, turned around to look at Ian once again. "Sure, fine, I'll remember that." And with that, he walked through the sliding glass door back into his house, leaving Ian standing there quietly.

Ian slowly turned, and showed himself out through the side gate of the yard. He wiped his eyes with his forearm, and drove slowly off down the street to head for home.

Lane, now in a state of stoicism, grabbed a glass, and filled it with ice. He walked over to the tall pantry, opened it, grabbed a full bottle of his favorite Rieger whiskey, and began to pour...he drank...he poured...he drank...he poured...

CHAPTER 20:

TERROR IN NUEVO LAREDO, MEXICO

Chico Alvarez spoke to a large crowd gathered outside the Nuevo Laredo police station. "I promise you, as your newly appointed Chief of Police, that I, Chico Alvarez, will no longer stand for the free reign of crime. The drug cartels have controlled our town for long enough, and it is high time we took a stand. As your new police chief, I swear to you today, that within ninety days, we will clean up the streets of Nuevo Laredo."

Cheers and shouts of approval erupted in support. Alvarez took a moment to enjoy the sound of so many agreeing with him. The press conference had been a last minute idea and he was certain no one would show up. If his father could just see him now. The shouts of support died down and he continued his speech. "We will not be intimidated, and we will no longer look the other way while these drug lords take away our children from us and turn them into their slaves. We will drive them away from our city, and make sure they never return…or face the consequences if they show themselves here again."

The crowd roared, happy to hear of the new chief's plans for their crime-ridden neighborhoods. At the conclusion of his speech, Alvarez climbed into his car to head home for a break.

As Chico pulled away in his car, he dialed his wife on his cell phone. "Hey baby," he said, after Anna answered the call.

"Are you pleased with how everything went?," Anna asked. "How did it go?"

"I feel great about everything, babe. Everyone seems to be supporting me, and you already know I've got some good plans going forward." He glanced in his rearview mirror as a black SUV passed the car directly behind him. The next thing he would address in this town would be stricter traffic rules.

Chico exhaled in disbelief as the same SUV cut in between Chico's car and another. "Some nutty driver is riding right on my tail," said Chico in a puzzled voice. "Like literally went around the guy behind me, and cut back in."

"It must be someone who doesn't know he's following the new Sheriff in town," Anna said laughing.

Chico swore under his breath, concern creeping into his voice. "Okay, well now another SUV has pulled up too, and he's coming up on my left side. Something isn't right. I'm getting off the main road, I need to draw these idiots away from the traffic."

Sheriff Alvarez pulled off onto the next side road, and hit the gas, testing his mysterious followers.

"What?" Anna called out. "Who's with you?"

Chico could hear the sense of panic in her voice. "I'm by myself," he said , his voice raising. "I need to hang up." He tossed his cell phone into the passenger seat, not taking the time to hit the end button. "Hang up with me right now, and call your men. Chico, please call them!" Anna pleaded into thin air.

Chico grabbed his radio handset. "Sheriff Alvarez here, I've got some maniacs on my tail, and need some backup…" Before he finished his head recoiled, as he exclaimed "What the…" A sudden jolt to his car knocked the handset out of his hand. He grabbed the steering wheel with both hands, trying to bring the car back under control, as he heard the voice of the police dispatcher confirming his position. He could not answer now. He looked up into the rear view mirror to see that his car had just been slammed from behind and the SUV was gearing up to try it again.

Chico heard a car honking at him, and he glanced to his right, spotting a man in one of the SUVs with the rear window down. From the backseat, he brandished a gun, while slapping it on the outside of the vehicle door. He grinned at Chico.

Chico tried to press the gas pedal harder, when a third SUV sped up from his left, turning hard into the front of his car, forcing him off the road. Grass, gravel and dried clods of dirt spun up as he traveled along the shoulder of the road. He slammed the brakes bringing his car to a spinning halt. Dazed, Chico tried to get his bearings. The bright sun poured through his windshield, and a cloud of dust swirled all around him.

"What the hell is going on, Sheriff?" shouted a voice from the police radio.

Chico grabbed the handset and began to shout "Get out here to…" He never had time to say more. The driver side door was flung open, and a pair of hands grabbed his shoulders, yanking him out of his seat. The man flung Chico, tumbling across the ground. His sunglasses came off, and his side arm was dislodged from its holster. He felt the rocks on the ground scraping across his body.

"Where are you, Sheriff!" continued the frantic voice on the police radio.

Another man opened the passenger door to Chico's car and grabbed the radio handset. "Uh, the Sheriff is busy now," he said laughing, as he yanked the handset, snapping it away from the radio.

Chico tried to scramble to his feet, coughing up dust. He felt the burning sun on his face, and the smell of hot car engines filling the air. His heart threatened to burst out of his chest, but he mustered his courage.

"Do you know who I am?" Chico said defiantly. His eyes finally came into focus, as he now saw a dozen men lined up about twenty feet across from him. His hand slid down to his side, but he realized that his gun holster was empty.

"Of course we know who you are, Sheriff Chico Alvarez," called out the large man standing in the middle of the group..

"Say hello to my little friend!" another man screamed from the right of the group. Immediately all the men started laughing, as they raised their guns and opened fire, launching a barrage of bullets. In a matter of minutes they completely shredded Chief Alvarez.

Alvarez was gasping for breath, covered in blood, unable to move; the hot, dusty, dry ground was trying to quickly lap up the last of his life. Next, the men turned around and began shooting up the sheriff's car, laughing as if having the time of their lives.

From inside Chico's car came a muffled voice. "No, not my Chico!" she screamed. Suddenly everything was silent. There came the heartbreaking sounds of her sobs.

All the men calmly climbed back into their cars, chuckling and chatting as if nothing in particular had happened. Just another day at the office for them. Everyone rolled down their windows to gaze upon their handiwork, and burst into laughter once again. Before they could pull away a white SUV barrelled toward them. It boasted a double-rack of emergency lights, and a siren blared.

"Reload!" commanded one of the men, as he opened his door. He called out to the men in the other vehicles. "Looks like we get to shred some deputies today too!" he said in a giddy voice.

Everyone jumped out of their cars quickly, and were lined up before the white SUV came to a full stop.

One of the men swore, and grinning said, "Welcome to the party!" The man cursed, then all the men opened fire, shredding the white SUV with another barrage of bullets. They emptied their cartridges, and looked at each other with big smiles, very proud of another victory.

The driver's side door of the white SUV creaked open, then fell off its hinges. The shooters stepped backward in astonishment as a single figure stepped out of the bullet-ridden vehicle. The huge figure, wearing highly reflective sunglasses, and a white cowboy hat, without even one scratch on him. Alvarez, barely clinging to life, weakly opened his eyes, astonished to see a stranger standing there. His mind could not wrap around what he was seeing. Apparently his assailants felt the same way.

Everyone stood still, looking at each other.

Finally, the stranger broke the silence. "The Lord hath opened his armory, and hath brought forth the weapons of His indignation," shouted the stranger.

The armed men could see he was twirling something around in the air with his left hand, which was creating a loud, whirring sound. Was it some kind of a slingshot? In the stranger's right hand was a fistful of smooth, round stones.

The men immediately began to scatter, trying to get back to their vehicles. The stranger began launching stones from his slingshot, with deadly accuracy, picking off each man with a single stone to the head. Moments later, the mayhem was done, and a dozen bodies were lying scattered on the ground. Suddenly, the stranger was no longer holding a slingshot, but instead, a sword. He cut off the heads of each and every one of the mortally wounded men.

Alvarez strained to lift his head. He heard the stranger speak once again. "Peace be with you now, Chico." The stranger looked away, and screamed "Vengeance is mine!", and he disappeared as Chico drew his last breath.

Thumos found himself flying over vast fields covered with the nodding heads of red poppies. A fury lit in his heart that these beautiful flowers, gifts from the Father, should be used in this way by the Nuevo Laredo drug lords. Flanking the fields were large metal buildings to warehouse the flowers and process them into opium and heroin. A flurry of activity caught his eye on the other side of the complex where workers busied themselves to produce the vile product. Thumos could stand no more. Hovering over the center of it all he waved his hands outward in a fanlike motion. Sprinklers in the field spontaneously sputtered to life, but instead of water, a red substance spattered the ground, the flowers, the people and the buildings where it oozed down the sides and pooled in thick, viscous puddles.

Thumos observed the workers running for cover, taking to their vehicles, diving into the buildings. Not this time, he thought to himself. No more cover for the peddlers of death. He raised his arms to the heavens and taking a deep breath exhaled and pointed toward the buildings and the complex beyond. The sky split open. Fire and ice, hail and lightning bombarded the area below him. Cars and machinery exploded, windows shattered from the hail and the buildings shivered at the onslaught.

Thumos descended, his feet touching the soft earth. Through the windows people peered at him where they had tried to seek refuge from the chaos. Many of them were covered in red, their eyes filled with confusion and fear.

A group of heavily armed soldiers ran outside from a nearby warehouse to face him.

"Stop right there, gringo," yelled a thickly muscled man holding a semi-automatic weapon.

Thumos stopped. Raising his hands as if in surrender, he snapped his fingers loudly. And then there was silence. Around them hail still fell, lightning still flashed and yet there was no sound. Some of the men lowered their weapons in confusion, looking around for an explanation that would never come.

From far away there came a low hum. Over the horizon, bounding over the tops of the rooftops large swarms of dark insects descended. Thumos stood unflinching, simply staring back at the soldiers who watched him intently. They began to shift on their feet nervously, their quarry forgotten as they began to see the approaching horde. The sound grew deafeningly louder, and the people who were still inside watching all this unfold, covered their ears in a futile effort to block the assaulting noise. Like a black cloud, moving in unison, an undulating wave of insects resembling locusts and flies swarmed around Thumos, creating a fantastic whirlwind that encompassed him. He could feel his hair blowing wildly, and his clothes rippling as though he stood in the middle of a violent storm. But these creatures left him untouched. Slowly he raised his arm to point toward the men with the guns. The swarm shifted and Thumos watched them engulf the soldiers.

They began to scream in terror as the insects began to feed. The thugs fired their guns futilely into the air.

Thumos calmly looked back to the buildings from where many of the workers had been watching in disbelief. The insects had reached the buildings and the walls came to life as the insects flowed like a living river up the walls and began to fill the buildings. He heard more screaming, and saw people trying to run from the buildings. The insects targeted those with weapons, encasing them.

Minutes later, the thick black cloud of insects poured out of the buildings and met with those in the yard. Then with one accord they zoomed off into the sky, disappearing. Dozens of bodies littered the ground, stripped to the bone. Many workers were left confused, terrified but very much unscathed. They had not taken up arms against the angel of the Lord, and had lived.

Thumos shouted at them "¡La venganza es mia!." Without a backward glance he charged into the sky leaving behind what looked like a war zone.

CHAPTER 21:

A BURGEONING ROMANCE

"Wow, such a beautiful place," exclaimed Lauren, as she sat down in her chair, which Ian had politely pulled away from the table, allowing her to be seated. Ian's olfactory senses detected a wonderfully scented perfume, noting it was not too heavy, but pleasantly detectable.

Should I say something about that? he thought to himself. *Or will I sound like an idiot, like I'm just giving her a line?* He opted to skip any perfume commentary for now. "I second that emotion," replied Ian, as he helped her slide her chair forward, to the table. He walked around to the other side. "This place is gorgeous, and I really do love the food here at OLA," he said with great anticipation, as he sat in his own chair.

"Oh, so you're a frequent guest here, eh *Detective Jelani*," said Lauren, grinning from ear-to-ear.

"On my salary?" responded Ian. "Let me just make this very clear, *Dr. Willis*. This is about a once-a-year event for me. I only come here on special occasions. *Very* special occasions," he said, with a broad smile on his face.

"I have always wanted to come here," Lauren said. "But I never had the opportunity. I've heard this is some of the best food you'll eat in town, and out here on Miami Beach. The view is just spectacular. And the smells here? The foods I am smelling are amazing. This is just heavenly."

"You know what?" Ian said, leaning in toward the table. "I really must agree with you. The view here is absolutely breathtaking," he said with a smile, staring straight into Lauren's eyes.

Oh boy, thought Ian. *So I skipped commenting on her perfume, and this is what I come up with? I'm such an idiot*, ridiculed Ian to himself in his head.

Lauren blushed. With a bashful grin, she shook her head. "You are too much, *Detective Jelani*. But you are very kind."

Okay, so maybe that worked, thought Ian. *Proceed with caution though*, he tried to reassure his nervous impulses.

A gentle, warm breeze was blowing in through the many open doors along the seafront wall of the restaurant. That helped Ian relax.

"Okay, *Dr. Willis*," quipped Ian. "I think we can drop those formalities here tonight, and just be 'Lauren' and 'Ian'. What do you say?"

"I'm just giving you a hard time, *Ian*," Lauren answered with an emphasis on his name. "I am perfectly fine with us using those names tonight."

"There is something about the way you say 'Ian', that I sure like to hear," he said. "You can say my name just as much as you want to."

Lauren smiled, and spoke. "Speaking of names, 'Jelani', I've always wondered about that last name of yours. It's kind of fun to say," she said with a chuckle. "Where is your family from?"

"It's a Swahili word," answered Ian. "It means 'full of strength'", he said with a confident nod.

"Well there you go," replied Lauren. "How apropos for you."

Ian laughed. "I guess so. My dad grew up in Uganda. He was such an excellent student, and some Catholic nuns saw some real potential in him. They were very instrumental in him getting connected to St. Louis University, Jesuit school, you know." Ian picked up his glass, took a sip of ice water, and set it back down.

"Wow, this is fascinating, Ian, go on," as she leaned forward, showing great interest.

"Oh gosh, there's a lot to his story, I could go on all night," said Ian. "But for now, long story short, he got a scholarship back in the seventies, arrived in St. Louis barely spoke any English, and eventually managed to graduate near the top of his engineering class."

Lauren could see Ian's eyes lighting up as he talked.

Ian continued. "He got recruited by Lockheed Martin, met my mama who was this awesome little music teacher at one of the high schools."

Now Lauren could see a whimsical look in Ian's eyes as he continued talking of his parents. It was obvious he had fond memories of them.

"And the rest, as they say, is history," Ian finished with a soft, reminiscing laugh, as he shook his head, taking another drink of his water.

"Big family?" questioned Lauren.

"Oh yes, very Catholic in that regard, was my family," Ian grinned. "I've got two brothers and two sisters, they're all over the place these days. Mom and Dad are both retired of course, still hangin' in there in St. Louis. I don't get time to go see them as often as I should," Ian said, now with a forlorn look.

Before Ian could turn the tables, and start quizzing Lauren about her family, she switched subjects on him.

"Now I bet you didn't think we'd ever get to this point, did you?" questioned Lauren. "How many times did you ask me out before I finally wore down, and accepted?"

"I pretty much lost count a long time ago," said Ian chuckling. "But you have to give it to me, I am a persistent man. I don't quit, never give up, just can't bear to take 'no' for an answer."

Lauren laughed. "Oh yes, I'll hand it to you. You are definitely…let's say, how can I say this…'pig headed.'" They both laughed out loud, and Lauren continued. "I told you many times I just don't like the thought of dating someone I work with. It just has the potential for too many headaches and obstacles. And especially in our line of work."

"Well I *will* give you that, but there's the key word, 'potential'" said Ian. "Handle a relationship the right way, and those 'potentials' won't happen."

"Oh, so you're a relationship guru, are you, Ian?" Lauren said with a giggle. "How many times have you dated someone you worked with from the same police precinct?"

"Well exactly, uh, zero times. But there's a first time for everything, right?" Ian answered with a big grin. "That's what I've *heard*, that it *can* work. And that comes from very reliable sources," he said, now trying to sound like a very astute professor.

"So why did you finally give in to my pestering you, my dear?" Ian continued.

"Well I just felt so sorry for you," Lauren said jokingly. "I mean I figured you must just be so desperate, since you kept asking a woman who rejected you dozens of times."

"I don't know if *dozens of times* is quite accurate to say," replied Ian.

Lauren interrupted him before he could say anything else. Her tone became more serious. "All jokes aside, you have always been very kind to me, Ian. And you do have a good reputation around the office; everyone likes you." She then leaned into the table, and spoke in a bit of a hushed tone. "And I happen to like the view here, too," she said, staring back into Ian's eyes, with a sly grin coming over her face.

Ian appeared a bit flustered now, as if not accustomed to a woman turning the tables on him. "Hey Miguel," Ian said, clearing his throat and waving his hand at their waiter. "I think we're ready for some drinks over here."

Miguel, a young man in his twenties, began to briskly walk toward Ian and Lauren's table. He was a sharply dressed waiter, in his white shirt, with a dark vest and dark dress pants. His black wingtip shoes were so well-polished, you might literally be able to see your reflection in them. His dark hair was perfectly arranged, and his goatee was trimmed with great precision. His dark eyes glistened with friendliness, as he arrived at the table where Ian and Lauren sat.

Miguel, smiling very attentively, exuded welcome and readiness-to-serve. "Greetings, Detective Jelani," he said. "Do you want your usual Corona in a frosted glass with a lime? And what can I get for the lovely lady?" he said, looking at Lauren, his bright white teeth sparkling a big smile at her.

"Uh, 'the usual'?," Lauren said questioningly, looking back across the table at Ian. She grinned like the cat who caught the canary. "What was that about a once-a-year event, *Detective Jelani*?"

Miguel looked puzzled. Ian looked back at Lauren sheepishly. "Hold on, wait just a second," Ian said defensively. "Now that bar over there," he said, as he pointed toward the restaurant bar, "happens to be a great bar, and it just so happens that Lane and I like to frequent *that* bar. But over here," he said pointing down with both of his index fingers, "Yeah, this is *in*frequent."

Lauren laughed, and looked back up at Miguel. "So tell me, Miguel, how many lovely ladies have you seen Detective Jelani 'over here' with?" she said, mimicking Ian.

Miguel looked back at Ian, and without missing a beat, said "You don't tip me well enough over at the bar, Detective Jelani, to cover for you." He laughed, and looked back at Lauren. "Based on his and Detective Madigan's crummy tipping habits, I can promise you he doesn't have enough money to be 'over here' very much," he said pointing down with both fingers, mimicking Ian.

All three of them laughed together companionably.

"Honestly, m'am" Miguel said looking back at Lauren. "I have never seen Detective Jelani here with anyone other than his grumpy partner, Detective Madigan. And by no means have I ever seen him graced by the presence of such a beautiful woman as you."

"Forget the usuals tonight, Miguel," Ian said quickly. "We'll take two glasses of your best cab."

"Very good, sir," Miguel answered, bowing his head, stepping away from the table.

"You'd better really tip him well tonight," said Lauren. "That is one smart kid!"

"Oh, you better believe it," Ian said, chuckling. "I think I owe him one. Okay, well grab your menu there," Ian said, pointing at the menu lying on the table in front of Lauren. "Let's see what's cookin'. You're right, the smells here are definitely amazing, and I'm anxious to try something new."

They both picked up their menus, and began to peruse them.

"Steak..seafood...so many choices, and it all looks delicious," exclaimed Ian. "Is anything sounding good to you, Lauren?"

"Oh, it all sounds fantastic," Lauren replied. "But I am certain I was smelling some salmon before, and that Panela Salmon sounds to-die-for. What about you?"

"I might be a little adventurous, and try the Pescado a lo Macho," Ian, with his best Spanish accent he could muster. "But the Sugar Cane Tuna sounds really interesting, too."

Miguel showed up beside their table once again, asking if they were ready to order, as he placed some bread and butter on the table. They placed their orders, and Miguel promised to be back shortly with their wine.

"So not to talk shop too much, but did you hear about everything that happened over in Wichita lately?" Lauren asked, in a more serious tone.

"You mean all that talk of a vigilante at work, then how he apparently was taken out himself?" Ian replied. "That is some crazy goings-on, for sure." He sliced a piece of bread off the loaf, offering some to Lauren. "This rye bread with the honey butter, it's the bomb, you've got to try some."

"Yes, thank you," said Lauren as she held up her bread plate. Ian placed a slice there, with a little bit of butter. "Everyone is talking about this 'Holy Terror,'" continued Lauren. "Do you think that's who took out this Whitaker kid in Wichita? Do you think this Holy Terror has been here in Miami?"

"It all seems a little paranoid, if you ask me," said Ian disgustedly, shaking his butter knife, while chewing a bite of bread in his mouth. Realizing his faux pas—Mom would be ticked, he thought to himself—he caught himself, swallowed quickly, and set his knife down. "No question, all the stories are sweeping the country, and it's really affecting people. The criminals are afraid, and now anyone who fancies himself as a vigilante is going to be a little worried, too."

"I've heard people are breathing a little sigh of relief, honestly," said Lauren. "It's like people feel more secure or something. And also, crime rates are actually dropping off, unlike anything anyone has ever seen before. No one is complaining about that."

"Well it's sure driving law enforcement crazy," said Ian. "And I don't blame 'em. Somebody is trying to do our job, and it isn't right."

Miguel walked up to the table once again. "Forgive my interruption, you two seem to be in the middle of an intense conversation, but here is your wine." He placed the glasses carefully in the exact right spot in relation to the dinner plates. "Please enjoy!" He started to walk away.

"Miguel," Ian blurted out, "wait a second. So, have you heard about the 'Holy Terror' news stories?"

"Oh, yes sir," said Miguel, with an excited tone, turning back to their table. "Is that what you two were discussing? I find all of that quite fascinating, myself."

"So you're okay with what this person is doing, Miguel?" questioned Lauren, as she took a sip of her wine.

"You bet!" he said happily.

"Now wait a minute," said Ian skeptically. "So you're telling me you're fine with someone or some multiple persons, taking the law into their own hands? What if they take out the wrong people, or what if they hurt innocent people?"

Ian took a sip of his wine. "Miguel, buddy, that is an excellent choice, delicious!"

Miguel grinned, very pleased with himself. "Caymus Napa Valley, 2018," he said quickly, then without missing a beat, continued with the previous conversation. "How do you know it's a *person*?" he questioned. He squatted down beside the table, looked around as if to see if anyone was looking, and continued in a hushed tone. "Have you heard of what happened in my home town of Nuevo Laredo?"

Lauren and Ian looked at each other questioningly, then looked back at Miguel.

"Nah, man," said Ian. "Never even heard of 'Nuevo Laredo.'"

"It's a town in Mexico, just on the other side of the border from Laredo, Texas," said Lauren. "A real hot bed of drug activity."

"Yes, exactly," said Miguel. "My parents moved us out of there when I was only a child. They were very afraid of the drug cartels. But just the other day, the 'Que Horror' went there. He wiped out all of the bad people there. My cousin is still there. She saw it with her own two eyes." A look of fear came over Miguel as he continued. "Apocalyptic, biblical events, she told me. It was something like the Israelites in Egypt, you know, the ten plagues." Miguel stood back up, crossed himself, and kissed the crucifix he wore around his neck. "I must get back to my other tables. I'll check on your food too," he said as he walked away quickly.

Lauren and Ian sat there dumbfounded, looking at each other with disbelief. They both quietly reached down, picked up their glasses of wine, and took long sips.

"Well, that was a little weird," said Ian.

"Kinda creepy even," said Lauren.

"I'm going to have to look up that story" Ian spoke again. "Wonder if he's exaggerating, or maybe his cousin was on something, you know, if that's a druggie hot bed."

Ian continued. "You know, Lane was working on something before *the incident*. He was looking at a bunch of stories in the National Criminal system. But he only mentioned it, and he never got to talk to me about it. Ever since Janie and Elizabeth died, he's not been the same."

"Oh, of course not," replied Lauren. "I can't imagine going through what he's been going through."

"No, me neither," answered Ian sadly. "More than anyone ought to have to deal with."

Miguel and another young man assisting him, showed up tableside with two plates of food. "Panela Salmon for the lady," Miguel said, signaling to the young assistant to set his plate in front of Lauren. "And Sugar Cane Tuna to the gentleman," he said, as he placed Ian's plate.

"Outstanding," Ian exclaimed, with his eyes wide open. "Miguel, Chef Castro has outdone himself. Lauren, yours looks incredible too."

"I don't know Chef Castro, but you can tell him I am spellbound, Miguel," Lauren said, as she stared down at her plate. She looked up at Miguel with a grateful smile.

"That smile is the only thing I need to tell the chef about, m'am", answered Miguel. "Thank you very much. Oh, another glass of wine?"

"Absolutely, both of us," said Ian, as he cut into his food. "That would be great, Miguel."

"Excellent, sir, I'll be right back with the bottle."

The conversation stopped for a bit, as Lauren and Ian eagerly ate their meals. Eventually, they both pushed away from the table, and at virtually the same time, looked up at each other.

"What was that you were saying before about this place having some of the best food in town, Lauren?" asked Ian, with an air of intense satisfaction.

"That may have been the best dinner I've ever eaten," said a very happy Lauren. "Normally, I enjoy conversing *during* the meal, but this was so good, I didn't want to stop to take time out to say anything," she said with a chuckle.

"I hear you," agreed Ian. "Truly an inspiring feast." Holding his wine glass out toward Lauren, she responded with a light tap to his glass with her own, nodding her head.

They both finished their glasses of wine. Ian paid the bill, they said their farewells to the very polite Miguel, and then they headed out of the restaurant.

"I can't stop thinking about what Miguel told us," said Lauren.

"Me too," said Ian. "Definitely need to check into that one."

They walked out into the parking lot. The air had cooled slightly after sunset, and the soft, cool ocean breeze brought a pleasant smell.

"I love that smell of lemongrass out here," said Lauren, as she inhaled deeply.

"I love that cool ocean breeze," said Ian. "Lane and I like to sit outside after the sun goes down, and look out over the beach while we have a beer."

"Corona, in a glass, with a lime," Lauren quipped.

"You got it, that's our favorite," Ian replied with a reminiscing smile. "I'd like to do that again with Lane one of these days. If he can come out of this."

Ian opened the car door for Lauren, and she slid inside. He walked over to the driver's side, and paused for a moment, looking back at the lights of the restaurant, where he could now see the outdoor patio. Under his breath, Ian said "God in heaven, please guide Lane through this time. He really needs you, Father."

Ian drove out of the parking lot, and pulled onto Collins Avenue.

A few minutes later, they arrived in front of Lauren's apartment. Ian parked out in the street.

"Regardless of any scary 'Holy Terror' stories, *Detective Jelani*, I had an amazing evening," said Lauren. She leaned over, and gently kissed Ian's lips, resting the palm of her hand on his cheek.

Ian, looking quite startled after the kiss, composed himself and spoke. "Uh, wait a second, my mind was kinda being blown, and I think I might've missed something here. Can we try that one more time?"

Lauren smiled and nodded her head. Ian leaned over to her, put his hand on her cheek, and they kissed for a much longer time.

Lauren opened the car door, started to step out of the car, then looked back at Ian. "And a good kisser to boot," she said. "Good to know. Good night, Ian. See you at the office tomorrow. Let's do this again." She stepped outside the car door.

Ian, in a stupor, completely mesmerized, finally managed to speak. "Really soon, yes, let's do this again. Good night, beautiful."

Lauren stuck her head down in the open door, and gave him that same embarrassed grin, shaking her head. "Next time, it's on me. Next time, I'll make you some dinner here at my place."

Ian shot her a big smile. "Now that sounds fantastic! Can't wait!"

Lauren shut the car door, and Ian watched her walk up to her front door, then disappeared inside. He looked straight ahead down the street, shook his head, and said "That is one incredible woman!" He looked upward, crossed himself, and said "Thank you Lord!"

Ian glanced back toward Lauren's house, and he could see the curtains pulled back slightly. He knew she was watching him out the window, and he gave his car horn a gentle toot. "Checkin' me out, is she?" he said out loud. A big smile came across his face, as he exhaled a sigh of satisfaction, and pulled away from the curb, driving away down the street. "Best date, ever."

CHAPTER 22:

TRYING TO TOUCH
THE UNTOUCHABLE

In a remote corner of the Twilight Realm, Satan walked toward his throne, with his head held high, as though he were parading in a royal procession. Kakos trailed closely behind him.

Just prior to seating himself, Satan ran his grotesque fingers over the elegantly decorated throne, gently caressing the various gemstones which covered it, with a glint in his eye. "Have you ever seen such majesty?" he said, glancing back over his shoulder at Kakos.

"Glorious, my lord," answered Kakos.

Satan eased slowly into his seat, with great fanfare, and let out a gentle sigh. "No king has ever sat upon a throne as splendid as mine," Satan said, as Kakos positioned himself to Satan's right hand, standing at attention, looking straight in parallel to Satan's view. "Why, even the *great* Yahweh

Himself," he said mockingly, "does not possess a magnificent seat as mine. He offers me no prestige, so I create it for myself."

"Of course you do," said Kakos, sounding slightly sarcastic.

"Watch your tone," growled Satan.

"I offer no *tone*, my lord, I only am in complete agreement with you," Kakos responded, in a less condescending way.

"Much better, Kakos, my servant," Satan said. "These red stones here," he said as he rubbed both hands over the red gemstones on the ends of each armrest, "are from a place you have never even seen, my dear Kakos. They are most impressive, for sure."

Kakos broke off his intensely outward stare, to look down where Satan was gesturing.

"Yes, I do not recognize those, my lord," Kakos said. "But I do recognize many of the other gemstones with which your throne is laden."

"Oh of course you do, Kakos, most of them are found on Earth where so many incredible treasures exist, but not all of these can be found there," Satan said boastfully.

Satan turned his head toward Kakos, trying to appear very stately. "All right, I am ready now, you may proceed," Satan said very calmly, then turned his head exaggeratingly, fixing his stare outward.

Kakos reached down beside Satan's throne, and picked up a black, twisted horn. He pressed it to his lips, and blew, causing the horn to emit a dreadful sound, as though some animal was dying.

A gnarled grin swept across Satan's face, as he watched his minion descending upon his throne room, from every direction.

"This vast multitude of angels, my Makria, once served Yahweh," mused Satan out loud. Kakos was the only person audibly able to hear him, as the motley crew of angels were noisy and chaotic entering the throne room. They all shrieked, screamed, fidgeted, pushed and struck each other.

"But now, they serve me. They bow only to me, just like you do," Satan said to Kakos.

They both continued to stare outward, across the gathering.

"Yes, my lord," was all Kakos would say.

"Look at them," Satan continued. "Once grossly garbed in brilliant white robes, issued by Yahweh, their appearance continues to grow darker, much more to my liking, naturally," Satan said, nodding his head in approval.

"No one is in attire as dark as yours, my lord," said Kakos. "Your clothing is blacker than the night. Why do we not all wear such blackness?" Kakos's concentration broke slightly, as if he had never thought about this before, and he looked down at Satan questioningly. "Some of them do not look well, my lord, they appear sickly, even weak," Kakos said with disdain, now looking up again at them.

"My dear Kakos, take no thought about such matters, they are all perfectly fine," Satan said, as though trying to be conciliatory. "It all depends on how long they have been in my service. You can tell that from the shade of their robes. The longer they serve me, the closer their robes are to turning completely black...like mine."

Satan finally slammed both hands down onto the armrests of his throne, creating a deep, booming sound. The mysterious red jewels emanated a blood-right light over the entire gathering, which sent them all groveling to the ground in fear. Even Kakos startled slightly, but he remained at his post.

"What shall we do about Thumos?" roared Satan. His eyes gleamed with anger, as his calm demeanor was now gone.

"Obviously Thumos will not join us, and his actions may very well jeopardize our own cause. Therefore, he must be condemned to the Banished Realm!" Satan shouted in a reverberating voice, slamming his fist down onto his throne once again.

At that proclamation, Satan's audience was plunged into a great frenzy. They all stood back up on their feet, screaming and shrieking once again.

Satan rose from his throne, and he began to pace frantically about the room. "I had to get permission from Yahweh to initiate my attacks against the great Job. We may be restricted from directly interacting with Yahweh's fleshbags, but *not* when it comes to the Agathon," he said, slamming one fist into the other.

Satan stopped his pacing in front of his throne, and he looked out over the minion. He held his arms up over them all, and his voice boomed over the raucous crowd. "All of you, seek out Thumos, hurt him, and send him to the Banished Realm!" Once again, the vast crowd erupted into screams, shrieks, and laughs. The throne room emptied in a flurry.

Satan was left alone with this most-trusted servant, Kakos. He sat back down on his gaudy throne, as Kakos began to speak. "My king, do you honestly think any of them stands a chance in hel…" Kakos broke off his comment, as Satan's eyebrow raised, while turning an irritated look at Kakos. He backtracked and modified what he was about to say.

"Uhhhh…I mean, stands a chance in the *world* of stopping Thumos?" Kakos asked with a tone of great doubt in his voice.

Satan frowned at Kakos. "You know how I feel about anyone using the h-word," he said, scowling. "No one is to ever mention that place in my presence."

"Kakos, my loyal subject," Satan spoke again, now more calmly. "As much as it pains me to even use the word, you must have more," Satan clears his throat, "*faith*," he finished, with an emphasis on that dreaded word.

"Thumos is but one angel," continued Satan. "And my following has grown to an all-time high. Yes, I am confident Thumos will suffer greatly, and be condemned to the Banished Realm," he finished in a very quick, dismissive tone.

Kakos mumbled under his breath, as he turned to leave Satan. "Let him who thinks he stands, take heed lest he fall," he said quietly.

"What did you say?" angrily questioned Satan.

Kakos paused, surprised that Satan heard him. He did not turn around, and said "I just said 'then Thumos must fall.'"

Satan spoke again. "Kakos, I want you to keep an eye on my minions. Report to me what is happening, and tell me immediately when Thumos has been dealt with."

Kakos, still facing away from Satan's direct view, rolled his eyes. Obediently, yet with an air of doubt and disgust in his voice, said "Yes my King. I will monitor the situation." Kakos disappeared, leaving Satan alone in his throne room.

Satan's vast array had scattered into groups of four to five. The various groups were even now scouring heaven and earth in search of Thumos. Satan laced his hands in front of him and allowed himself a moment to be proud of his impressive network. He was able to remain very informed of activities both in heaven, on earth, and any other worlds the Father had created.

Thumos sensed them long before they struck. He thought to himself, *Where the dark ones certainly excel in finding information, that is not nearly enough to compensate for their lack of intelligence and fortitude. They may possess the right information, but being organized and knowing what to do with that information is beyond their capacity.*

Like bees buzzing in his ears, their negative energy flowed. Based on what he knew of Satan's trackers, these four could only be Raca, Zeus, Chernibog, and Xena. Thumos calmed his breathing so he would not give himself away and continued to act as though he was meditating. With angelic spies everywhere, working on both the dark and the light sides,

Thumos' allies had notified him of Satan's orders. He rather enjoyed setting himself up to bait the Makria, and engage them in battle. This is what he was made for.

Zeus motioned to the other three silently, instructing them to spread out in order to surround Thumos.

Suddenly, Thumos heard Zeus shout "Now!" Instantly, Thumos back-flipped over all four of them as they tried to converge on him. He chuckled as he watched them all collide into each other.

Raca was first out of the pile. He looked back at Thumos and shouted "You're mine, Thumos," as he lunged toward Thumos.

"I think not, Raca!" exclaimed Thumos, easily dodging Raca's swings. With two quick strikes, Thumos sent him flying off out of his view.

Zeus attacked Thumos from behind, bringing his rhabdos over Thumos' throat, trying to choke him. Xena and Chernibog quickly ran over and each landed quick hits of their rhabdoses on Thumos's legs, trying to knock him down, to gain an advantage over him.

Grunting in pain, Thumos began to spin, lifting Zeus off his feet. Zeus's legs slammed into each of the other two Makria, sending them sprawling to the ground. Thumos reached over his head, grabbed Zeus by the hair, and flung him back over his own body. Then, Thumos slammed him to the ground, face-planting Zeus. Wasting no time, he grabbed his rhabdos, and plunged it right through Zeus's back.

"That was for Armada!" he screamed upwards into the blackness, hoping Satan could hear his cry. He looked back at the other two, with a fire in his eyes, and yelled "Which of you wants to follow Zeus into the Banished Realm next?"

Thumos heard Raca charging from behind, and without even a backward glance, he thrust his rhabdos backwards right through Raca's abdomen.

Seeing how Thumos had dispatched Zeus and Raca so quickly, Xena and Chernibog glanced at each other with a look of fear in their eyes, and both instantly turned in the opposite direction and fled in fright.

Group after group of the Makria met with the same fate at Thumos's hand, as did that first group. None of them proved a match for him, as each time he faced more foes, he more easily conquered them. They all either were condemned to the Banished Realm by Thumos' rhabdos, or they turned tail and escaped that impending doom.

Back in Satan's hall, the Dark One grew increasingly frustrated with the obvious lack of success against Thumos. He slammed both fists down onto the highly polished, dark black surface of his table.

"Kakos!" he screamed in an out-of-control shrill.

Kakos appeared, sporting an obviously devious grin. "I hate to say it, my king, but 'I told you so'!" Kakos spoke sarcastically.

"You know what, Kakos? Sometimes I wish you would just shut your big mouth!" Satan screamed into Kakos' face, before slapping him violently to the ground.

Kakos rose back to his feet. "Forgive my insolence, master," he said with his eyes lowered.

"What are we going to do about this?" Satan asked harshly.

Kakos replied in a calm, matter-of-fact tone. "Thumos is a very powerful warrior with great passion for his 'craft', Master."

"Do not tell me the obvious," Satan retorted. "Tell me something I do not know about him. His passion is the one quality about him I hate the most!"

Kakos continued. "He is not like a man who has a family or friends who are dear to him. No weapon has been fashioned that can defeat him. He has no weakness to exploit; no apparent vice. He cannot be reasoned with."

"Okay, okay," Satan spoke impatiently. He put his hand to his chin, as a big grin came over his face. "But you are wrong, my dear Kakos," he said in a decidedly calmer tone. "That is it, my friend. He *does* have a weakness."

Kakos looked puzzled. "What is it? What are you talking about?"

"Thumos actually cares about what happens to the children of that egotistical, over-inflated Father. Surely we can use *that* against him," Satan said eagerly.

"Aha, very good point, my king," said Kakos, nodding his head in agreement. "I will have to investigate this," he continued. "But wait," he said excitedly. "My king, do you know who Roberto Valenzuela of Miami is?"

Satan laughed out loud. "Are you kidding, of course I know who that is. He is one of my favorite people of all time. He is ruthless, spiteful, foul—a truly evil person."

Kakos continued. "I know assuredly that Thumos has taken an especially keen interest in an incident involving Valenzuela and a Miami police detective whose family was killed by Valenzuela in a car wreck. I believe that is the key to getting at Thumos."

"Who is this police detective?" Satan questioned.

"His name is Lane Madigan," Kakos answered

"Oh yes, I do know of him a little bit," Satan responded. "I have also heard things about his irritating partner as well, Ian Jelani; some sort of goodie-two-shoes flesh-bag," Satan said dryly.

"So, yes, excellent idea Kakos," Satan continued. "We must use this against Thumos. You will pursue that situation, Kakos," Satan commanded.

"Oh, and please, do something about that Jelani character while you are at it," Satan added. "He could really interfere in this if you are not careful.

Yahweh's faithful can actually be quite powerful when aligned with His will, and definitely have a propensity to throw a wrench into our works."

"They are weak, pathetic creatures, my Lord," replied Kakos flippantly. "There is no reason to be concerned about their abilities."

"Trust me, Kakos," answered Satan harshly, leveling a finger into Kakos's face. "I have seen it time after time throughout man's history. Make no mistake, they are utterly capable of interfering. And if the Spirit of Yahweh fills them, they are especially irritating."

"By your command, then, my king," replied an obedient Kakos, slapping his arm across his chest. He disappeared into the darkness.

Satan sat back down on his throne. "Now we are finally getting somewhere, he said as a huge grin slinked across his face.

"Thumos thinks he has no chinks in his armor, but his care for the Father's children will be his downfall," Satan continued. He kicked his feet up, threw his hands behind his head, and began to laugh maniacally.

CHAPTER 23:

A MATCH MADE IN HEAVEN... OR MAYBE HELL

Thumos's senses had been great at detecting impending battles with Satan's forces who were hunting him. He was always confident in his abilities to defeat the Makria, and maybe his recent victories had given him a taste of overconfidence.

He felt quite proud of his skills as he roamed the Twilight Realm once again. Suddenly a mysterious figure appeared before him, much to Thumos's surprise. He had not sensed any of Satan's minions approaching this time, yet there before him stood one of them. Oddly enough, this time there was only one. Normally there had been at least three.

"Well this is going to be easy," Thumos thought to himself. "And who are you?" Thumos shouted boastfully.

The mysterious figure stood there silently, staring back at Thumos.

"Are you speechless?" Thumos spoke again. "Are you overwhelmed to be standing here in the presence of the mighty Thumos?"

The unknown opponent grinned slightly, shaking his head, but still said nothing.

"Well you shall be overwhelmed momentarily," said Thumos matter-of-factly, as he began to walk toward his opponent. He drew out his rhabdos, spinning it masterfully in his hands.

The mysterious figure drew his weapon. Thumos stopped momentarily looking very puzzled. The stranger was armed with a weapon that looked more like a sword than a rhabdos. "Odd," he thought to himself. "I have never seen an angel display his rhabdos as a sword in the presence of another angel."

The stranger was also looking at Thumos, very puzzled as well. Finally, the stranger broke his silence. "What weapon do you wield?"

"What do you mean?," Thumos answered, almost offended by the question. "This is my rhabdos of course. Why are you presenting yours as a sword?"

The stranger responded with great surprise. "This is the only weapon I possess."

Thumos shrugged. "It is of no consequence. You can pretend to fight me with a sword, I will still send you to the Banished Realm regardless." And he began to move toward the stranger, this time charging quickly.

Thumos noted this Makrian did not show any fear in his eyes, as the others nearly always displayed. The stranger began to charge toward Thumos as well.

The two met with a colossal blow, rhabdos to sword. The two angels stood toe-to-toe, as their weapons met repeatedly, with neither gaining advantage.

Thumos spun down low, finally landing a glancing shot of his rhabdos to the stranger's leg. It gave off the usual sizzling sound and a few dark streaks emanated from the point of impact.

The stranger screamed in great pain, as they both took a couple of steps backward away from each other. The scream actually surprised both of them.

Thumos thought to himself "A minor blow like that normally would not inflict so much pain."

The stranger shouted. "What did you do to me?" With that, he yelled in anger, and stormed toward Thumos.

Thumos successfully defended all the stranger's sword strikes, but he was now feeling far less confident. "I have never seen a Makrian fight with such ferocity," he thought to himself in a panic. "Maybe Kakos, or Satan himself, but not one of these second-rate losers!"

Suddenly the stranger's sword sliced across Thumos's upper right arm. Thumos screamed in pain, but also in anger, as he looked at his arm in disbelief to see his angelic flesh laid open. Once again, both angels took steps backward away from each other, with surprised looks.

"How in the universe did you do that?" Thumos shouted. "What manner of sword is that?"

The stranger just looked completely puzzled, not understanding why Thumos was so shocked.

Thumos, now feeling pure rage, screamed and charged at the stranger. He flung his rhabdos spinning furiously right for the stranger, who looked utterly shocked by this maneuver. He swung his sword wildly trying to defend himself, but Thumos's rhabdos struck him in his gut and his back, before circling back to Thumos.

"To the Banished Realm with you!" Thumos shouted, as he attacked the stranger furiously.

"What are you talking about?" retorted the stranger, fighting off Thumos's attack as best as he could.

Thumos tried to spin, and just as he came back about face, the stranger met him with his sword blade plunging all the way through Thumos's left shoulder.

Thumos screamed louder than he ever had before. He actually went forward toward the stranger, allowing the blade to pass farther through him, so that he was now close enough to land a massive head butt into the stranger's face. The blow sent the stranger backward, unable to hold onto the sword any longer.

Thumos grabbed the sword, pulling it out as far as he could, but of course his arms were not long enough to remove it completely. He leveraged his rhabdos against the sword guard to push it all the way out. Thumos grabbed the sword and flung it off to the side, and advanced toward the stranger, who was now looking a bit panicked.

"You can go wait for your master, Satan, in the Banished Realm, Makrian!" shouted Thumos. He swung his rhabdos at the stranger, who grabbed it with both hands.

The stranger shrieked as both hands began to sizzle. Thumos kicked him in the gut, sending him flying. But unfortunately, his kick landed the stranger within inches of his discarded sword.

"Great," said Thumos unenthusiastically, speaking to himself. "You had to kick him in *that* direction."

The stranger grabbed his sword, but was barely able to hold it with his injured hands. He glanced at Thumos, and put his right hand up to his forehead, giving him a slight salute. "We shall meet again," he said calmly, and disappeared in a flash.

"You can count on it!" shouted Thumos upward. "I know not who or what that was, but he and his master, Satan, will pay dearly for this treachery."

Thumos also was gone a moment later.

CHAPTER 24:

CALLED INTO QUESTION

Fresh off the most recent battle with Satan's minion, then this newest, more powerful stranger from Satan's ranks, Thumos had decided to visit the Neutral Realm where he could rest and recharge. He stood quietly, arms crossed in front of him. No one else was there. He closed his eyes, and began to think to himself. He began to ponder what was next.

This stranger, highly unusual.. Satan must have had him in hiding for quite some time, training him, arming him with some new weapon. I thought I knew all the angels of the Makria, but obviously as his ranks continue to swell, I am not able to keep up with them all.

He winced in pain a bit, opening his eyes slightly, glancing downward to both of his shoulders. He saw the odd wounds, the cut on his right arm and the more severe left shoulder wound, thinking how his flesh had never been pierced before. "What a strange sensation," he said to himself, then slowly raised his head level once again, slowly closing his eyes. Though in pain, he also could sense that the wounds were already starting to heal.

Satan obviously grows desperate, Thumos continued his silent thoughts. *He cannot win me to his side, so he sends his dark warriors after me, then this even more skilled dark warrior. But I must not let his distractions deter me from my mission, there is so much more to do.*

His thoughts continued, as if trying to win an argument with himself, or convince himself of his position. *Satan will never fool me with his duplicity. I am nothing like him, my work is of utmost nobility, I am functioning as the right arm of Yahweh, just as I always have.*

Apparently the archangels just do not understand, he thought, shaking his head, closing his eyes tighter. *They think they know better, they want to protect these horrible criminals rather than put a stop to them. Why do they try to stop me?*

Suddenly, a voice broke the silence. "Thumos, why are you doing this?" Krino asked sternly, in his deep, resonating voice.

Thumos's eyes popped open in surprise. Standing before him were several angels. He recognized most of them, some of whom he had fought alongside in the days of old. Some of them he only knew of, but did not know them personally. He saw Krino, the stately looking angel who was much taller than Thumos, and who had addressed him first. The look on his face was stern and unyielding. Periago was there too, another fellow soldier from some ancient battles. He was shorter than Thumos, but very stocky and muscular; someone you always wanted at your back in a fight. Eleos, the quiet one, was also there. He rarely spoke, but when he did, it was usually something very profound. He too was frowning. Then there was Kategoreo. Thumos had heard of him, and he was definitely recognizable because of his large size, but Thumos knew nothing about him.

Periago, chimed in next, taking a tentative step forward...."Yes Thumos, we want to know what you are thinking; what is behind all of these attacks on Earth."

Without hesitation, Thumos exhaled in irritation, saying. "I am exacting the Father's vengeance upon the guilty."

"Then the Father sent you on this mission?" Krino replied as if he already knew the answer, crossing his arms over his chest.

Thumos answered. "The Father did not *specifically* send me on this mission...,"

Perigo interrupted, throwing his hands upward in disgust. "What about the Father's policy, 'Vengeance is mine, I will repay, says the LORD'?"

Thumos answered angrily. "I have fought far more battles than all of you put together. I have seen the Children suffer in ways that none of you can imagine." Thumos emphasized his statement and made a sweeping motion over them with his hand. "You have no right to call me into question—I know what I am doing!"

Krino spoke again, uncrossing his arms as he took a couple of steps toward Thumos. He shook his hands in a pleading way. "But you are in direct violation of the Father's non-interference policy, are you not. Angels are not to interact with humans unless specifically commissioned by the Father to do so. Satan and his followers are even bound by that restriction. How can you excuse yourself from that basic edict which the Father issued at the original quickening?"

Periago agreed, saying. "None of us are even capable of interacting with the humans apart from the Father's will, right?" he spoke in a puzzled tone, looking around at the other angels. "You and the archangels have been granted special access to carry out such interaction, and you are obviously abusing that." Periago propped his hands on his hips, almost in a challenging gesture.

Thumos stood speechless. He could feel his anger reaching a boiling point, and based on the looks in the other angels' faces, he knew his face revealed his intense anger.

Eleos, quiet until now, spoke. "And what about all the people you are not helping, Thumos? Why do you not respond before a human dies? Why not intervene before a cruel death is exacted on one human by the other?" he said harshly.

Thumos, now barely able to contain his anger, replied "I am not the Father, so I am not able to know the future. I do not know with certainty that a human is about to die, only that he or she *has* been killed. Hence, I do not act until something worthy of vengeance has been done."

Exasperated, Thumos turned away, no longer facing the group.

"But you are being so inconsistent," said Kategoreo, now stepping forward. He raised an accusing finger, pointing it toward Thumos. "You have taken upon yourself too much responsibility. Your actions are not just in how you execute judgment. This is why such matters must always be left up to the Father."

Thumos turned back toward them once again, covering his ears. "ENOUGH!" screamed Thumos. Reaching for his rhabdos, he held it above his head. "I do not answer to any of *you*, and I will be happy to prove it to you with rhabdos."

All the angels took fearful steps backward, at Thumos' show of force. None were willing to experience his prowess as a warrior, he knew. Not all angels had been quickened for the purpose of battle, not like he was. He knew they were reviewing all of his previous battles and victories. By now, they all also knew about his encounters with the Old Red Dragon, and they certainly knew they were no match for him in this scenario.

"Obviously many other angels must appreciate what I am doing, as they are helping me watch for opportunities," Thumos snarled. "Without their help, I cannot see what is happening all over the earth. Surely you can understand!" he finished forcefully.

Kategoreo spoke, as he began to pace back and forth. "On Earth, we all know that each country has an angel stationed to keep watch over it, then several others are appointed to assist that angel." He paused to lend weight to his statement, glancing at Thumos.

Thumos stood staring at Kategoreo, but begrudgingly yielded an ever-so-slight nod of the head, in agreement.

Kategoreo resumed pacing, his huge feet making loud thudding sounds. "Some countries are overseen by an angel of the Agathon, and unfortunately, some countries have fallen to the oversight of Makrian forces. There is a constant struggle for supremacy, Thumos, and clearly your efforts are distracting for the Agathon."

Kategoreo's tone began to grow more heated and upset. "Some of them who are helping to keep you informed of activity, are neglecting their duties to help maintain their hold over the nations." His voice rose. " Why, even the prince of the kingdom of the United States of America now is barely clinging to his oversight, while the Makria are hard at work *everywhere*, trying to take possession. The Evil One would love nothing more than to seize full control there." Kategoreo stopped, looked at Thumos, angrily his fists clenched tightly at his sides.

Eleos began to speak once again, in his normal calm, steady voice, in stark contrast to Kategoreo's tirade. "Yes, and that is yet another problem with your current course of action, Thumos. You are causing problems with the Father's faithful angel corps. You are dragging many of them into all of this!" he said, now starting to raise his voice too.

That change in Eleos's tone really caught Thumos's attention. He remembered occasions of fighting shoulder to shoulder with Eleos in the past, being amazed at his calm demeanor even under heavy fire. He had never seen this angel get very excited about anything. He was rather stoic, in fact, which made this display very surprising.

All these angels were now feeding off of each other's increasingly agitated tone. Even so, Thumos could still see a slight tinge of fear in Krino's eyes, and fear in angels is extremely rare. Thumos felt he still had the edge, he knew that he was still intimidating to these angels, and had no reason to think this would turn into some sort of a brawl.

Krino mustered the courage to speak once again. "Please, Thumos, consider our questions. And think about your answers. We too seek justice, but only the Father's justice—not yours, not man's, not our own. Think about what you are doing!" This group of angels now formed into a solid wall of angelic beings, facing Thumos with a bolstered sense of confidence in themselves.

Thumos's temper had steadily risen, while he had listened to all their "feedback", and yet, in the back of his mind, he also pondered what these comrades had said. "Enough!" He huffed, stomping his foot down powerfully, sending shock waves around him.

This reaction yielded its intended result, as the group of angels struggled to remain standing. They looked at each other with a renewed sense of trepidation.

With his teeth clenched, he shouted "I am the right arm of Yahweh. I *know* what I am doing." He looked at them all with fury in his eyes, although he detested the sense of doubt in his own voice. He could not bear that thought. He fought the inclination, and shook his head in disgust. In a flash, he was gone.

Krino's shoulders relaxed, and his head fell, as he let out a sigh of relief. "I was not sure what was about to happen."

"Agreed," retorted Kategoreo. "But I think we could have taken him."

The others turned their heads slowly toward him, with puzzled and doubting looks.

Eleos voiced what the others were thinking in silence, now reverting back to his signature dry tone of voice. "Are you familiar with the Children's old phrase 'when hell freezes over'?" He did not crack a smile.

But everyone else, besides Kategoreo, chuckled. And the Neutral Realm was suddenly left empty once again.

CHAPTER 25:

TERROR IN SEATTLE, WA

† humos reappeared in the Twilight Realm, where he hoped he could find some solace, away from anyone else. He paced angrily, in the dim dusky light. *How could they call his good works into question? Had the heavenly host spent too much time away from Earth? Obviously they have lost touch with the predicament of evil rampaging across the world.* He smacked his fist into his open hand, as if to punctuate his thoughts. He would be an instrument of God. He would exact God's vengeance once again. He would drown out the echoes of Krino's final words of castigation.

As Thumos entered the earthly realm again, he came upon the city of Seattle, Washington. Down by the docks, at Fisherman's Wharf, the breeze was cool, and the smell of fresh fish hung in the air. Rain engulfed the city, as it so frequently did. He maneuvered down the street through the rain, carrying no umbrella of course, unlike most everyone else. The day's dark gray clouds were giving way to the purple of twilight, as a steady stream of oversized raindrops continued falling.

Kim Hui Shin threw open the front door of a local Chinese restaurant on Fisherman's Wharf, followed immediately by three of his gang members. Shin glistened in gold jewelry, adorning his custom tailored Gucci black suit. All four men sat down at a table menacingly, as Shin snapped his fingers, demanding attention from the restaurateur.

"Hong Foon, we are waiting to be served," he demanded impatiently. The gang members all chuckled, as they watched an older Asian gentleman, quivering behind the cash register, a look of great distress in his face.

Hong, the restaurant owner, grabbed a pot of hot tea and several cups, and quickly dashed over to the table. With his eyes to the ground, in an apologetic bowing posture, he distributed the cups and began pouring tea for Shin and his men. His hands shook nervously as he tried to fill their cups, but he spilled some over the table.

"Welcome to my restaurant, Mr. Shin," said Hong with a broken voice. "Excuse my clumsiness, I can clean that up right away."

"Forget about the tea, where is my money, old man?" yelled Shin. "You want me to continue to protect you, don't you Hong?"

"Yes, of course, but business has not been very good lately," spoke Hong feebly, with his eyes averted in respect. "Please be patient with me, Mr. Shin."

Shin spat. "I'm not here to listen to your weak excuses, old man. We've been more than patient with you. Are you telling me you're not paying me what's owed tonight?" Shin smiled and slowly rose to his feet, "We aren't leaving here tonight with empty hands. Over five years ago I set you up in my building here, and let you open this restaurant as a favor to your brother. You remember your brother, don't you Hong?" Shin said, now looking intently into Hong's face. Shin reached into his pocket, and drew out an ornate switchblade knife. He purposely waved it slowly right in front of Hong's nose, and gently laid it down on the table.

Without looking up, Hong gave a quick nod in acknowledgement.

"And you remember what happened to your brother, right?" Shin said, with a sinister grin.

Once again, Hong gave a quick nod, while still looking down at the floor.

"Where is your brother, now?" Shin continued to press. He shot a sly grin toward his men. They all chuckled once again.

"You know very well, Mr. Shin, that he is no more, no thanks to your men," Hong said, now sounding a bit more defiant, and finally looking back up into Shin's eyes.

Shin nodded at one of his men, who grabbed Hong by the back of the neck. Pinning Hong's left hand to the counter, a second man stood up, and grabbed the ornate switchblade lying on the table. The stroke was so quick that it took Hong several seconds to realize he no longer had a ring or pinky finger. The fingers now sat adjacent to his hand in a pool of rich red.

Hong screamed and drew his hand to his chest, slumping to the floor in agony.

"No!" screamed Hong's daughter who ran from the kitchen. "Leave him alone, you monsters!"

Shin reached out, grabbed her by the throat, then threw her like dirty laundry to land by her father on the floor.

Suddenly a young man came running out of the kitchen waving a butcher knife. "You're going to pay for this, Shin," he yelled. "Leave my father alone!"

"Ling! No!" screamed Hong's daughter.

Ling swiped at Shin with the butcher knife, but it was a futile attempt and contacted only the air. The momentum brought him closer to Shin, who grabbed him by his collar. With a practiced karate kick, Shin snapped Ling's leg at the knee. Shin caught Ling as he was going down, spun him around to face Hong and Pei, then he grabbed the bloody switchblade off the table.

Shin smiled as he spoke. "Know that I was only defending myself, Hong." And with that, he drew the blade across Ling's throat, as his family screamed in horror. Shin let go of the lifeless body, the blood circling the body like a halo.

"We'll be back this weekend, old man," said Shin, handing his blade to one of his men to clean. "I suggest you have your money by then, or your pretty little girl will become your next payment." He took a moment to size her up, licked his lips and laughed. Taking their cue from him, the other men laughed as well, and started to follow Shin out the door.

"Should I take care of those two witnesses sitting over there?" said one of Shin's trained thugs, motioning toward a couple of restaurant patrons, who had slinked down into their seats during all the commotion. Shin and all the men paused at the front door.

"No," said Shin casually. "They are like frightened little children, and will say nothing." Grinning, and now looking at the couple, Shin spoke again, this time in a very loud voice. "I have no disagreement with them. And they know if they do say anything, I will hunt them down, cut out their tongues, then kill them."

All the men nodded in approval, and left the restaurant.

The couple sat back up in their seats, and looked at each other, horrified. The woman said "Oh my god, I can't believe what just happened. And we just sat there letting it all go down without lifting a finger."

The man threw his hand in front of her face, as though he were trying to shush her. Then he replied. "Those guys are from the 'Fighting Tigers'. They do that kind of stuff all the time. You so much as even look cross-eyed at them, and you're done." He glanced around, as though making sure the coast was clear. Then in a more hushed tone, he leaned in closer to the woman, and continued. "They think they're invincible, above the law. I've heard they've got all kinds of military-grade state-of-the-art weapons. And besides all that, they are supposedly these super-duper martial arts masters.

They would rather kill people with their bare hands than use guns and all. We don't want to get involved, babe. You heard what they said about us. Just pretend like we didn't see anything."

At that, he grabbed her by the arm, and stood up, pulling her with him. They left some cash on the table for their bill, threw on their raincoats, and scooted out the front door. They were almost running out the door, when they crashed into a passerby right outside the front door.

"What's the rush?" the stranger spoke.

"Uh, you don't wanna know, mister. Active shooter kind of thing. Save yourself," said the gentleman. Then, the couple dashed down the street ignoring the rain which had increased in intensity.

Thumos watched them race away, then glanced inside the door, which hung ajar. He stepped inside the building, which was wafting with the pleasant smells of teriyaki sauce, soy sauce, and a variety of delectable hot spices. But accompanying the pleasant smells was the unmistakably unpleasant smell of blood. His ears were accosted with the sounds of moaning, crying, and pleading. As Thumos looked toward the back, where the kitchen was, he could now see blood splatters covering the floor, walls, and ceiling. He now saw bodies lying on the floor, and some women crouched down holding one lifeless body.

"What in God's name happened here?" he said.

"The Fighting Tigers," shouted a woman, who was wrapping a dish towel around an older gentleman's hand.

"All I needed to know," said Thumos, as he darted back out on the sidewalk.

"I have seen enough. The Fighting Tigers' reign of terror ends now." Thumos said angrily.

The door of an abandoned warehouse on the pier crashed open. At least a dozen men looked up, stunned to see someone so easily penetrate their heavily locked down warehouse. Kim Hui Shin, without saying a word, nodded at his men to attack.

Thumos landed a massive head butt to the first attacker. Like a watermelon exploding when it is dropped on the floor, he watched the man's head blow up in pieces. Thumos took note of several other men charging at him, hands and feet flailing. Despite their best attempts, no man was unable to land any strikes on Thumos. He watched their feeble attempts, as if they were all in slow motion, and he had not yet gone on the offensive at all. He was simply dodging them all, as if in some orchestrated synchronous dance.

Thumos stood in a defensive posture, while all the other men bent over sucking wind. "Are you kiddies done now? My turn," he said confidently, with a cat-caught-the-canary smile.

Like a bullet out of a gun, Thumos moved to the nearest man, snapping his neck. As he dropped that man's body, he roundhouse kicked the next man, ripping his lower jaw off. The next man had just enough time to put his hands up to try to block Thumos, but Thumos grabbed both of his hands, snapping his elbows downward where now his forearms were bent toward the floor. Thumos's right jab caved in the man's chest, as he crumpled to the ground.

Thumos delivered a flurry of blows and kicks to several other men, and moments later, the floor around him was strewn with the bodies of the Fighting Tigers. Some were dead, others were badly beaten and bloodied.

Kim Hui Shin surveyed the carnage. He had stood back, simply observing everything, as if plotting his next move in a game of chess. He had watched all of his men receive the beat down of their lives, but he had not lifted so much as a finger to help out.

Kim suddenly leapt like a panther out of a tree, and kicked Thumos square in the back. It was the first time anyone here had landed any punch or kick. Kim watched him stumble forward several steps, but Thumos never hit the ground.

Thumos spun around quickly. "I guess I lost track of *you*, little man," he said condescendingly. *But that really makes me mad that he actually touched me.* Thumos thought to himself disgustedly.

"Your skills are very impressive, stranger," said Shin. "But now it is time to show you who is the true master of this dojo. Then, once I have broken every bone in your body, I will rip out your throat, and watch you die on the ground."

Standing on the opposite side of the room, listening to Shin's threats, Thumos stood poised. At the moment Shin finished his little speech, Thumos actually laughed out loud. He did not say a word, but with a Neo-like hand gesture, right out of the movie "The Matrix", he motioned for Shin to come to him.

Shin felt his blood boil in anger over that gesture. He whirled around, grabbing an ornate sword from its wall mounting, and turned back around toward Thumos, only to see that he was already holding a katana sword which had appeared out of nowhere.

Shin screamed, and charged toward Thumos. The sound of metal against metal clashed and rang throughout the whole building. Shin felt the sword in his hand reverberating like never before. With every strike, it grew harder and harder to hang onto it, from the ferocious vibrations. He felt Thumos's sword land an incredible blow, and he watched in disbelief as his ornate sword disintegrated into nothing. Just then, he found himself flying backward through the air from Thumos landing a kick into his chest.

Shin stood up wearily, and spit a wad of blood out of his mouth. "I am going to kill you.", he screamed with rage in his eyes.

Shin ran to his weapon wall again, and grabbed a bokken. He turned around quickly, only to find that once again, Thumos was able to match his weapon.

Shouting something in Chinese, he once again charged toward Thumos. Their bokkens collided, and once again with every strike, the overwhelming force coming from Thumos made his hands ache trying to hold the weapon. Thumos swung downward one last time, slicing Shin's bokken into two pieces. Shin watched Thumos's bokken swipe across his head, and he felt himself fall to the ground.

He pushed himself up onto all fours, and looked up at Thumos, to see him reach behind his body, and produce a pair of nunchucks. He watched an impressive display put on by Thumos spinning the nunchucks around all parts of his body. He could not believe that his foe did not even seem out of breath, not at all.

Shin, now feeling extremely weakened, put his hand to his ear. A stream of blood was flowing down the side of his head. He shook his head as if trying to shake off the blood. He turned toward his weapon wall once again. This time the best he could muster was a slow stumble over to the wall. He caught himself against it, almost falling, and feebly reached up to retrieve his own nunchucks.

He turned around, and this time, he saw his foe standing right there in front of him. He swung his nunchuck at Thumos, but Thumos caught the nunchuck in his left hand. Now, like a puppet dangling from a string, he was suspended there holding one end of his nunchuck, while Thumos held the other end up. He felt Thumos's nunchuck strike his right knee, smashing the kneecap. He watched the nunchuck sling into his left hip, cracking the joint. He felt one last hit come up into his lower jaw, knocking several teeth out.

Shin's grip loosened on his nunchuck, and he face-planted into the floor. He propped himself up on his elbows, in excruciating pain, and said "Truly, you are the master here."

The other Fighting Tigers who were still breathing, had finally managed to get back on their feet. They were all shouting out, as they assumed they were about to witness the final execution of their leader, who now barely clung to life. Thumos waved his hand at them, floating upward into the air, and the floor beneath them began to quake. A great crevasse opened up in the floor right where Shin was laying, and he slid into the blackness of a great hole, screaming as he fell. The entire floor behind him was sloping toward the crevasse, and all the other men started screaming as they tried to no avail to scramble away. Soon they all slid down into the gaping hole, screaming as they went.

The crevasse closed with a deafening slam. And then there was silence.

"Vengeance is mine, I will repay saith the LORD!" shouted Thumos.

CHAPTER 26:

TERROR IN CHICAGO, IL

The TV news anchor from WMAQ spoke somberly. "A seventeen-year old young man was shot and killed by two officers from the Chicago Police Department last night, when those officers believed the young man matched the description of someone who had just robbed a nearby Warehouse Liquors store."

"Damn, worthless cops," screamed Raymond Dreyfuss, as he watched the morning news. "I am sick of these dirty cops getting away with any and everything. This country would be better off without these stupid cops getting in the way."

Sporting an untucked flannel shirt, over dingy blue jeans, Raymond stood staring at the TV. He ran his fingers through his disheveled dark hair with his right hand, then reached down to stroke his matching unkempt beard with his other hand.

Raymond thought about his own run-ins with some of Chicago's police force. He walked around the house, nervously checking all the windows, as if expecting someone was spying on him. He glanced at his mutt of a dog, Charlie, lying on the couch, who was completely oblivious to Raymond's ramblings. "They have been after me ever since I was a kid, just never leaving me alone, you know it Charlie?"

Charlie raised his head up off the couch when he heard his name, and perked up his ears. Once he realized his master was just talking out loud again, and had no treats or food to offer, he plopped his head back onto the couch.

"I mean, okay, so I shoplifted here and there, what kid hasn't done that?" continued Raymond. "I got into a few fights in school, then at work, big deal. Hitting me up with speeding tickets, parking tickets, drunk and disorderly citations, haven't they got better things to do? Go chase the real criminals, do somethin' important."

Raymond stomped back into the kitchen, his very large belly shaking all the while, and grabbed a cup of coffee. Then he walked over to his liquor cabinet, and added a little bit of Wild Turkey to his hot coffee. "Yeah, that's what I'm talkin' about," he said out loud, directing his comments back at the dog.

"Menace to society," he said , pausing to draw out his self-styled moniker, putting just the right emphasis on menace. He walked back over to the front room window, and peered out into the street, then pulled back his closed blinds. "That's what that idiot judge said about me last time the cops hauled me into their courtroom," he said, angrily swearing. "What a crock. Well just you wait, I'll show you all what 'menace to society' really means", he yelled sarcastically. "You ain't seen nuthin' yet!"

Raymond muttered to himself, as he walked over to some locked wall cabinets. He unlocked the cabinet, and opened the door. Grinning from ear to ear, he continued talking to Charlie, who continued to ignore him.

"Tonight's the night. I am gonna make the Chicago PD pay for everything they've done wrong." Behind the doors of the locked cabinet, he stared at the arsenal he had been amassing for several months now.

Raymond gave out a sinister snicker. "Yeah, that's what I'm talkin' about," he said.

After dark, Raymond slipped off to the corner of 73rd and Halsted. He parked his old Lincoln Continental in a dark alleyway, popped the trunk, and stepped out of the car. He walked to the rear of his car, looking up-and-down the street, then opened the trunk lid. He began tunelessly whistling quietly, as he pulled some thin gloves onto his hands, stuffed a couple of pistols in the back of his pants, stood two different rifles leaning up against the open trunk, and loaded his pockets with some extra ammunition. He then picked up the two rifles, again peeking up and down the street to make sure no one was around, then stepped onto the street.

The night was brisk, and Raymond shivered as he walked up the street, still whistling quietly. He looked up into the sky, to see there was no moon out tonight. It was a new moon, just as he had timed this night, to help eliminate another potential source of light. He passed by an infrequently used warehouse, with a row of bushes out in front, running alongside the street. Raymond gently laid one of the rifles on the ground inside the cover of the bushes. Then he continued walking another block or so to a curve in the road, which angled to a dead end. No one could come from that direction, at least not by car. There was a stone wall off the shoulder of the street, here at this curve. He carefully leaned the other rifle against the wall, on the opposite side away from the street.

Raymond started walking back toward the warehouse. "Aha, now that's what I'm lookin' for," he said in a hushed voice, as he spied a big rock lying on the ground. He knelt down, looking around to be sure still no one else was watching, picked up the rock, and rose back to his feet slowly. Raymond continued his stroll, until he was now standing in front of the warehouse.

The sound of breaking glass broke the silence of the night, as he heaved the rock through the window of the warehouse.

Raymond walked back up the street, this time a little more quickly, to the stone wall, and crouched down behind it. From here he would have a clear view of any arriving police officers. He had studied their habits for weeks, studying distances on maps, listening to his police scanner, timing out drive times in his own car. From behind the stone wall, he waited for approaching officers to arrive. A few minutes later, a single CPD squad car came driving slowly up the block. A broken out window, generating an alarm at an insignificant warehouse, would not warrant more than one squad car. He grinned as he saw a lone squad car pull close to his hiding place. They were so close he could hear them on their radio, and he felt a slow grin slide across his face.

"Officers Cohen and Hammond here, responding to that possible 10-62 in progress over at 73rd and Halsted," said Officer Bill Cohen, letting the police dispatcher know they had arrived.

They heard the police dispatcher radio to another pair of CPD officers on patrol that night, to provide backup. "Officers Carney and Mendez, you're fairly close by. Wrap up what you're doing, and head over to back up Cohen and Hammond."

"Yeah, don't strain yourselves Carney and Mendez. As soon as you finish your donut mission, see if you can find time to head this way!" said Officer Cohen over the police channel.

"Oh sure" said Officer Sheila Carney sarcastically, pretending to be speaking with a mouthful of food. "We'll get there one of these days."

Officer Cohen put the car in park, and left the flashing lights on. They had opted for no siren of course, for a call like this. He glanced at his partner, officer Rachel Hammond. "Well, I'm sure this is some kind of stupid false alarm, but I guess we'd better check it out" he said disgustingly.

"Let's go get some hot coffee after this," said Rachel. "It's getting cold out tonight."

"You big baby," said Bill. "This is great weather—will make a man out of you!" he joked.

"Well obviously you must need some more cold weather then, you loser," Rachel razzed back, laughing.

Rachel's laughing was drowned out by the sound of a bullet piercing the windshield of their car. The bullet had struck Bill right in the chest, killing him instantly. Officer Hammond frantically grabbed at the police radio to call for help.

"Officer dow…" and Rachel's voice fell silent before she could finish her sentence. Her call for help had been interrupted by yet another deadly bullet fired through the windshield. The precision headshot killed her.

Raymond chuckled to himself quietly. "Two shots, two dead" he quipped to himself, pleased. "That was easy. Now to bag a couple more before I call it a night. At this rate, I should be able to make a big dent in the CPD over the next few weeks," he said to himself proudly.

Leaving his long rifle behind, Raymond jogged down the street quickly, stopping by the bushes to grab the assault rifle he had stashed there a few minutes ago. He then walked carefully toward the quiet squad car. With his gloved hands, he opened the passenger side, and Officer Hammond's body slumped over outside the door.

"This will make a nice little trophy," Raymond said as he reached down and pulled Rachel's shield off her uniform. "Worthless piece of garbage," he said, as he kicked her in the head. Then he walked around to the other side and retrieved Officer Cohen's shield as well.

"Cohen? Hammond? Someone answer!" shouted the police dispatcher over the radio.

"Officer Mendez here, we're on our way, double time!" Raymond heard another respond.

The "Menace to Society" heard the siren and saw the lights of the approaching squad car, carrying the Officers. "And once again, all according to plan," said Raymond, as he quickly scooted off the street to a dark spot behind some bushes, very close to the first squad car.

"Officers Mendez and Carney arriving on the scene," radioed the officer, as they pulled up and stopped about thirty feet away from the other squad car.

The officers carefully emerged from their squad car, with guns drawn. It was a peculiar scene, as both officers walked on the street, their shoes scraping across the pavement; the only sound in the area. It was still…very still. The emergency lights of the first squad car spun around, eerily flashing streaks of red over the quiet street.

"Bill? Rachel?" called out one officer.

"I can't tell what's going on here," said the other. Raymond watched as this officer scanned the area. "I see Bill sitting upright in the car, but I can't tell what's wrong. Rachel's car door is open, but I don't see her anywhere."

"I don't like the looks of this," said his partner nervously.

"Cohen!" shouted the first officer. "What's going on; where's Hammond?"

Both officers closed in on the car, one from either side.

"Blood!" called out the officer on the driver's side of the car. Looking frantically around, he clearly saw Rachel's body lying limp, half out of the car. Blood was everywhere.

"Officer is *down* over here," shouted the woman officer, nearly simultaneously, as she could see the bullet wound in Bill's head. Her eyes darted around, trying to find a shooter.

Raymond quietly stepped from the dark bushes, firing his assault rifle. "They can't hear you anymore!" he said sarcastically, laughing, as he continued to fire.

The woman was hit first, as a bullet to her leg sent her sprawling to the ground. Her gun slid under the car. The other officer fired off one round, hitting nothing, before he was hit in the shoulder of his shooting arm. He lay sideways on the ground, unable to operate his weapon any further.

Raymond tossed aside his assault rifle, and pulled out his Glock 357 pistol. He sauntered toward the woman where she laid writhing on the ground.. "The assault rifle doesn't do enough damage. I'm gonna use my 357 and put a big hole in you. Any last words, you stinkin' cop?" Raymond said, swearing at her.

"Excuse me, sir, but I think you dropped something," said a young black man from behind Raymond, who had appeared out of nowhere.

"Huh, what?" Raymond spoke, spinning around in surprise not knowing anyone else was around.

"This is a really nice rifle that you dropped over here." The young man continued speaking calmly, casting a smile over at both officers lying helplessly on the ground.

"Kid, get outta here! We're hit! Go find help!" yelled the male officer.

Raymond shot a grim look at the young man. "Boy, I sure am sorry, but I can't have any witnesses." He raised the 357 pistol up level with the boy's face, and started to squeeze the trigger.

"Not the kid!" screamed the woman officer, as she grimaced in pain, holding her hand up.

The boy's smile turned very stern, and he simply said, "No!" as he raised his hand up, palm toward Raymond.

Raymond grinned and pulled the trigger. Excruciating pain rocketed up his arm, before his mind could wrap around what had just happened. He looked down where his pistol should be, and there was now nothing. No pistol, no hand. His head jerked back up to the boy who still stood in front of him.

How is he not dead? thought Raymond, wrestling with the question in his head. He felt himself sink down to his knees, with the overwhelming pain radiating up his arm, as the boy stepped toward him.

This small-framed young man grabbed Raymond by the throat, and pulled a sixteen-inch serrated blade knife from the back of his pants, and plunged it into the top of Raymond's chest. He slid the knife down Raymond's body like he was made of butter, until the knife disappeared into the man's fat gut. The young man dropped Raymond's lifeless, split body down onto the pavement, and stood there dispassionately.

The male officer, still lying on the pavement in his own pool of blood, watched the shocking scene unfold. His thoughts turned from pity for the young man and fearing for his own life, to terror over what the young man was doing. His attention flashed over to his partner as she screamed in horror, her eyes fixed on the young man. Still wincing in pain, he held one hand tightly over his wound.

"Carney, get a hold of yourself, we've got to calm down here," he said. He looked back at the young man in utter disbelief. He was uncertain of what to say or do.

"Help is on the way," said the young man coolly, calmly moving toward the two officers.

The wounded officers watched the young man look over the lifeless body of Raymond Dreyfuss, and they saw his face dramatically change. He had looked upon them with eyes of sympathy, but now they saw the squint of anger in his eyes.

"Vengeance is mine!" shouted the young man with his fists clenched, looking over the carnage around him. He had shouted it so loudly it startled them both, even though they were looking right at him. The young man quickly disappeared into the darkness, just as more emergency vehicles finally arrived on the scene.

CHAPTER 27:

GRAPPLING WITH GUILT

Back in the Neutral Realm Thumos sought relief and rest. He was weary from these last encounters and in addition to this, he could not shake Krino's statement from their last encounter: "We too seek justice, but only the Father's justice—not yours, not man's, not our own."

Thumos flung his rhabdos to the ground in disgust, and began to pace. He clenched his fists as he walked. *The Earth is so full of evil. The violence humans commit against one another is so shameful.* He stopped his pacing for a moment, placed his hands on his hips, and his head fell downward. He stared at the ground for a moment, let out a huff of disgust, then resumed his pacing.

I feel like I am fighting a losing battle. How can I possibly stop it all? Thumos's pace grew more frantic and erratic, overwhelmed with feelings with which he was not accustomed. *I am an angel of Yahweh, a fierce warrior, commissioned to rain down terror upon His enemies.*

Thumos stopped pacing again, and pressed the palms of his hands to either side of his head. All the faces of those whom he had dispatched on Earth flashed before his face. That was joined by the voices of Krino and the other angels who had called him into question. He was still haunted by the words of Satan, who had tried to convince him that he somehow had something in common with the Old Red Dragon.

This is what I was created for. Why am I starting to have all these second thoughts?

In his mind, Thumos kept replaying all those conversations, and thinking about his next steps. *What am I going to do now? What's the use of it all?*

Thumos sat down on the ground, dejected and tired. He propped up his knees, and rested his elbows on them. For a moment he allowed his memories to resurface, latching onto the names and faces of his brother warriors and all the battles he had fought. He and the archangels had battled Satan on countless occasions. This brought a wry smile to his face. On one particular occasion, when the tide of battle seemed unsettled, he had heard Michael's powerful voice, barking out commands to everyone during battle. The Host had rallied and the day was won.

Thumos shifted a bit, feeling his muscles uncoil, beginning to regenerate and restore themselves. He still had vivid memories of his original quickening, the surge of energy, warm, light and deep abiding love. Most of all he recalled the pride he had in being created by Yahweh for a special purpose.

Thumos relaxed further, sliding his legs to a flat position. He pressed his hands onto the ground at his side, lifting himself a little higher, as he started to well up with feelings of pride.

Thumos thought of all the solo missions Yahweh had sent him on, to vanquish enemies of the Israelites, the likes of Egyptians, Canaanites, Assyrians, and Babylonians. He thought about defending many other righteous chosen ones of the Father, and even aiding the very mother of Jesus and her parents.

Then Thumos began to remember so many occasions where he begged Yahweh to let him go to the aid of those he saw suffering. Sometimes Thumos was allowed, sometimes he was denied.

Thumos stiffened a bit, and crossed his arms, as his thoughts began to turn to more unpleasant memories. Visions of the Son of God being tortured and killed, while he could only stand by helplessly flooded his mind—and the same thing happened for many of Jesus' followers. He thought of many angels who now sided with Satan, with whom he had once fought along-side and counted as friends as part of the Agathon, who now had become betrayers of Yahweh. He thought of all the Makria whom Satan had sent to destroy him, and he thought about Armada. Dear Armada, his faithful friend who had taught him so much while they served with the Warriors together for a short while.

Thumos bristled, and began to feel pangs of anger take over. *Lucifer. A name I have not thought about nor uttered for eons.* Faint, nearly forgotten memories of him, began to materialize in his mind. *What happened to you, another one who taught me so much, how could you?* As quickly as those distant memories began to emerge, his thoughts then quickly went back to Armada. *My dear Armada, whom Satan mercilessly beat and banished to the Abyss. That was my fault, all my fault. I failed you.*

Thumos finally buried his face into his hands, and he began to weep. He had seen other angels weep before, he had seen the Son of God weep as well. He had never before wept himself; it was a very strange sensation.

Suddenly, one of Thumos' informant angels, Phluaros, appeared nearby. No angel had actually stood at his side during any part of his quest, but many of them certainly did sympathize with his efforts, and had tried to help him in less direct ways. Phluaros had done so frequently.

"Thumos, I have some information for you," said the broad shouldered Phluaros. Thumos, surprised to see his visitor, momentarily glanced away, trying to hide his sorrow. He reasoned with himself. *I have an image of being stoic and stalwart to maintain, I cannot allow him to see me like this.*

Thumos spoke in a deep, monotone voice. "What is it?"

"I have information about Roberto Valenzuela," replied Phluaros.

This must surely be a sign. Thumos jumped up to his feet quickly. "Tell me what you know."

CHAPTER 28:

AN ANONYMOUS TIP

"Well top o' the mornin' to ya, Dr. Lauren Willis," said Ian as Lauren approached his desk. She smiled as she passed him. Quickly, he jumped from his chair, dropping his pen in the process, and followed her down the hallway.

"Good morning, Detective," Lauren said without slowing or looking over her shoulder. She sounded determined and ready to get to the grindstone.

As he moved to catch up with her he did take the time to appreciate the blue power suit she was wearing. He almost told her so, but held back. No one knew about them yet. If there was even a "them". He exhaled in frustration. There were probably a hundred things he could say that would sound suave and caring, but instead, this is what he heard coming out of his mouth: "You are, uh, looking smart and in charge this morning. You have that determined look about you."

Lauren finally stopped, and slowly turned around, grinning. Ian thought to himself how breathtaking she looked. He loved it when she wore her hair up like she had today. She was the total package...beautiful and smart.

"So Dr. Willis," said Ian, shoving his hands in his pockets, "What kind of fru-fru coffee are you having today?" He grinned and pointed toward the drink she was carrying.

"Oh, it's good," answered Lauren. "It's a heck of a lot better than that black mojo you drink," she said laughing.

Ian laughed saying, "No, now that is *real* coffee, m'dear. What you're drinkin', that's not real coffee. It is sugar and cream and other junk with a wee bit of coffee mixed in there."

Lauren countered, holding her drink out toward Ian. "Why don't you just try some of this, instead of making fun of me? I bet you'd like it, *especially* since this is my favorite. Iced coffee—two pumps of vanilla syrup, two pumps of toffee nut syrup, and a little cream—extra shot. It's delicious!"

"Okay, okay," agreed Ian, as he politely took the drink from Lauren's hand. "I'll try a sip..." as he started to bring the cup to his mouth. He suddenly stopped. "But only a sip, I can't have my image tarnished by drinking this fru-fru stuff." And with that, he took a big, long gulp of Lauren's drink.

"Hey now, don't be drinkin' all of my drink," Lauren said with a laugh.

Ian stood, with an inquisitive, thoughtful look in his eye. He nodded his head slowly, after a momentary delay, handing the cup back to Lauren. "Well...I must admit...it's almost...tolerable," he said with a smirk.

"Tolerable?" Lauren said with a playfully irritated voice. "Now that is the best coffee drink you are ever gonna have."

"So, this is your favorite, eh?" Ian said, without acknowledging her comment. "I think I'd better mark that down. I am going to want to remember Dr. Lauren Willis's favorite morning drink...just for future reference," he said with a wink and another grin.

"Oh, is that so, Detective Ian Jelani?" said Lauren. "Well your drink is easy to remember—pour some black sludge into a mug, and you're good to go!"

They both laughed at each other, just as Lane stormed through the precinct door.

"Lane, what's up?" said Ian. Lane, sporting a sour frown, did not even acknowledge Jelani, and strolled right past him without so much as a word.

"So, which Lane do we get today?" asked Lauren under her breath. "Dr. Lane Jekyll or Mr. Lane Hyde?"

"Your guess is as good as mine, doc," sighed Ian. "Every day is a crap-shoot. Roll the dice, let's see which version of Lane is going to come through that door. I'm telling ya, he has got to pull this together. The Cap is none too happy about him."

A sympathetic Lauren interrupted Ian. "But this is a terribly traumatic event, Ian. Every day must be a constant battle between depression and utter fury. None of us has ever been through anything like that. To lose your wife and daughter, in that kind of way? I mean I can't even imagine what that would do to a person."

"I know, I know, none of us really gets it," continued Ian. He then started pacing back and forth, then said "And hey, I am his biggest advocate, and I will continue to be. All I know is that he has spent the last sixty, maybe seventy days, trying to track down and catch Roberto Valenzuela, to the point of ditching his normal duties." Ian stopped for a moment, looking up at Lauren, expecting to see a sympathizing look from her. He didn't wait for it and continued.

"When he does try to work on one of his actual caseloads, he always tries to make it somehow connect to Valenzuela," Ian continued, now throwing his hands up in the air as if at a loss. "Everyone around him has tried to be patient and polite to the guy, but in the end, he's got a job to do just like all the rest of us. Some of the guys are now making bets as to how long it will be before the Cap fires him."

As if she might have been overhearing their conversation, Captain Julie Franklin stepped out of her office. "Jelani, get in here!" she demanded.

Ian looked at Lauren, holding up both hands, palms out. "Stay right here," he mouthed. Lauren shook her head, denying his request, and tapped her watch.

Lauren mouthed back at him, "Too much work to do." She held her hand up to her face, mimicking a phone call, indicating for him to just call her later. Then she spun around, and continued on down the hallway.

"Shut the door behind you," said an obviously irritated Captain, as Jelani turned to enter the office. "Look, Ian, Madigan is on thin ice."

"M'am, I know he is, and I am at a loss as to how to help him," said Ian.

"I have covered for him long enough. He has either got to start getting some *real* work done around here, or the brass is calling for him to get the heave-ho," said Captain Franklin. "I feel really bad for Lane, and I'm not asking him to forget about his wife and kid. He can stay angry as long as he wants, but he's got to start working down his caseload."

"I get it, Cap," said Ian. "I have tried to help redirect him, and it hasn't worked so far. Trust me, I'll keep on him, and he's going to get his head back on straight any day now."

Captain Franklin could see the doubt in Ian's eyes, then retorted "Are you sure about that, Detective, because I sure am not." She waved a hand at Ian dismissively, and looked back down at the paperwork on her desk. "Get back to work."

Jelani stepped out of the captain's office, closing the door softly.

Ian pulled out his phone, and began typing a text message to Lauren. "That did not go well..." he sent to her.

A new text message quickly popped onto Ian's phone. "Sorry about that." Lauren had replied.

"I will bring you up to speed later, TMTT." Ian sent back to her.

"TMTT?" Lauren's text popped in.

"Too much to type", Ian replied, adding a smiley face emoji.

"What are you, a teenager?", with a laughing emoji, Lauren replied.

"I hate texting; would much rather talk in person." Ian replied, with a rolling-eyes emoji.

"Okay, okay, we'll talk later." Lauren replied. Ian slipped his phone back into his pocket, and headed over to Lane's desk.

"Ian, I'm glad you're here," said Lane, as he glanced up from his desk.

"Man, you walked right past me back there a few minutes ago" said Ian. "I spoke to you, and you didn't even look at me."

"Oh, sorry, I guess I'm just really focused. Ummm...yeah, okay," answered Lane, rubbing the back of his head. He looked down at his desk, wagging his head. Sitting down in his chair, he started picking up papers, shuffling things around on his desktop.

"You're obsessed, my friend. That's what I would call it," Ian blurted out. "I am going to lay this out as simply as I can, Lane." He leaned forward on Lane's desk to make his point. "I just talked to Cap. She is at her wit's end with you. You have to pull yourself together, and quick. I know you miss Janie and Lizzy..."

Lane stiffened and glared at Ian, but remained silent.

"No one is asking you to do anything but get focused on your caseload," continued Ian. "We will get Valenzuela..."

Every muscle tightened in Lane's face, as Ian watched Lane's face redden in anger. "I don't want to hear that name spoken out loud, Jelani, you know that." he said, his voice starting to rise in pitch and volume.

Ian could see the veins beginning to bulge in his friend's forehead and neck. He immediately felt bad for having mentioned Valenzuela's name.

As calmly as possible, Ian continued his hands raised, palms out. "We will nail that slime ball, but we also have other cases to work on. How many times have I warned you about this? When you don't carry your weight around here, it creates a drag on the rest of us."

Lane sat back down, running his hands nervously through his hair. He began to speak as if he had heard nothing Ian just said, then looked back down at his paperwork. Calm once again, Lane started waving both hands up-and-down slicing the air, saying, "I've been wracking my brain, trying to figure out how to bring down Valenzuela. Every lead I get just goes cold. His attorneys are as high paid and crooked as they come, but I'm going to get to him. If anything dirty is happening in Miami, his hand is in it."

"Seriously, bro?" Ian said disgustingly. "You're not even listening to me. Look at your desk, man. It's a mess. You're a mess. You really need to get it together, my friend." Ian looked around, to check for anyone listening in, and he continued in a hushed tone. "I told you my story from St. Louis. I shared that with you to try to help you understand, to keep you from going down *that* path. I know what I'm talkin' about here, and you just aren't listening." Ian turned around angrily, and walked back to his desk.

Lane looked across his desk, and spotted his "Holy Terror" file. He opened the file, glancing at some of the crime scene photos previously associated with this Holy Terror figure. "If only Valenzuela's face were on one of these victim photos," he muttered out loud to himself. "But on the other hand, I want the pleasure of taking my revenge out on him myself."

Just then, Lane's phone began to ring. "Detective Madigan, here," he answered.

"I have an important tip for you, Detective Lane Madigan," said a dark, mysterious voice on the other end of the line.

"Who is this?" Lane said inquisitively.

Ian looked up at Lane, to see him signaling. Ian immediately knew Lane wanted a phone trace.

"Trace it," Ian said in a loud whisper toward several officers, who scurried about frantically, and the phone trace was started just seconds later.

"Did I give you enough time to start your trace, Detective Madigan?" the voice said, speaking very slowly and methodically.

Lane acknowledged nothing about the caller's insights, and continued talking. "So, tell me about this all-important tip. What's it about, and who are you?"

"You must get to the waterfront tonight by sunset. Sometime after that, Roberto Valenzuela will be conducting some special business there," the stranger's voice finished abruptly.

"Well, I appreciate the information, but how do I know this is legitimate?" questioned Ian, trying to stall the caller for time so the phone trace could work. "Tell me who you are, and what's your interest in Valenzuela?"

"You know who I am, Lane," the voice said in a hushed tone. "You know who I am." The call ended.

Ian could see a look of great trepidation on Lane's face.

"You look spooked, man. So who do you think *that* nut case was?" said Jelani.

The officer tracing the call chimed in. "It was one of the few pay phones left here in Miami—that does us no good. It's way across town."

Ian could see the wheels turning in Lane's face, but Lane was not saying much.

Lane looked up at Ian, and shrugged his shoulders. "I don't know, Ian," Lane said unconvincingly. "Everybody in town knows how much I hate Valenzuela. Probably just a hoax."

"Well maybe so, but shouldn't we still check it out?," said Ian.

Lane spun around, looking Ian squarely in the eye. "We?" he said in an obvious tone suggesting there would be no "we" about this. "What do you mean 'we'? Yes, I am going to check this out, but no one else needs to bother with a likely false alarm. You said it yourself, I've been wasting too much time on trying to track down Valenzuela, so I'll just spend my own personal time on this."

"Aha, so you have been listening to me," shouted an excited Ian, grinning.

"I may be bullheaded, but I'm not deaf," Lane said.

Ian, sensing that maybe his partner was easing up a bit, tried inserting some levity into his conversation.

"Bullheaded, lunatic, nut job, plus a lot of other insulting things I can think of—and a lousy actor, I might add," answered Ian. "You've got some idea about this caller, and you think it's a hundred percent legitimate. I don't really know why, but I know you, buddy. If you think I'm letting you go check on this alone, you're crazy. I am not takin' *no* for an answer. I'm your partner, and partners always have each other's back."

"To the bat cave," Ian said, in his best attempt at a Batman voice.

"Seriously? Now who's the nut job?" said Lane. Wagging his head, and a slight grin breaking over his face—for the first time in a long time. "Okay, *'Batman'*. Holy terror, Batman, let's go gettum!" Lane said.

Ian, following behind Lane, slowed his pace for a moment. "Holy Terror?" he thought to himself. "Where in the world did that come from?"

Leaping into the squad car, they sped off down the road.

"Na, na, na, na-na-na-na-na, na-na-na-na-na, Batma-a-a-a-n," Ian's voice trailed off, singing out the theme song from the old 1960s Batman television series.

"I may be a bad actor, but you are one lousy singer!" yelled Lane.

Following behind Lane, Ian grabbed his jacket, thankful to finally see him able to relax some. But despite the levity, he felt an eerie sense, as if the two of them were heading into something very intense.

CHAPTER 29:

CONFRONTING THE VILLAINS

The unmarked squad car, carrying Lane and Ian, pulled up to an abandoned warehouse at the waterfront. Ian shut off the car, killing the headlights. The last few rays of sunlight spilled over the horizon as the sun set. Both men opened their car doors at the same time. The air around them was hot and muggy.

Ian broke the silence. "Man, it stinks down here. What is that god-awful smell? It's like some lethal combination of a high school locker room stench and dumpster rot."

Drawing a deep breath, ignoring Ian's comments about the smells, Lane said skeptically, "This anonymous tip better pan out."

"Well, there's only one way to find out, partner" replied Ian, as he unsnapped his seat belt. He drew his 38 special out of its holster and held it in front of his face. "Think we'll need more than these? Or should I grab the shotguns in the trunk?"

"Look, we don't even know if there's anything worthwhile to find here," answered Lane, as he drew his Desert Eagle 357 magnum pistol, popping the magazine to make sure it was full. "Let's just take it easy first, and go check out this sleepy little quiet area."

"You can say that again, " said Ian, checking his pistol as well. This place feels pretty dead, doesn't it. Sure doesn't look like a hot bed of criminal activity. But it's a crime how *bad* it smells," Ian said as he grinned at Lane.

"I'd have to agree with you on that," Lane said, returning the grin "Alright, let's go…quietly," he said quietly. Ian nodded, without saying a word.

Both men slowly pushed their doors the rest of the way open, and stepped out of the squad car with their pistols drawn. They stopped short of shutting the car doors, scanned the area, then paused to look at each other across the hood of the car. Ian could feel his adrenaline starting to flow. Nothing appeared out of the ordinary, yet he knew his body was telling him anything but that. He glanced back at Lane, and he could tell his partner was less tense than he was feeling.

Lane spoke first, straightening. "You were right, a real sleepy town," he said, lowering his gun, no longer trying to be quiet.

In a burst of sound, causing both detectives to instinctively duck for cover behind their car doors, as bullets from an automatic rifle peppered their car.

"What the hell?" yelled Ian. "I think we spoke too soon, man," he screamed.

"I guess that anonymous tip *might* end up being something!" yelled Lane sarcastically.

"Oh, you're real funny," shouted Ian. "What now, Captain Obvious? Did you see anything?"

"No worries, I got him. Single shooter," Lane replied, now speaking more calmly and gesturing toward the edge of the building. "He's to our right."

Lane moved to the right with precision. He quickly raised his gun, and with laser focus, fired two quick rounds. The automatic weapons fire ceased, to the sound of a body thudding onto the ground.

"Okay, nice shootin', Tex!" said Ian with a grin, as he stepped out from behind the car to inspect Lane's handiwork. "Hey, in case you were wonderin', I'd say that phone tip was definitely legit." Ian shot a grin at Lane.

"Uh, do ya think so?" Lane replied in a goofy voice.

His goofiness faded quickly, as he looked back over at Ian, and noticed him limping. "Dammit, you're hit, buddy!" Lane said, as he ran over to catch Ian, who was starting to go down to the ground.

"You're bleeding pretty good—no, no no," exclaimed Lane. He pulled his jacket off, wrapping it around the bullet wound in Ian's leg.

"It's just a flesh wound" Ian said, in his best Monty Python Black Knight voice.

"Ian, quit clowning around!" Lane said worriedly, as he assisted him back over to the back seat of the squad car.

Lane grabbed the radio handset. "Officer Madigan here," he shouted. "We've got a 10-108 here, officer down. We need backup and an ambulance right now. Get as many officers as you can down here at the end of Rockerman Road, near Kennedy Park, the abandoned warehouses. Do it!" he commanded, and dropped the handset.

"Help is on the way, my friend," he said to Ian. "You'll be fine now. I'm going to go nail that worthless Valenzuela," said Lane. "I know he's here somewhere."

Ian saw a fire in Lane's eyes now. "Hey man, just hold up," said Ian, grabbing Lane's arm. "Wait a few minutes for backup to get here first. Then they can help you get that crackpot."

Lane shook Ian's grasp. "Valenzuela must've heard the gunfire, and knows someone is here. I'm not letting him get away again," he shouted, as he turned to run back toward the dark building.

Ian pulled himself up to a standing position, hanging onto one of the squad car's open doors. "Don't go all 'Paul Kersey' on me, man," Ian shouted.

Lane shot a puzzled look back at Ian, shaking his head questioningly.

"Ah, you're too young to remember that movie, I guess," Ian said, recognizing Lane did not understand the innuendo. "Never mind," Ian said, his tone becoming more matter-of-fact. "Just remember that vengeance belongs to God, Lane, not you—*remember* that!" he shouted as loudly as he could after Lane. Then he slumped back into the seat of the car, pain overcoming him.

Ian fumbled around, and finally found a first aid kit. He unwrapped the jacket from around his leg, and could clearly see the exit wound of the bullet that struck him. He splashed the wound with some disinfectant solution, and wrapped some gauze tightly around his leg. "I'm not leaving him alone in there," he said through gritted teeth. Somehow hearing it out loud gave him strength.

With that, he hobbled to his feet, and made his way after Lane. "Please God, don't let me be too late," he prayed audibly, struggling to make his way into the dark building.

Lane, maneuvering with stealth and caution, was well ahead of Ian at this point. As he entered another warehouse room, he encountered dead bodies strewn around the area.

Obviously a botched drug deal, thought Lane. *More carnage left behind by Valenzuela and his goons.*

Just then, another of Valenzuela's henchmen sprung out of nowhere, guns blazing. With cool precision, Lane fired once, and another man was added to the body count.

"Roberto Valenzuela!" shouted Lane. "This is Detective Lane Madigan, Miami Vice. Give yourself up. Dead or alive, you're coming with me!" Lane thought to himself, *But dead is fine with me.*

A third assailant began to fire at Lane from above. Firing blindly upwards, Lane ran for cover. Safely behind a stack of large metal boxes, he reloaded his pistol, as the henchman continued firing around Lane's location. When the gunfire dwindled, Lane emerged from behind his barricade, coolly strolling into the open, fully upright. He fired three quick shots, two striking the shooter, who fell off the stories-high catwalk.

Ian peered from around the corner of a hallway, which led into a much larger room. The light was not great, but enough that he could see his way around. Hearing no sounds, he cautiously crept into the larger room, and crouched down behind some boxes. He saw several open doorways leading to other places in this huge warehouse.

Ian breathed deeply, trying to remain as quiet as possible. The stale, humid air and the pain from the gunshot wound in his leg made breathing more and more labored. As his eyes adjusted to the dimmer light, he saw an endless sea of crates, barrels, and drums piled around everywhere.

Ian noted that all these containers displayed various companies' logos and countries' flags. He saw writing, some in English, some in other languages. *A lot of places for the bad guys to hide out.* That thought concerned him. These objects cast varying shadows around, creating an eerie atmosphere. As he looked about, was he seeing movement? *Are my eyes playing tricks on me?*

Ian decided there really was no movement. He wiped some sweat off of his forehead. *Plenty of cover here for me too*, he thought to himself. He had heard a barrage of gunshots just moments ago while coming down the last hallway, but it came from elsewhere. But without any shots being fired anymore, he had no idea which direction to go.

He scanned the room and thought, I heard automatic weapons fire, like a 9mm Uzi. Also, there were 357 magnum gunshots, and that's what Lane is carrying. He shifted his gun to his other hand and flexed his fingers. Hopefully no one else is carrying one of those, as that will help me figure out where Lane is...if I hear another shot, that is.

Ian strained to hear anything, but with no clues on which to base a decision, he chose a hallway nearest him, to his left, and carefully hobbled along the corridor.

Once again, he found himself in another large warehouse room, with catwalks above, and more dim lights everywhere. All the windows were painted black, but weather and time had chipped away at the paint, allowing tidbits of sunlight to come in. The installed industrial lighting sported old bulbs, gunked up by dirt and soot. All that combined with the lighting being so high off the ground, seeing anything clearly was challenging. Ian noted some of the lights looked like they were hanging on by a thread, ready to tumble down on top of him at a moment's notice. *What the heck, can they not install decent lights in these places, clean up a little bit now and then, holy smokes?* He then noticed several bodies lying around the room.

"God, no," Ian said quietly. He glanced around, looking for signs of movement, anything to indicate that anyone was alive. Seeing nothing, he made his way around to each of the bodies. They were all dead. *God, please don't let one of these guys be Lane, I'm begging you*, he thought to himself as he rolled another one over to expose the face

After inspecting all the bodies, finding them all dead, none of them were Lane. *Well, now I know I'm on the right trail. Body count. It's like some outlandish Arnold Schwarzengger shoot 'em up movie—except, this is real.*

Ian looked around, faced with another tough decision. More doorways, more directions to choose from. *Now which way? There was no answer to his silent plea except the drip of ancient pipes.* He knelt down, and began to do what he knew he could do best for now—he began to pray.

CHAPTER 30:

CONFRONTING THE
ULTIMATE VILLAIN

"Satan, where are you, you filthy scum?" shouted Thumos. Thumos, now walked through the Twilight Realm. He continued "It's time for you to pay for what you did to Armada!"

Satan emerged from the darkness, calmly grinning at Thumos. His dark robe flowed about like snakes slithering all around him.

"Where are the rest of your worthless fools?" Thumos questioned.

"Why, they are out looking for you, my...*friend,*" Satan answered, sarcastically. "It would seem they have done a poor job in fulfilling my directives, since, right here you are."

"Wrong," said Thumos emphatically, with a slight grin. "They found me. And now they are with Armada, in the Banished Realm, which is where you are headed now, you pathetic traitor. That is the price you will pay for putting Armada there."

"I guess we shall see about that," Satan smirked, lacing his fingers in front of him.

Satan watched Thumos grasp his rhabdos tightly with both hands, and it began to glow bright white, as though absorbing the heat of the anger building inside him. He also saw Thumos's eyes emanating a brilliant white light. *I have not seen him like this before*, he thought.

Satan saw Thumos charging straight toward him. He felt the ground shaking beneath him with Thumos's every step. He threw off his dark robe as something like black smoke billowed from around him, revealing his jet black rhabdos. Satan barely managed to raise his rhabdos up, one hand on either end, in order to block Thumos's first overhand strike. He slid backwards in the process, barely able to stay on his feet. His eyes darkened, as he summoned all his own strength.

Satan swung his rhabdos back at Thumos, catching a glancing blow on Thumos's left arm. To his amazement, Thumos did not even wince, giving no indication he felt anything. Before he could strike again, he felt Thumos's large foot kick him in the gut, sending him stumbling backward. Barely stabilizing himself once again, avoiding falling down to the ground, he looked up just in time to feel Thumos's white-hot rhabdos swipe across his back.

Satan shouted in pain, as he dropped to one knee. He quickly bounced back up to his feet, facing Thumos. He began to slowly walk backwards away from Thumos, trying to stall for time. "Thumos, why must we fight like this?" he said, coughing.

"I intend to destroy you, you Old Red Dragon, right here and now," retorted Thumos.

Showing no signs of slowing down, Satan saw Thumos rushing him once again. He managed to block several back-and-forth swings of Thumos's rhabdos, but felt himself slowing down.

Halting his attack momentarily, Thumos spoke, spinning his rhabdos around like a baton. "Your powers are growing weak. How does that feel?"

Satan saw a sinister grin on Thumos's face. His eyes remained as white hot as ever. "Now look, Thumos, I do not want to see you end up like Armada," Satan said, gasping for breath, looking down trying to gather his composure.

Satan looked back up just in time to see Thumos swinging his rhabdos with a single hand, allowing it to extend much further than normal. He felt searing pain across the right side of his face, sending him tumbling to the ground.

"You shall not speak that name, ever again!" shrieked Thumos.

Satan managed to stagger back to his feet once again, but his vision was blurred now. "Do not think you can defeat me, Thumos," Satan said, wheezing and winded, no longer holding his rhabdos.

Satan suddenly felt himself flying backward, off his feet, his chest in utter pain from Thumos having swung at him like a baseball player slugging a homerun. He landed hard on his back. Rolling over, he pushed himself up onto all fours. In agonizing pain, he looked down his torso only to see dark streaks streaming down his body.

"I am the Prince of the Power of the Air", Satan muttered weakly. He rolled back over off all fours, sprawled out on the ground. "I am the Evil One. I am the Father of Lies. I am invincible," he sputtered.

He watched Thumos walk over to him slowly, silently, and stand over him. "You are defeated!" shouted Thumos. He watched Thumos's muscles bulging as he bent his white hot rhabdos with both hands. The rhabdos finally snapped in half with a monstrous explosion.

Just as that explosion sounded, Satan could see behind Thumos that Kakos had finally appeared.

Thumos raised both pieces of his broken rhabdos up over his head, both with sharp, jagged edges.

Satan heard Kakos shout "Noooooooooo!"

"Vengeance is mine, saith the Lord of Hosts," Thumos bellowed in a booming voice, drowning out Kakos's scream. Then plunged his rhabdos pieces downward with all his might to thrust through Satan.

Satan balled up into a fetal position, crying out in sheer fright. But suddenly, he found himself engulfed in some kind of force field, and the two halves of Thumos's rhabdos vaporized into a bright light as he attempted to drive them into Satan's body.

Thumos stumbled backward in shock. "What? How did…", he said bewildered, unable to finish his own sentence. He looked at his empty hands, he looked at Satan, he looked around searching for an explanation.

Satan slowly rose to his feet. He felt himself quivering, still engrossed with fear. He watched Kakos running to his side.

"Well done, my king, I have never seen anything like that before," said an admiring Kakos. He picked up Satan's robe, and draped it over him. "You truly are amazing. I thought you were surely banished to…".

Satan raised his hand, signaling Kakos to stop. He cleared his throat, and feigned gathering his composure. "Uh, well, yes," he stammered. "It was nothing."

Kakos whisked his master off into the darkness, and they both disappeared.

Several other angels, mostly from the former Warriors group, had arrived on the scene moments before Kakos, and were quietly standing back awaiting to see Satan defeated. They all stood speechless, also in shock over what they had just witnessed.

Thumos stared blankly at all these other angels, when all three archangels, Michael, Gabriel, and Raphael flashed in from above. They stood between Thumos and the other angels.

Michael demanded, "What in Yahweh's name has happened here?"

Tachu answered first. "You are not going to believe this, we do not even understand."

"Silence," said Michael, raising his hand toward Tachu. "Thumos, explain yourself."

Suddenly, interrupting everything, Phluaros appeared on the scene, and called out to Thumos from behind the crowd of angels. "Thumos, Lane Madigan is in peril."

Thumos, looking over at Phluaros, sensed the distress in his voice, and the look in his eyes. He knew something bad was happening. Despite his utter confusion over what had transpired, and now the Archangels appearance, demanding information from him, he disappeared straight upward, to the sound of a sizzling lightning bolt.

CHAPTER 31:

A FINAL SHOWDOWN

Lane stood quiet, motionless now, after the latest commotion, his eyes methodically scanning the room, on high alert for any surprises. His ears stood at attention, listening for any signal of movement. He breathed steadily, all he could hear—all he could feel—was the strong palpitation of his own heart, beating much faster now, his adrenaline coursing through him.

Lane eyed the dead bodies lying about, which were there thanks to his marksmanship. Without remorse, no emotion of any kind over the slaughter around him, Lane ejected the now empty clip from his 357 magnum, reached into his pocket, and grabbed a full clip. He inserted it into the gun, gave the bottom of the clip a firm pop to ensure it was fully engaged, all in one fluid movement.

Lane crept stealthily. *No Valenzuela here*, he thought. He spotted another hallway seeming to lead into another room. Carefully stepping around a pile of boxes, which had been scattered across his path from the man who had fallen from the catwalk, he maneuvered toward the door on the other side of the room.

Just before he stepped into the next hallway, Lane heard the single click of a leather soled shoe striking the floor subtly from behind him. Without hesitation, he whirled back around toward the sound, just in time to see the spark of a gun firing. Lane felt the intense burn from a bullet piercing his left shoulder, and passing cleanly through the tissue.

Despite the searing pain, Lane fought back the instinct to look over at his injury. Instead, without speaking a sound, he quickly fired his weapon, having no time to even take aim. Lane now felt like he and everything else was moving in slow motion. He saw his quickdraw shot striking Valenzuela somewhere, but where? Lane saw Valenzuela drop his 9mm pistol, as his assailant crumpled downward, collapsing onto the floor.

Lane would not have been surprised in the least to see his own heart come right through his rib cage. He glanced down at his chest, just to make sure. Lane thought, *I have never felt my heart racing like this before.* He thought for a moment he might pass out, as his knees buckled, only momentarily though.

Lane gathered himself, keeping his weapon up in front of his body, squarely taking aim at the motionless body of Valenzuela laying across the room from him. Cautiously, he began to slowly walk toward Valenzuela.

Is he dead? questioned Lane to himself. He said nothing, only continuing to walk slowly toward Valenzuela, but despite his cautious approach, his adrenaline showed no signs of slowing down.

Lane began to feel a wave of varied emotions coming over himself, and a flood of thoughts filled his racing mind. He was angry. *I can't believe I let his idiot get the drop on me.* He was enraged. *I hate this man. Finally, he will get what he deserves.* He was worried. *Is Ian okay?* He was in pain. *My shoulder, I can barely move it.* Lane's hodge-podge of thoughts was interrupted, as he finally received an answer to his own question about Valenzuela's status.

"I can't believe you shot me," groaned Valenzuela, as he rolled over, facing toward Lane. With difficulty, he tried to push himself into a seated position.

Lane looked down at the disarmed Valenzuela, noticing a mangled right hand. *I only shot him in his gun hand; it wasn't a kill shot,* he thought to himself, disappointingly.

Valenzuela stared down at his own injury. "You should be dead, you stupid cop," speaking with great difficulty, grimacing in pain. Propping himself up against a nearby floor pillar, Valenzuela finally looked up at Lane.

To the sound of a gun hammer click, Valenzuela found himself staring at the end of the barrel of Lane's 357 magnum. Lane saw Valenzuela swallow hard, then he saw Valenzuela look past the gun barrel, up into his own eyes.

In cool detachment, Lane stared back into Valenzuela's eyes. He felt a great sense of satisfaction welling up inside, as he could see the look of surprise and fear staring back at him.

"You took away my life, you animal!" screamed Lane. He pressed his gun barrel into Valenzeula's forehead. Valenzuela's eyes looked down, as Lane saw him tense up, expecting the worst.

"You murdered my wife, my baby girl—my poor little girl," Lane railed, as tears began to fill his eyes. Now, he no longer felt any pain in his left shoulder, though it hung limp beside his body, as blood continued to ooze down from the wound.

"And because of you, I'll never meet the unborn child my wife was carrying," screamed Lane, as now he bounced the end of the barrel of his gun off of Valenzuela's forehead repeatedly. Lane saw Valenzuela look up in desperation at him, at hearing that news. He apparently did not know about Janie's pregnancy.

"That's right, you worthless lowlife, you killed *three* Madigans," yelled Lane, emphasizing the number three. He took a shooter's stance, stepping back just slightly, positioning the gun directly at Valenzuela's face. " You don't deserve to live," he said with a shout. Then in a suddenly calm, stoic voice, Lane added "The only thing you deserve is a bullet to the head."

Thumos finally arrived on the warehouse scene, just as Lane prepared to shoot Valenzuela. He stood off to the side, watching the exchange between these two mortal enemies. *Relief*, thought Thumos, seeing Detective Madigan gain the upper hand over Valenzuela. "Hopefully he can finish what I was unable to do against my own foe," he said under his breath, anxiously waiting to see Lane finish the job.

Thumos relaxed his tension a bit, seeing that Lane had the situation well under control. Invisible to any human eyes, he crossed his arms in satisfaction, glad to witness firsthand Valenzuela receiving his just recompense of reward.

Lane's eyes filled with rage, as he began to slowly squeeze the trigger of his gun.

"Wait!" screamed Valenzuela, as he tried to scoot backwards along the floor. "What do you want? I'll give you anything you want. I'll give you as much money as you want. I'll give you names. Whatever you want, I'll give it to you, just tell me," he said desperately. Valenzuela's eyes darted around the room, looking for some way of escape. Lane saw sweat pouring profusely from Valenzuela's nervous face.

Lane did not hear anything Valenzuela said. All he could hear in his head were the words of Ian; those words he had heard time and time again over the years. *Vengeance is mine, I will repay, says the LORD.* Those words echoed now through his head, and slowly, his disposition toward Valenzuela was changing. Lane felt his anger mysteriously melting away.

Vengeance is mine, I will repay, says the LORD. Lane was hearing a female voice repeating that same line. *Janie?* he thought. Startled, Lane stepped backward away from Valenzuela, rising up to a fully standing stance. He glanced around the room, but saw no one.

Bewildered, Lane looked back at Valenzuela. He saw a puzzled face staring back at him. "No one else is hearing all this," Lane said out loud.

"Hearing what?" Valenzuela said, looking back and forth around the room, very confused over what was transpiring.

Lane began taking yet a few more steps backward away from Valenzuela. Quietly, he began repeating what he was hearing in his head, to no one in particular, "Vengeance is *not* mine; it is God's." Lane could hear his own voice saying that, and yet he could also almost hear his partner, Ian, saying it to him just as he had done so many times in the past.

What an odd feeling this is, Lane thought to himself, then he spoke out loud again. "Vengeance is not mine, it is God's."

Thumos uncrossed his arms, and took a couple of steps toward the two men. He squinted his eyes, and his gaze fixed on Lane. *What is happening here?,* he questioned. *What voices does Lane think he can hear?* Thumos knew full well that no one else was there in the room, but he also found himself looking around the room. Obviously seeing no one, his eyes again fell to Lane. Thumos, in awe, became oblivious to everything else. He was watching and listening to Lane intently.

How could Lane possibly have found the slightest shred of mercy in his heart for this Valenzuela? He could not believe what he was witnessing here. Lane seemed to be prepared to spare the life of his most hated enemy. *He has a chance to exact a fair and just punishment on his family's murderer, yet he apparently is about to turn down this golden opportunity.*

Lane felt calm, a peace that he did not fully understand, and the rage that had once flamed within him only moments ago, that had fueled all of his days since his family's death, departed from him. He glanced back to Valenzuela, and said it to him very calmly. "Vengeance is not mine; it is God's."

Lane saw Valenzuela staring at him in disbelief. It was clear to Lane that Valenzuela must be thinking he was a *real whacko, just plain messed up.* Lane felt a slight smile form at the corner of his mouth.

Is this what it feels like to be filled with the Spirit? Lane questioned himself in awe. He lowered his weapon, and stepped backward. Holstering his gun he began to read the Miranda rights in a confident voice.

Lane took his eyes off of Valenzuela for a moment, as he reached around his waist for his handcuffs. Valenzuela sneered, saying "You are really out there, man, you are freakin' nuts!"

Lane ignored Valenzuela's chiding. *This truly is justice, far better than simply shooting this criminal in the head, as he had envisioned doing.* His thoughts then rushed to his family. *I need to visit their gravesite as soon as this is over.*

Lane extended his hands toward Valenzuela, ready to slap the cuffs on this dirtbag. He heard a small explosion and a flash of light that caught him off-guard. Lane looked at Valenzuela, and saw a shaking hand pointing a small snub-nosed gun back at him. Confused, Lane glanced down at his chest, and saw red blossoming through his shirt. Just as everything began to register in his brain, he fell backwards, crashing to the floor.

Ian heard a single gunshot that made him spring into action, despite his body's protestations. *That's no 357 magnum, not automatic weapons fire; that was something smaller in caliber.*

Ian panicked, struggling to move forward. Lane's gun had not returned fire. A shot of adrenaline and fear propelled him to his feet. His eyes quickly darted around the room, looking for something that would lead him toward the sound. He saw yet another corridor, and headed that way. Ian knew the pain was worsening, and he could feel blood flowing more freely down his leg. Lightheaded, he used the wall to steady himself and half walked, half slid down the hallway, propelling himself forward with his one good leg.

God, help me, became his mantra.

Thumos stood dumbstruck at the turn of events that now unfolded in front of him. He had been so puzzled by Lane's change of heart, that he never saw Valenzuela sneaking a gun from the bottom of his pant leg.

Thumos burst from the shadows, a scream on his lips. Racing to Valenzuela, Thumos ripped the gun from his hand, and shoved him to the ground. Then Thumos threw the gun to the ground at Valenzuela's feet with such force, it exploded into powder. He watched Valenzuela shield his eyes from the explosion of the gun, as he clenched his fists, glaring down at Valenzuela.

Valenzuela, dazed, looked up in shock. "Wait, the guy from the cemetery, from the funeral of Madigan's family," he exclaimed, as he recognized Thumos. "That was you. And now you're here?" he said, confused. Valenzuela struggled to get to his feet, now speaking in a calm, business-like tone. "Nevermind all that, just get me out of here. I'll give you whatever you want." He looked into Thumos's eyes, and saw a rage like none other he had ever seen in his life.

"A wise man holds his tongue," Thumos said sternly, eyes blazing.

Thumos reached into Valenzuela's mouth, and felt for the man's flailing tongue. He grasped it in his hand, closing on it with satisfaction as Valenzuela's eyes bulged. In a swift motion, Thumos stood with the man's dangling tongue. Before Valenzuela had time to react, Thumos returned the man's tongue to him, placing the bloody stump into Valenzuela's hand.

Thumos allowed his human appearance to begin fading away, to reveal his true angelic image. His human attire began to disintegrate into nothingness. He could see the look of sheer terror in Valenzuela's eyes. Thumos could feel his brilliantly shining brass-like skin emanating its natural heat, as if he were made of lightning, and he heard Valenzuela now groaning in panic.

Thumos shook his head, and his once long, flowing white hair floated away as multiple horns began to now appear out of his head. His once human-like ears stretched into elongated leathery appendages. His mouth expanded outward, creating almost a snout, with long, white fangs. With every breath, Thumos felt bursts of flame pulsating from his mouth. He almost resembled something like Anubis, out of ancient Egyptian mythology.

The light from Thumos's brilliantly bright sun-like eyes enveloped Valenzuela's face, and he saw Valenzuela trying to cover his eyes. He heard Valenzuela shrieking out in guttural screams of fright. Speaking in a voice so powerful, as if it were multiple voices of varying pitch, he loudly shouted. "Then he hewed him into pieces before the LORD!"

Thumos, now fully revealed in his completely unobscured angelic form, raised his flaming sword over his head, and swung his first blow at Valenzuela, which severed his right arm. "For Janie Madigan!" Thumos screamed in his bone-shaking voice.

Thumos's sword raised again, and delivered another blow to sever Valenzuela's left arm. "For Elizabeth Madigan!" Thumos yelled.

Thumos swung his sword again, cutting off both of Valenzuela's legs at his knees. "For the unborn Madigan child," Thumos screamed.

"And for everyone else you have ever victimized," thundered Thumos. As Valenzuela's body began to fall to the ground, the final swing of Thumos's sword decapitated Valenzuela's body before it could hit the ground.

"Vengeance is mine!" roared Thumos's terrifying angelic voice, shaking the entire building.

Thumos stood for a moment, breathing heavily, his entire body heaving up and down, as he glanced over the pieces of Valenzuela's body which lay scattered around on the floor now. He began to summon himself back into his previous human form.

Thumos's flaming sword slowly faded away, and his dark colored human clothing began to reappear over his body. His skin, his hair, his face—everything about him reverted back to his human appearance now. He glanced over at Lane, who laid where he had fallen. He was not moving.. Thumos quickly moved toward Lane, knelt down and gently slipped his hand under the back of his head, lifting him slightly.

"Lane Madigan, are you still with me?" Thumos spoke calmly.

"Who, or what, *are* you?" Lane said, in a faint, weak voice.

"I am Thumos, an angel of the LORD Most High," said Thumos in a calm, gentle voice.

"It was you all along, wasn't it?" said Lane, his voice rasping and thin. "An angel vigilante? What a story that would have been." He inhaled a labored breath. " But I'm not going to be the one telling this story, am I?"

Suddenly, Lane's eyes focused past Thumos. "Janie?" His voice caught in his throat as he said, "And Elizabeth too?" Tears of joy flooded his eyes. "How…"

Thumos turned to see the ethereal spirits of Lane's wife and daughter. He saw two other figures as well, a very small person, and a taller person in a traditional priestly brown robe. He took several steps backward to remove himself from this reunion.

Lane watched the robed figure walk toward him. This person knelt down next to Lane, gently reaching over to hold his right hand.

The man now spoke. "Our Father in heaven, hallowed be Thy name."

Once Lane heard what the man was saying, he immediately joined with him, and the two spoke together in unison. "Thy kingdom come, Thy will be done on earth as it is in heaven. Give us this day our daily bread, and forgive us our trespasses as we forgive those who trespass against us. And do not lead us into temptation, but deliver us from evil, for thine is the kingdom and the power and the glory now and forever. Amen."

The robed man continued, and now Lane only listened. "Have mercy on me, God, according to your loving kindness. According to the multitude of your tender mercies, blot out my transgressions. Wash me thoroughly from my iniquity. Cleanse me from my sin. For I know my transgressions. My sin is constantly before me. Against you, and you only, have I sinned, and done that which is evil in your sight; that you may be proved right when you speak, and justified when you judge."

Lane interrupted the robed man's recitation. "Oh yes, I recognize this. Psalms 51," he said weakly.

The robed man smiled patiently at Lane's interruption, nodding his head in agreement. Then he continued. "Behold, I was brought forth in iniquity. In sin my mother conceived me. Behold, you desire truth in the inward parts. You teach me wisdom in the inmost place. Purify me with hyssop, and I will be clean. Wash me, and I will be whiter than snow. Let me hear joy and gladness, That the bones which you have broken may rejoice. Hide your face from my sins, and blot out all of my iniquities. Create in me a clean heart, O God. Renew a right spirit within me."

Lane could feel his breathing growing more shallow, but he smiled, feeling a sense of calm and relief. His pain was dissipating, as he continued listening to the robed man's recitation of the 51st Psalm.

"Do not throw me from your presence, and do not take your holy Spirit from me. Restore to me the joy of your salvation. Uphold me with a willing spirit. Then I will teach transgressors your ways. Sinners shall be converted to you. Deliver me from bloodguiltiness, O God, the God of my salvation.

My tongue shall sing aloud of your righteousness. Lord, open my lips. My mouth shall declare your praise. For you do not delight in sacrifice, or else I would give it. You have no pleasure in burnt offering. The sacrifices of God are a broken spirit. A broken and contrite heart, O God, you will not despise." The robed man finished speaking.

Lane felt the man grasping his hands, and once again saw the man smiling at him as their eyes connected. Lane once again felt an overwhelming sense of peace and serenity flow through his body. He watched the robed man rise slowly to a standing position, and then watched him walk away, disappearing behind the other spirits.

Lane looked up at Thumos, and motioned for him to come closer again. "Who was that man?" he asked weakly.

Thumos moved closer to Lane, and knelt down next to him. Surprised that Lane did not know, he answered "Oh, that was the Apostle Jude, patron saint of lost causes. The Father allows this to happen sometimes when an earthly priest is not able to celebrate last rites."

"And who is the little boy I see standing there?" asked Lane.

Now Lane could see a bright light glowing from behind Janie and Elizabeth. Lane's pain was completely gone now, and at the appearance of the bright light, he also began to feel a great comfort flow through him. The silence was interrupted by a deep, powerful male voice. "Elizabeth, tell your Daddy that it is time for him to come home with us," a voice spoke from the light in a stern, yet gentle tone. "And introduce him to your little brother."

Elizabeth took the hand of the little boy, and excitedly stepped toward her father, smiling. "You heard Jesus, Daddy. You get to come home with us. We get to be together again," she said laughing. She pushed the little boy forward toward Lane. "This is William, Daddy. You never got to meet him before. William, say 'hello' to your daddy."

"Hello daddy," said the little boy, in a quiet voice. "My name is William."

"William?" said Lane, as tears of joy streamed down his face. "Really, that is our son?" Lane questioned, looking back to Janie.

"Yes, my love," said Janie, smiling sweetly, placing each of her hands on the heads of the two children. "Let's go", and she reached out both hands for Lane. He watched as the three of them moved toward him.

Thumos rose back to his feet, and took several steps backward as Lanie, Elizabeth, and William drew closer to Lane.

They grasped Lane's hands, and pulled him up. He felt completely healthy and rested now. Lane looked back, to see his lifeless body lying on the floor. Surprised to be standing up, yet seeing his own dead body lying on the floor, he looked down to his arms, torso, and legs, and saw a spiritual glow emanating from this new body of his. Lane knelt down before the light, crossing himself, and said "Thank you, Lord Jesus, I am ready to be with you all."

Thumos saw several other angels now appearing on the scene. He had seen these angels before, but he was not familiar enough to know them by name. Thumos smiled approvingly, as he knew why they were here. He watched them join hands, forming a circle, surrounding the Madigan family, and a warm, gentle glow of light began to envelope them all.

Thumos shielded his eyes, as the brilliantly bright light surrounding Jesus began to rise slowly upward. The group of angels, along with the Madigans, began to also rise slowly upward following behind Jesus. Within a few moments, they were all gone.

Thumos looked back over in the corner near some refuse and other discarded boxes to see Valenzuela's spirit standing there, witnessing all of this in the backdrop of everything that had just transpired. He could see Valenzuela looking around frantically at the pieces of his physical body strewn around the area. Then his eyes met with Thumos's eyes. He could see a speechless look of shock and horror in Valenzuela's face.

Thumos noted that the once feared crime boss appeared nothing like the Madigans. Instead of white, glowing garments, he was dressed in clothing that hung in tatters around his frame. A host of Makria suddenly appeared, surrounding him. They slapped shackles and chains on him. The dark host grabbed the chains, and began to drag his spirit off. His screams of pain and terror far exceeded those of his gruesome death. Thumos listened with satisfaction as Valunzuela's cries faded into the distance.

Thumos stood alone momentarily, then was instantly joined by the three archangels, Michael, Gabriel, and Raphael.

"Come with us now, Thumos," Gabriel spoke gently. "The Father wishes to speak with you."

Thumos, perplexed by this, spoke. "The Father? The Father wants to speak with *me*?"

"Yes, said Michael reassuringly. "He wants you to come home to Him now, Thumos."

"Raphael, you go deal with Ian Jelani, and we shall escort Thumos to the Father," Michael commanded.

"By your command, brother Michael," said Raphael. He turned away, and began to make his way toward Ian.

Thumos nodded compliantly, and for the first time in several recent encounters with the archangels, he obeyed their command without question.

Ian Jelani stood in a corner unnoticed by anyone. He had seen everything from the moment Thumos sprung into action. What he saw then, had sent him cowering to the floor in sheer fright. No man, he knew, righteous or not, could stand before an angel of Yahweh without trembling in complete fear. All Ian had been able to do was watch. He rose to his feet, as sirens finally began to sound off in the distance, signaling the approach of police and emergency support.

"*I'm not sure I know what to do with all this,*" Ian thought to himself. Then he spoke out loud to himself. "No one is going to believe this, it's too overwhelming. I'm not sure I believe it myself."

"Believe what you have seen, Ian Jelani," Raphael spoke, walking up silently from behind Ian.

"What?" Ian shouted, nearly jumping out of his skin, as he looked around to see where that voice came from. "Uh, who, or what, are you?" he questioned, as he recognized this was no ordinary man walking toward him.

"I am Raphael, an archangel of God the Almighty," Raphael said in a lofty voice. "You need to get to the hospital, then home to rest. You will survive these wounds."

Raphael's calm voice switched to a more stern tone. "But speak to no one of what you have witnessed here today."

Ian fell down to a kneeling position. "I am already speechless, my lord," Ian said in a reverent voice.

"Rise up, Ian Jelani," commanded Raphael. "I am not your Lord; you have only one Lord. You have found favor in the eyes of the Father, Ian Jelani."

Raphael had sounded very official to this point, but seemed to revert to a less formal approach as he suddenly winked and added, "And keep up the good work, Jelani. We angels have taken a liking to you. We are all rooting for you!"

Ian heard a sizzling sound, as though lightning was about to strike, and with a thunderous pop, suddenly Raphael was gone. He looked up, still down on his knees, and through the fading image of where Raphael had been standing, Lauren ran toward him.

Falling to her knees beside him she wrapped her arms around Ian, weeping. "I was so worried, Ian. When I heard the call had come in, officer down, and they said it was Lane calling in...I panicked...my mind was racing. I couldn't bear the thought of you being gone." She pulled back, looking into Ian's eyes, tears streaming down her face. She kissed him.

"Goodness, I was so worried about you," Lauren said. She hugged him again, even tighter.

"Nope, not dead yet," Ian quipped. "I suppose God ain't finished with me just yet."

"I'm not done with you either, Detective," Lauren replied with a grin. She finally noticed his wounded leg. "Oh my God," she said, looking back into his face again. "Why didn't you say something? Medic, get over here!" she yelled over her shoulder in a commanding voice.

Ian looked surprisingly at Lauren's change of tone. "Remind me to never get in *your* way," he said, chuckling.

Ian found himself surrounded by paramedics, fellow officers, and fire crew. He was on sensory overload with everything happening around him. He then felt himself being pulled abruptly onto a gurney.

"IV fluids, now," he heard one paramedic demanding. Ian felt another person grabbing his arm, wrapping a blood pressure cuff around it, quickly pumping it up. Someone else tied a tourniquet around his leg, and he winced in pain as it was tightened.

"Pulse is at 75, BP is 140 over 80, not too bad," shouted a paramedic. "But get some bandaging on this wound," she shouted, pointing at Ian's leg.

"Jelani," shouted Chief Franklin, who was making a B-Line toward Ian's gurney.

Ian saw a red-faced, angry Chief Julie Franklin bearing down on him. "What in God's name has happened here, Detective?" she questioned. "This is like some kind of war zone! The Mayor and the media are breathing down my neck already."

One of the paramedics intercepted Chief Franklin, blocking her path. "Not here, not now, Chief," said a paramedic. "You can talk to Detective Jelani later. Now get outta our way."

"All right, all right," answered Chief Franklin, calming down, wagging her head. "I just need some answers. This place is a madhouse," she said, throwing her arms up in the air. "And where is Detective Madigan?" she demanded.

Another officer walked up from behind Chief Franklin, and took her by the arm, pulling her away from the gurney. "We found Detective Madigan's body over here, Chief, he…didn't make it," the officer said sorrowfully.

"Dammit," said Chief Franklin, running her fingers through her hair. She looked back inquisitively at Ian lying on the gurney, wanting to ask him more questions, but the paramedics were wheeling him away. "We'll get to the bottom of that later, I suppose," she said with a grimace.

Ian felt the bounce of the gurney rolling along the rough roadway. Lauren walked beside him. *"Don't tell anyone about this,"* Ian thought to himself. *"Inexpressible words, which it is not lawful for a man to utter. Now I know how the apostle Paul felt."* Despite the flurry of activity around him, and the Chief railing at him, Ian felt a big grin coming over his face.

"You must be some kind of crazy man," Lauren said.

Ian looked at her calmly. "Me, crazy, why?"

"All this happening around you," Lauren said, waving her hands around. "And you're just lying there smiling like a goof ball."

Ian laughed. "I was just thinkin'," he said. "Lot to process here, ya know." He winked at Lauren, still grinning at her, as the paramedics lifted his gurney into the back of the ambulance.

"Let's go. Get him to Downtown Medical ASAP," shouted the ambulance driver.

"I'm following you there," called out Lauren, waving at Ian.

Another paramedic jumped into the back of the ambulance next to Ian, and slammed the rear door shut. The vehicle quickly tore away down the street, sirens blaring, lights flashing.

CHAPTER 32:

LIFT UP YOUR HEAD, O YOU GATES

humos felt the firm grip of each archangel, as Michael grasped his right arm, and Gabriel grasped his left arm. In only a flash of time, they had streaked past the first heaven, Earth below was but a pale blue dot. Thumos looked around as a menagerie of celestial objects blurred past him.

"I have witnessed this scenery countless times in my existence," Thumos thought to himself. *"But this time feels so much different. For such a long time, I have traversed this path with the heavy weight of anger and vengeance, but this time I am overwhelmed with an incredible sense of peace and tranquility."*

Thumos watched the second heaven disappearing behind them, as they now approached the third heaven. Below, the Twilight Realm streamed past them, then the Neutral Realm followed suit. As they breached the edge of the Neutral Realm, Thumos raised his hands as best he could, to shield his eyes from a bright white light. It was as if the most brilliant sun that ever shone was rising in grandeur from an eastern morning sky.

Thumos's eyes acclimated to the brightness, as Michael and Gabriel gently glided him down to a vast surface of a light blue brick walkway. Hefelt the archangels' grips loosen, releasing him onto the surface. His feet touched down on the hardened ground, and he instantly felt a soothing warmth under his feet.

"What am I to do now?" Thumos questioned. But just as he looked over his shoulder to speak to Michael and Gabriel, they were both already disappearing into the distance, returning the way they had come.

Thumos shrugged and shook his head, then looked back in front of himself once again. His gaze followed the sky blue pathway, which led to three large gates. Extending out from the gates, as far as his eyes could see in both directions, were high walls, like fortress walls, rising 144 cubits high.

Thumos stood motionless for a few moments, gazing in awe at the massive structure before him. He walked the pathway toward the wall. He looked down at the bricks of the walkway, then stopped abruptly, looking up and down the pathway.

"Blue jasper?" he questioned out loud. "Incredibly rare. How beautiful. It is like walking across the sky back on Earth."

As he got closer to the wall, he could see the blue pathway wrapped around the walls as far as he could see. Thumos diverted himself from the gates momentarily, and walked up to the wall, placing his hand on it.

"More jasper, but clear," Thumos said out loud, as he brushed his hand across the wall. "These walls are stacks of one cubit square, solid bricks of jasper, with no evidence of any mortar." He could feel that same gentle warmth emanating from the walls, that he felt under his feet.

"Incredible," Thumos said out loud. "Each stone has a precious gem in the center." He passed his hand over one of the gemstones. "A red jasper stone," he said. After closer inspection, he noted several different gemstones in each of the jasper bricks.

Thumos recounted out loud all the gemstones he could see. "Jasper, sapphire, chalcedony, emerald, sardonyx, carnelian, chrysolite, beryl, topaz, chrysoprase, hyacinth, amethyst. Twelve different types of gemstones, repeated throughout all these jasper bricks."

Thumos smiled, then pressed his face up against one of the jasper bricks. "Translucent, but not transparent," he said, trying to spy through to the inside, without success. "But something inside is glowing."

Thumos walked back toward the three large gates, sliding his hand all along the wall until reaching the first gate, where he took a few steps back away but continued his stride until he reached the center of the middle gate. Thumos stared up at the monstrous gates for a moment, then he walked toward the middle gate, once again reaching out to touch.

"Incredible," he gasped, as his hand slid over the surface of the gate. "Each of these gates is made from a single pearl, as pure white as white can be." He looked closely at the ornate carvings in the gates. He saw a variety of symbols, some he recognized, others he did not.

However, at eye level, Thumos did clearly recognize some larger writing. In fact, he looked at all three gates, and could see each gate had a name carved into it. "Dan," he read out loud, as he looked to the left gate. "Judah," he read out loud, as he looked back to the center gate. "Naphtali," he read, as he looked to the right gate.

"The Ancient of Days is expecting you, Thumos," said a booming voice.

Thumos startled slightly, not expecting to hear anyone speaking to him. He looked around puzzled, not seeing anyone.

"We stand guard, up here," declared the same voice.

Thumos finally looked up, toward the top of the gate. He was shocked to now see three ominous creatures, one standing atop of each gate. Each stood at attention, holding a revolving flaming sword. *"How in God's creation did I not see them before?"*, Thumos thought to himself.

"Are you cherubim?" Thumos asked, trying to maintain his composure, but still sounding timid.

"Indeed, we are," said the same one who had spoken before. He was the one standing over the gate of Judah.

"I have never seen cherubim before, but of course, I have heard of them," Thumos responded, feeling slightly less intimidated now. Then he glanced back and forth at the other two cherubim, who remained silent. Their gaze was fixed on him. *"I can almost feel their stare,"* Thumos thought to himself, subsequently reverting back to a less confident version of himself.

Thumos looked back to the one in the center, who seemed slightly more cordial. "Are there others here?", he asked. *"I have always wanted to ask these guys some questions,"* Thumos thought to himself. *"Not going to blow this opportunity."*

"Here, yes, and many other special places, we are commissioned to guard," answered the middle cherub. "You are at the Eastern gates of the City of the Most High. On each side of this perfectly square city, at the center, are three gates just like these," he said, as he motioned, sweeping his hand across the three gates. "Three gates on the south side, three gates on the north side, and three gates on the west side. Over each gate is stationed one of us, to guard it."

Thumos noticed that the other two cherubim simultaneously looked at the one in the center, almost as if to say "you are telling him too much".

The center cherub looked at both of them, and waving his hand, said "Do not be troubled, Thumos will soon learn many things." Both of the other cherubim resumed their cold stares at Thumos.

"You saw three of the names of the twelve tribes of Israel on our gates," continued the middle cherub. "Each gate has one of these twelve tribes inscribed upon it."

"Did you see the twelve courses of stones at the foundation of the walls?" questioned the middle cherub.

Thumos did not speak, but only shook his head. *"Yet something else that I missed,"* Thumos thought to himself, feeling embarrassed.

The cherub made a gesture toward the foundation of the walls, offering Thumos the opportunity to go inspect that part of the wall.

Thumos walked over closer to the wall again, and now noticed large white stones of granite, several cubits in length, which formed the base of the wall. He walked along the wall, noting a different name on each of these foundation stones. The names appeared to repeat every twelve stones.

Quickly, Thumos walked back to where he was once again positioned below the middle cherub. He looked up and said "Each stone is inscribed with the name of one of the twelve apostles of the Lamb. That pattern repeats with every twelve foundation stones."

The middle cherub nodded, slightly grinning at Thumos.

Just then, each of the three massive gates began to slowly rise upward. Thumos heard the sound of chain links pulling tight, metal on metal grinding in conjunction with the rising gates. Once the gates were a few cubits off the ground, Thumos could see three muscular cherubim straining with great effort, each one pulling a large chain to raise the corresponding gate.

Finally, the gates reached their fully open positions. The three muscular cherubim stood fast, their arms rippling from the weight of the gates, and they all looked at Thumos. Thumos looked at them, then glanced back up to the cherub over the Judah gate.

"Enter now," the cherub said, gesturing gently, offering Thumos passage through the gate.

Thumos hesitated for a moment, looking back again to the cherubim holding the gates open, then cautiously stepped forward. Just before passing through the threshold, he paused, glancing up at the middle cherub one last time, and noted he was smiling approvingly, nodding his head. Thumos continued, and stepped through the gateway.

Instantaneously with stepping to the inside of the gate, the three cherubim released their grip. The chains rattled loudly as they recoiled, and the gates slammed to the ground with a thunderous clap. Thumos spun around quickly to look behind, caught off guard by the ferocity of the gates closing. Just as he turned back around to face frontward again, his ears were assaulted by a reverberating chorus that practically pinned him up against the pearly gates.

Thumos covered his ears, but even that could not drown out the myriad of voices he heard chanting "Holy, Holy, Holy." He pressed himself to step away from the gate, to continue moving forward. Pulling his hands down from his ears, since covering his ears was not softening the tremendous sounds, he then looked up. Circling high, above the center of the complex, he saw an incredible sight.

Thumos could see a host of creatures flying about, high overhead. Each one had six wings. With two they covered their faces, with two they covered their feet, and with two they hovered. They all cried out to each other "Holy, Holy, Holy is the LORD of hosts! All of creation is filled with His glory!"

"Seraphim!" Thumos yelled out loud. Even yelling loudly, he could barely hear himself. "More of the heavenly host I have never seen before!"

Thumos looked around, marveling as his visual senses tingled. He breathed in deeply, his olfactory senses overwhelmed as well.

"Incense," Thumos said, still speaking in a shouting tone. "The prayers of the saints."

Thumos looked down to see the sky blue jasper brick walkway continued before him, stretching out in every direction. But one path was different. He saw a wide path, like a city street.

"The street of gold, transparent as glass," Thumos said. His eyes followed that golden pathway, straight in front of him. Thumos gasped. Now he saw, at least one hundred cubits away from him, the source of the glowing which he had seen from outside the walls.

"The city of gold, clear, just like the street," Thumos exclaimed.

Thumos could see the golden street led right up to the opening of a large structure, which resembled an ancient castle. Through an open doorway, intense smoke poured out from inside the structure. Thumos's head slowly lifted upward, as his eyes scanned up the clear-as-glass gold brick walls, and the intense smoke was billowing from up high as well. He could not see the tops of the walls, for the smoke.

Having stood motionless for a long time, as he had tried to absorb everything around him, Thumos finally began to walk the golden pathway. He was unsure if he should, but he also felt an irresistible draw toward that doorway up ahead. Thumos also had finally acclimated to the loud chants of the seraphim, so he felt less disoriented now.

Thumos noted great spires along the walls of the castle structure, cascading upward, also disappearing into the smoke. Even those spires were made of the same transparent gold. The closer he approached the open doorway, the aroma of the incense grew more and more intense.

Thumos got within just a few cubits of the open doorway, when he abruptly stopped.

"The tremendous glow of the city is not coming from the clear golden walls," he thought to himself. *"It is coming from* inside *the structure. Something else is giving this city its light."*

Thumos began to tremble, and he dropped to his knees. "The city had no need of sun or moon to shine on it, for the glory of God gave it light, and its lamp was the Lamb." Thumos quoted out loud Revelation 22:23, in a shaking, wavering voice.

"But nothing unclean will enter it, nor anyone who does abominable things," Thumos continued, quoting Revelation 22:27, as he now bent over forward with his face to the ground, covering his head with his arms. "I cannot do this, I cannot enter this place," Thumos wept.

"Thumos, come forward," spoke a familiar voice. Despite the continued loud chanting of the seraphim, Thumos heard this very clearly. He looked up, still cowering on his knees, and saw Michael the archangel now standing at the doorway.

"Michael, please, I am not able to go in there," Thumos pleaded. "I am not worthy."

"Thumos, even the most righteous person still appears in filthy rags, before the Most High," Michael replied. "Of course you are not worthy. No one is."

Thumos watched Michael walk toward, with sympathetic body language. He had not seen Michael look this way before. Then Thumos felt Michael grasp his arm, gently lifting him up to his feet.

Thumos stood up straight once again, and looked over at Michael. Their eyes locked.

Michael smiled softly, yet another surprise to Thumos. "You must go. Everything will be fine," Michael said, as he gestured toward the doorway.

Thumos looked back toward the doorway, looked back at Michael and gave him a single nod. Michael let go of Thumos's arm, and Thumos looked straight ahead once again as he began to walk cautiously toward the doorway.

Thumos reached the doorway, one step short. The smoke was pouring out from the doorway intensely, and he found himself engulfed by it. He paused, took a deep breath, and put his head down, stepping through the doorway.

CHAPTER 33:

IN THE THRONE ROOM

Thumos had crossed the threshold with his head tilted downward, his eyes averted in respect. After a couple of steps into the room, he stopped walking, surprised by what he found...or actually what he did not find.

Silence. "What?" Thumos said out loud. Dumbfounded, his eyes darted back and forth, without moving his head in the slightest. He no longer heard the chanting.

Thumos looked up. No seraphim. He looked down at the floor, to the left, to the right. No smoke. He turned 180 degrees to look behind. *"No doorway?"* he thought, which gave him a bit of a shock. All he saw where the doorway used to be was the same transparent golden bricks as the rest of the city.

Thumos reached out with his hands, to touch the transparent gold, then moved up to the wall where the doorway used to be. He looked through the transparent gold, expecting to see Michael, or the cherubim who raised the pearl gates. Instead, Thumos saw nothing.

Just as Thumos turned to face the front, a gale force wind came out of nowhere, knocking him right to the ground on his back. He looked up, and saw nothing above except sheer bright white. His ears were filled with the sound of that unbelievably strong wind, which was so powerful, and arrived so suddenly, it utterly stunned Thumos.

Thumos struggled to roll over, and with all his might, he managed to push himself onto all fours. The incredible magnitude of the wind force continued to drive Thumos downward, as he pushed with all the strength he could muster, he tried to stand. But the rushing wind was so powerful still, even his super strength was insufficient against this wind which was clearly more powerful than any hurricane or tornado he had ever seen on Earth. Thumos's long flowing white hair whipped about behind his head, and he squinted his eyes, barely able to keep them open. His lips and cheeks rippled from the force of the wind. Finally, he could take it no longer and let out a billowing scream in defiance of the wind.

Thumos's voice echoed off the walls of the structure, as he shook his head. As suddenly as the wind had appeared, it abated. He was still down on all fours. Thumos looked back and forth. Nothing else happened, and he slowly rose to his feet.

Thumos looked around to still see a large, empty room. The walls of the perfectly square room were still the clear-as-glass golden bricks, and he looked up to see the walls rose high only to give way to a white vastness. Still, nothing except for him in this room. No other beings, no objects, no smoke, just nothing. Thumos did not know what else to do, so he began to walk toward the center of the room.

Thumos found himself having to throw his arms out in front of him, to avoid face planting into the floor. This time, a powerful earthquake was shaking the entire room. He felt like a ball in a playground parachute game, tossed about the shaking floor. Thumos would not have been surprised if the floor had disintegrated, and he plunged into nothingness below.

Thumos screamed again, in another show of defiance, now against this earthquake. Once again, it ended in an echo off the now completely still walls. He found himself lying on his back, staring up into the vast whiteness above. Thumos pushed himself up onto his elbows, looking around, shaking his head in disgust.

"I knew I should not have come in here," Thumos thought to himself. *"I will not be able to stand before the power which dwells in this place. Skin-ripping winds, and bone-crushing earthquakes…what is next?"*

Thumos pushed off his elbows into a sitting position on the floor, then braced his hands down to push back onto his feet. *"Am I being punished?"* Thumos thought to himself, as he resumed walking toward the center of the room.

Thumos found himself throwing his arms instinctively up to his face, because the entire room exploded all around him into a raging fire.

"I see fire, but I feel nothing. What is happening to me?" Thumos thought to himself. Maintaining his composure, he put his arms down and continued walking. He stopped in the dead center of the room, and as quickly as the wind had ceased, then also the earthquake had quieted, the fire dissipated.

Thumos stood still and quiet in the middle of the room, still accompanied by no one and by nothing. He had no idea of what he should do next, so he simply stood still, waiting.

"Now what?" Thumos said, still remaining completely stationary. *"It seems like forever that I am just standing here, but it is probably not."*

Thumos cocked his head slightly. *"Wait, did I hear something?"* he thought doubtingly. He moved his head side to side, looking around the room, seeing nothing.

"There it is again," Thumos said, turning 360 degrees in place, scanning the room for someone or something. *"I know I am hearing a voice, but it is so soft, I do not know what it is saying."*

Thumos continued turning around in place, searching the room. Suddenly, another large doorway appeared in the center of one wall. Thumos sniffed. His pulse quickened at the scent of incense wafting through the air.

Now Thumos heard the voice more audibly. It seemed to be calling out his name. Despite a strong sense of aversion to that newly appearing doorway, Thumos was also inexplicably drawn toward it. He began to walk toward it.

"Thumos," called out the voice once again. The voice was a deep, resonating, commanding voice, yet it was calm, not angry.

Thumos's pace quickened slightly, as he neared the doorway. The billowing white smoke he saw before was now pouring through the doorway. He could hear his own heart beat, and felt his pulse surging throughout his body. Thumos felt terror at the thought of stepping through the doorway, but simultaneously felt unable to stop himself from doing so. He swallowed hard, closed his eyes, and stepped through the doorway.

"Holy! Holy! Holy!" reverberated throughout the space and inside Thumos's mind. Instantly he clinched his eyes closed as he felt panic mounting inside him. Reasoning to himself he slowly determined to open his eyes to continue his journey.

Thumos saw the seraphim once again, this time much closer overhead than before. He threw his hands over his ears, overwhelmed. He felt the sound waves of the chanting reverberating through his body.

Thumos looked straight ahead, to see pure white footsteps, like solid ivory, leading upward. The large train of a tremendously large purple robe, which shimmered in interweaving gold thread, spilled down the steps. Thumos looked all around and saw the great white smoke covering the floor all around him, as the seraphim continued their deafening chorus of praise.

He dropped to his knees, unable to speak, unable to move. The chanting suddenly ceased, and there was absolute quiet. The sounds around Thumos had gone from assaulting his ears to now completely gone. He winced, as he heard an echo of ringing in his ears, which slowly dissipated.

"What are you doing here, Thumos?"

Thumos felt his body going completely limp, as he bowed and placed his forehead to the ground, his forearms framing his face. In complete supplication. He had no question about whose voice was speaking to him. Thumos heard gentle footsteps approaching but he dared not rise. "Thumos, rise up!" the voice commanded authoritatively.

Thumos, now paralyzed with his fear, could not obey the command. He continued to bow, maintaining his position. *"How can I possibly even think about standing up and speaking to Yahweh?"* Thumos thought to himself.

"Thumos," the voice spoke again forcefully. And although the voice was forceful, it was simultaneously very gentle and calming. "Everything is as it should be. You may rise up and face Me now. Be not afraid, but trust in Me."

Finally, Thumos felt his strength returning, and slowly he rose to his feet. He still could not lift his eyes, but kept his gaze on the floor, arms hanging limply at his sides.

Thumos mustered the courage to speak. "Speak my Lord, for Your servant hears."

"Thumos," boomed Yahweh's voice, now not quite so calmly. "Do you know why I have summoned you here before Me?"

The change of demeanor in Yahweh's voice jolted Thumos slightly, causing him to lift his eyes while keeping his head bowed. "I have a few ideas about that, my Lord, but I do not wish to presume," Thumos replied.

Just as Thumos finished his sentence, his eyes now fully fixed on Yahweh. From the facial expression of Yahweh, he knew he looked shocked. He saw Yahweh smiling ever so slightly at him.

Yahweh spoke gently. "Am I not what you were expecting, Thumos?"

"Indeed, He is not what I was expecting", Thumos thought to himself. Thumos saw, for all intents and purposes, a man standing before him. Thumos looked intently up and down, visually taking in everything he could see. *"He does appear like a man, but He is not like any other man I have ever seen."* Thumos noted first of all, He is a behemoth. *"His shoulders are so broad, and He must be twice as tall as me. His muscular arms and legs make mine look tiny, and His hands are so large, He could easily wrap them around my body."*

The most noticeable thing that jumped out to Thumos was Yahweh's eyes. They gleamed with an intense emerald green, as though his eyes were made of shimmering gemstones. He was robed in a stunning purple garment with that golden threading, what Thumos had seen on the ivory staircase. Also, Yahweh's skin shone brightly, like that of brass, and his long, flowing gray hair poured out from underneath a spectacular golden diadem, which sported a variety of gemstones.

Thumos also noted sword hilts protruding from underneath Yahweh's robe. Apparently Yahweh wore a sword on each hip. The hilts of the swords were ivory white, carved like the head of a lion, studded with emeralds and rubies. Yahweh wore a bronze breastplate, engraved with a fascinating image which Thumos had never seen before, like some kind of sigil.

Thumos took a half step forward, gazing intensely at the image. *"Mesmerizing,"* he thought to himself. *"I see the Star of David, but I also see the cross of Christ. Then there is the Ark of the Covenant, the great mountain, a flaming sword. Many familiar images, as if all combined together."*

Then Thumos detected that if he shifted his stance left or right, each of the combined images would come clearly into view, and each image seemed to come to life, to animate. He found himself nearly forgetting in whose presence he stood.

Yahweh finally spoke again, repeating his previous question. "Thumos, are you surprised by My appearance?"

Thumos shook his head, disengaging his stare into the dancing images of Yahweh's breastplate. "Um, yes My Lord. I have never looked upon You, only heard Your voice," Thumos said, as he cast his glance downward once again.

"Thumos, I am Spirit, I am not a man," Yahweh spoke authoritatively, folding His hands in front of His body. "I only appear in this prophetic form, to help ease your mind, to make it easier for you to converse with Me."

"Yes, My Lord, I understand," Thumos said timidly. "I am merely your humble servant."

Yahweh continued. "Thumos, where have you been, and what have you been doing?"

Thumos answered, "My Lord, I am confident that You already know where I have been, and You know what I have been doing. Nothing under Heaven nor Earth, nor anywhere in Your creation can be done without Your knowledge…" Thunder interrupted his response, and he bowed his head quickly.

"Do not patronize Me!" roared Yahweh, in an angry voice. "Just answer my questions!"

Thumos's demeanor changed to a much more genuinely apologetic tone. "Yes, My Lord, I will answer You. I have been on Earth, exacting Your vengeance on the unholy wretched of humankind."

"That sounded pretty decent," Thumos thought to himself, momentarily forgetting that Yahweh could read his very thoughts.

"Maybe to you it did, but not to Me." Yahweh responded out loud to Thumos's unspoken thoughts.

Thumos glanced up to look at Yahweh, and saw Him now standing with his arms crossed in front of His chest, looking very stoic.

"Did I commission you on this quest?" Yahweh questioned.

Thumos took a deep breath, and exhaled, not wanting to say what he was about to say. "Well, not exactly, My Lord," Thumos responded quietly.

Thumos timidly watched Yahweh cross His arms, and heard Him groan. He saw Yahweh looking back at him with a slight air of contempt, as he heard a faint, distant clap of thunder.

"It is a 'yes' or 'no' question, Thumos," Yahweh demanded.

Now the idea of a quest for vengeance in Yahweh's name was not sounding like a very good idea. Thumos could feel his shoulders slumping downward, as he folded his arms. He wagged his head, and looked back down to the ground.

"Then how can you claim to be exacting *My* vengeance?" Yahweh continued questioning. "Do I take pleasure in the death of the wicked, or would I not rather rejoice over them turning away from their wickedness?"

"But My Lord," Thumos interjected, starting to sound slightly irritated. "You used to send me on all sorts of such missions down through the ages. As a right hand of Your justice, I carried out those missions under Your instructions. I only thought…".

Yahweh threw His hands to His hips, and a deafening clap of thunder sounded. "You *thought* what?" Yahweh questioned angrily, with a fiery look in His eyes.

Thumos remained silent, with his head still bowed. He could not contemplate any sort of response to this.

Thumos, keeping his head bowed, lifted his eyes slightly, to see Yahweh clasp His hands behind his back, and He began to pace a few steps back and forth. But when Thumos saw that Yahweh kept His eyes fixed on him, despite the pacing, his eyes quickly diverted back downward.

"To whom then will you liken Me? Who is my equal?" said Yahweh. "Lift up your eyes on high, and see who has created everything. I have named everything, and set it all in motion. By the greatness of My might, and because I am strong in power, nothing is lacking. Do you doubt this, Thumos?"

Again, Thumos could not answer, and kept his eyes averted downward, away from Yahweh.

Yahweh asked another question. "Have you considered My servant, Detective Lane Madigan? Through his life and behavior, have you learned anything for yourself, Thumos?"

Thumos replied timidly. "Yes, My Lord, he has taught me much. In one act, at the end of his life, I have learned much, and yet, it is still difficult for me to comprehend. It is very hard for me to tolerate evil having any hint or glimmer of gaining any ground.

"You remember the man after My own heart, David?" questioned Yahweh. "So many times, Thumos, he could have taken the life of his enemy, King Saul. Yet time after time, he spared him, even after the king attempted to kill him so many times. You were there, Thumos, you saw that with your own eyes."

"Oh yes, I can never forget that about the mighty King David," answered Thumos. "His continued mercies on King Saul were painful for me to watch, since I wanted to see the Benjamite king pay for his treachery."

"Showing that mercy was part of King David's calling, Thumos," Yahway continued. "I desire mercy, even more than sacrifice. David was extending My own mercy, which I continue to show toward so many. That was his calling, Thumos. And what Lane did was also his calling. It was his destiny. Many have learned, and many more will learn, valuable lessons because of him," Yahweh said. "What he has done will honor and glorify Me before many people."

"Vengeance is mine, I will repay," Yahweh continued. "No one aside from Me is capable of properly exacting vengeance. I alone am the one who is able to truly classify what is to be called 'good' and what is to be called 'bad'. I alone know the hearts of My creation, and therefore, vengeance can only be delivered by My hand, whether that be through you, Thumos, or any number of other ways which I see fit. It is all at the good pleasure of My will."

Thumos unfolded his arms, starting to raise his head up once again, taking a step forward. He looked up at Yahweh, spreading his hands out in front of him, palms facing up. "But, my Lord," Thumos began to speak. "It does not seem fair...", then he paused. He caught himself, his tone with Yahweh sounding frustrated. Then as he further examined his body language, he realized he was overstepping his bounds. He dropped his hands back to this side, and once again looked down at his feet.

Yahweh, obviously irritated with Thumos, broke the awkward silence. "Who framed the foundations of this universe? Who brought the light out of darkness? Who created the Earth and all that is on it? Who formed humans from the dust of the Earth? Who created you, Thumos?" Yahweh stopped speaking, as if waiting for a response from Thumos.

Thumos pondered whether he should respond or not. For now, he remained silent.

Yahweh, obviously knowing Thumos' thoughts, continued speaking. "Do you believe My arm to be so short that I am unable to do anything about what is happening on Earth? Do you suppose My vision is so shortsighted that I am unable to see what is happening? Do you suppose that My plans are so disorganized that I am not in control of My creation? Do you believe that any part of My creation, even to the minutest, most insignificant piece of matter, falls outside of My control?" Yahweh paused again.

Thumos lifted his eyes slightly once again, to note that Yahweh had stopped His pacing, folding His arms back across His chest, casting a hard stare at him. Thumos continued to remain absolutely silent. Of course he knew what the resounding answer to each of Yahweh's posed questions were.

Yahweh raised His right hand up to His chin, and began to speak again. "Thumos, are you aware of what My servant, the apostle Peter, wrote in his epistle…"

For the first time, Thumos felt less intimidated, and grew a bit excited. He looked up toward Yahweh with a gleam in his eye. This time Thumos was the interrupter, as he said "Oh yes, my Lord. The Mystery—that is a most fascinating and intriguing passage in Your revelation to humankind."

Thumos knew very well what Peter had written in his first epistle: "Things which angels have longed to look into." Thumos said excitedly, "Every angel in existence was well-acquainted with that interesting statement which Peter wrote."

Yahweh waited patiently for Thumos to complete his interruption. Thumos stopped talking , and could see Yahweh's patience, but also, His irritation with the interruption.

"Then listen to Me carefully," Yahweh said with even greater authority in His voice now, sounding very stern and serious. "Because I am going to tell you something which Peter wrote. Only My archangels fully understand what I am about to tell you. This is for your ears only. Do you understand what I am saying to you?"

Thumos felt a huge grin coming over his face. He felt like a child on Christmas morning, first spying the Christmas tree overflowing with gifts. He was giddy with excitement, but tried to disguise his enthusiasm. He could not believe that he was having a conversation like this with Yahweh.

"What could this be?" Thumos thought to himself. He felt both amazement and terror. He could not even begin to fathom what would be a revelation to which only the archangels were privy. He stood at attention, as he waited to hear Yahweh's next words.

"Please, My Lord, proceed—I am definitely ready." Thumos said anxiously.

Thumos could see yet another slight grin coming over Yahweh's face. *"What a fool I am,"* Thumos thought to himself. *"Yahweh knows what I am thinking, how I am feeling. It is futile to try to hide my enthusiasm."*

"Alright Thumos," Yahweh spoke again. "I know the excitement welling up within you. I am pleased to see you, my mightily enraged angel, finally allowing your guard to come down a bit. Walk with me."

CHAPTER 34:

A TRIP DOWN MEMORY LANE

Thumos followed behind Yahweh, toward a doorway which surprisingly appeared out of nowhere. He watched Yahweh walk right on through it without missing a beat. Thumos noted a thick, cloudy mist which prevented him from seeing what was on the other side, nor could he see Yahweh anymore. He paused for a moment right at the doorway, and apprehensively stepped through himself. He felt a softer surface beneath his feet, and he looked down to see what he had stepped on. The thick mist still hung in the air, and he was not yet able to see his feet.

Thumos waved his hands in front of his face to clear some of the mist from his face. As the wispy tendrils of the mist parted he found himself startled beyond belief. In front of him emerged a lush, green landscape without end. Thumos saw perfectly manicured grass walkways spidering out in all directions. As he cast his gaze about him, he beheld towering trees, the like of which were long gone from the face of Earth. A gentle breeze stirred their leaves and it was warm and pleasant on his face.

Thumos looked in amazement at Yahweh, who had stopped walking a few paces ahead of him patiently waiting for him. He saw Yahweh's long, flowing gray hair rustling softly as the breeze gently wafted tendrils across his shoulders. Yahweh sported a huge smile, exposing His perfect, pearly white teeth.

Thumos smiled back at him and continued to look . He noted beautiful shrubbery, dotted with brilliantly colored flowers of all shapes and sizes. Deep forest green colored bushes with glossy leaves shone in stark relief to the bright hued flowers. Some were white with red throats, others were pink with green throats. He saw some of the most startling colors of blue, yellow, orange, purple, and all that in various shades. Then it occurred to him with a startling shock. *There are no shadows. None. Light emanates in all directions.* He turned an astonished glance toward Yahweh.

"This is incredible," Thumos said in a hushed voice, trying not to disrupt the quiet serenity of this new environment.. "What is this place?" he questioned Yahweh.

Yahweh only continued to smile at him, and then motioned for Thumos to follow him down one of the paths leading to the right.

Beyond the Father's form in front of him, Thumos saw another stunning sight. Ahead of them, were more of the Cherubim. These Cherubim held flaming swords and stood guard in all directions.

Thumos drew in a quick breath as understanding washed over him. "The Garden of Eden," Thumos said out loud, in the most reverent tone he could muster. "This place still exists?"

Yahweh continued walking ahead of Thumos, but finally spoke. "Of course, Thumos," He said, almost sounding surprised that Thumos would ask such a question. "It is no longer in the original place as when I created it, but it still exists, just the same as it did back then."

They continued their same pace, passing by the Cherubim. Thumos tried to catch their eyes as he passed by, but he noted they refused to take their gaze away from their watchful post, paying him no heed whatsoever.

As the Cherubim faded into the distance behind, Thumos continued his euphoric sense of awe at this lush garden. Now he noticed magnificent fruit trees surrounding them as well as the other foliage he had initially seen upon entering the garden area. All the varieties of fruit looked perfectly healthy, not one was rotten or fallen to the ground. *They all look so delectable, I have never seen such perfection before,* Thumos thought to himself.

"This is how humankind was meant to exist, Thumos," said Yahweh, as He waved His hands upward, motioning to their surroundings. "This is a place of true beauty and unadulterated perfection. It truly is right to call it 'good.'"

Just as Thumos was starting to wonder if they were the only two beings in this place, he noted a short distance ahead the form of another figure coming into view. He continued to remain silent, walking behind Yahweh, his curiosity mounting. Thumos thought this was a female as they walked closer, noting dark hair, and a long flowing white robe. A sense of recognition began to course through his mind. *Could that be her?* He wondered to himself.

Yahweh stopped in front of this person, and He said, "Do you recognize My servant…"

But before Yahweh could finish His sentence, Thumos interrupted Him. "Mary," Thumos said in a whisper. "Of course I know who *she* is," Thumos said. "I initially did not recognize her looking like this," he said, motioning his right hand toward her.

Mary stood before them, rosy red cheeks, smiling graciously, saying nothing. She was in a long, white flowing gown that shone brightly like the sun. At Mary's feet was an image of the moon, and she wore a sparkling crown of twelve stars. Her dark hair fell about her shoulders.

"Hail, favored one, the Lord is with you," Thumos said enthusiastically, with his head bowed.

"You remember how Gabriel greeted My servant Mary, so long ago," Yahweh said. "Very good Thumos, very good."

Thumos raised his head, and gasped, taking a step backward in startled fashion. An object glowed brightly before him, Mary's hand now resting upon the object. It was a rectangular object overlaid completely in gold. Four gold rings were on top, one at each corner. Two golden cherubim were affixed to the top, facing each other from both ends of the object, and their wings were depicted as stretching over the top of the box.

"The Ark of the Covenant," Thumos said, once again in a hushed voice.

"Yes," said Yahweh in His deep, forceful voice. "The Ark bore My word throughout the Old Testament, and then Mary bore My Word which was made flesh. Now here they are, together."

Yahweh continued, with a sound of excitement in His voice. "Eve, the mother of humankind, failed the test in this very garden. My servant, Mary, answered My call and fulfilled the destiny I gave to her. She is the new 'Eve', the spiritual mother of all My children. Hence, her presence now glorifies My beautiful garden, the very place where began the fall of humankind. And yet, through Mary's obedience, and the subsequent perfect obedience of My Son, humankind was brought back to Me."

"Thumos," Mary said, speaking softly. Thumos remarked that her voice sounded sweet and gentle, like a wondrous melody. A complete calm washed over him as she continued.

"I never have been able to thank you for being my guardian angel when I was a child. You, and so many other of the Agathon, the Archangels, all of you did so much to protect me and my parents, Anne and Joachim, from Satan and his Makria."

Thumos watched Mary pause, looking verklempt, tears welling up in her eyes. She smiled at him, meeting his eyes, said, "I just had no idea what all was happening back then, all of it happening in the heavenly realm, being beyond our mortal ability to see. It was not until after my assumption that I learned of all that had transpired. Truly amazing, and I am eternally grateful for you, for all of you, and of course for the Father who sent you to me."

Thumos watched Mary glance lovingly at Yahweh, then she sighed as she looked back to Thumos, comforted in being able to express her appreciation. He stood silently, staring down, not sure how to answer her, but her words brought back a flood of memories he had not contemplated in such a long time.

"Come, Thumos, we must continue," Yahweh said, gesturing with His hand, encouraging Thumos to follow him as He turned to continue walking the path.

Thumos bowed in reverence to Mary, and standing back up, he said "You are very kind, Mary. May you continue to magnify the LORD, and may all generations continue to call you blessed." He smiled, taking a step backward, then turned and joined Yahweh as they resumed walking once again.

"Come, Thumos, we must continue," Yahweh said, gesturing with His hand, encouraging Thumos to follow him as He turned to continue walking the path. Thumos and Yahweh resumed walking once again.

"My Lord, I have so many questions," Thumos said excitedly. Yahweh said nothing, He only kept walking, with hands folded behind His back.

Thumos did not let Yahweh's silence deter him.

"The Ark," Thumos continued. "I thought the Ark was lost to the Babylonians."

"I may have appointed the Babylonian nation to execute judgment on My people," Yahweh said. "But of course, I would not allow them the pleasure of even setting one finger on My Ark. The archangels led My faithful prophet, Jeremiah, on an expedition to hide the Ark for a time. Now, it is here."

"I never knew the archangels did that," exclaimed Thumos.

"You are not the only one sent on secret missions, My dear Thumos."

"What about Joseph; where is he?" asked Thumos.

"Oh, Joseph is around somewhere, probably building something," said Yahweh.

Thumos chuckled. "So others are here?"

Yahweh stopped walking, so Thumos stopped also. He watched Yahweh turn around to face him, crossing His arms.

"Of course," Yahweh said, shrugging one shoulder. "You will see."

Yahweh turned around and resumed walking, uncrossing His arms, once again folding His hands behind His back.

Thumos stood still for a moment, then realizing he was falling behind, quickened his pace to get back to within a step or two behind Yahweh.

"What about Jesus?" Thumos said. "Will we get to see Him?"

Yahweh did not break stride, and said "Thumos, so many questions," He said, clicking His tongue. "Not likely. My Son is very busy. All things have been placed under His feet. He is reigning as you know. He has much to do before the coming of the Great Day. He has much to do before humankind's death, the final enemy, is conquered."

The two walked silently for what seemed to Thumos to be a very long duration. They eventually came into something of a clearing that extended as far as he could see, with a floor like marble. It was covered in fabulous topiaries.

Yahweh stopped walking, placing His hands on His hips, as Thumos passed Him by, walking into this new area.

Thumos now could see that the topiaries were in a variety of shapes, sizes, and configurations. The first one he saw, at the edge of this area, was beneath a gorgeous leafy tree which had more branches than he could easily count. Lovely fruit was dispersed throughout the branches, and below the branches were topiary figures of a single man and a single woman. The figure of the woman was reaching up into the tree, as if she were plucking one of the fruit from a branch.

Thumos looked to his right, and saw another topiary. This one was not of people, but rather what appeared to be like a large boat. On the top, flat part of the boat, were all kinds of miniature topiaries depicting a huge variety of animals. Thumos looked back at Yahweh, who was still just standing there, smiling at Thumos's fascination.

"Welcome to the Epic Courtyard," boomed Yahweh's voice, as He threw His hands proudly up into the air.

"Epic Courtyard?" Thumos said in a questioning voice.

"Yes," continued Yahweh. "All throughout this courtyard are *epic* moments in humankind's history, depicted in this unique way. Some of My other angels are commissioned to come here periodically to create these topiaries, which forever record important moments in My creation's history. Moments when my people spoke or acted, that would create epic events for the rest of humanity. Why Thumos, even events revolving around the activity of My angels may appear here."

"The first scene you were looking at," Yahweh continued, pointing where Thumos had been staring initially. "Do you not recognize Adam and Eve, eating of the forbidden fruit? Or that second one there, Noah's ark?"

Yahweh walked into the courtyard area next to Thumos. "Over there," He said, once again pointing in another direction. "Moses, at the burning bush, where he first met Me."

"But for whom are these made, My Lord?" Thumos asked.

"Why, they are for everyone else who is here," Yahweh said, spreading His arms and hands over the area.

Thumos looked around, and now saw all sorts of people walking around throughout the courtyard. *They had not been there a moment ago.*

"Come, come," Yahweh said, motioning for Thumos to follow Him. "Let us go deeper in."

Thumos saw these incredible topiaries all around, each depicting some key moment in history. Many others were observing these depictions, pointing at, and talking amongst themselves about these impressive displays.

Thumos pointed toward an empty spot of the courtyard. "I have seen a few empty locations, My Lord," he said inquisitively. "What about these empties?"

Thumos was greatly surprised by Yahweh's reaction, for He gave out a laugh that reverberated all around him.

"The blank areas are for events that have yet to transpire, Thumos," Yahweh said with a gleam in His eye. "Obviously *I* know what is to be placed in those spots, but I love a good surprise, so I will not send the angels to create those depictions until after-the-fact."

"So is this place the same thing as 'heaven'?" asked Thumos.

"Oh no, of course not, Thumos," answered Yahweh. "It is a special place for My faithful ones to visit, to reminisce, to learn, to be inspired."

Thumos glanced back around the area, and was surprised to now see many people wandering in and out of the courtyard. He could hear the faint sound of a variety of conversations, and people stopped to observe various depictions. Thumos also could now detect a familiar scent once again.

"My Lord, am I detecting the scent of incense here?" Thumos asked.

"Why yes, you are, Thumos," answered Yahweh. The prayers of the saints are constantly rising up before me as incense from an altar. Many of these are prayers directed at Me, but many are also simply those who are still living asking for those who are here to pray on their behalf."

Thumos tilted his head slightly, revealing his puzzled state.

Yahweh continued. "Thumos, why would that puzzle you? I am the God of the living, not the God of the dead. All these who have gone before, who have crossed to this side ahead of those still roaming the Earth, can still petition Me, the same as when they themselves walked the Earth. They are very well cognizant of the predicaments on Earth, and are a great cloud of witnesses, still desirous to help those whom they have left behind."

Yahweh changed the subject. "But now, Thumos, come along, we have much more to discuss together."

Yahweh motioned at Thumos to return the way they had entered into the Epic Courtyard. As they stepped off the courtyard floor, back onto the neatly manicured grass path, Yahweh pointed at another path, one different from where they had arrived here. Yahweh headed along that path, and Thumos followed close behind.

With the Epic Courtyard now out of view, they came upon another clearing, much smaller. Thumos looked about, and noticed the path they had been traveling on actually ended here. He could see the path ended at a very small marble pad, with two marble bench seats that sat across from each other, at either end of the pad.

Yahweh motioned for Thumos to sit down on one of the bench seats. Thumos sat down as directed, and carefully watched Yahweh walk to the other side, and take a seat on the bench opposite him.

CHAPTER 35:

UNSPEAKABLE REVELATIONS

Yahweh spoke again. "Thumos, I, the Lord God of Hosts, reign sovereign over all My creation." There was a long pause, almost as if He was not going to say anything else.

"Is that all?" Thumos thought to himself. He looked back at Yahweh, tilted his head, squinted one eye, and began to fidget in his seat.

Yahweh nodded His head in a short, bobbing motion. "You have consternation over that, Thumos?" He continued. "No, that statement is not all I have to say."

Yahweh placed His feet squarely in front of Himself and crossed His arms. "Every part of My creation, every creature, every molecule in every world in the universe, is under My command. From before the foundations of the universe, I predestined everything that has been, everything that is, and everything that is yet to be. Inside the boundaries of time is the past, present, and future. But they are all the same to Me, Thumos, for I planned it all. Nothing happens that has not passed through the fingers of My hand. Do you understand Me thus far?" He paused, waiting for Thumos to give an answer.

Thumos was pondering over what the Lord had said. "Yes," he answered, "I do understand thus far." Thumos continued, speaking very methodically. "So what you are telling me is that everything I have done has happened because You planned it this way? Even this very conversation, my very words, Your own words, You have orchestrated all of this?"

Yahweh began to show His excitement that Thumos was on track. "You are correct, Thumos. You may find this difficult to accept, difficult to understand. Humankind has struggled with this concept since the Earth was created, even though My word has clearly revealed it to My children. Yet even they, My elect, have often failed to comprehend it."

A flood of questions began racing through Thumos' mind. He was so inundated by his own thoughts, he was unable to find the words to continue speaking for now. In particular, he was thinking back to his last encounter with Satan, and that whole situation had been very puzzling to him.

"What about Satan being spared from my rhabdos?" Thumos questioned. "Did You protect him from my strike?" he added to his first question.

Yahweh spoke firmly. "Satan's time has not yet come. The punishment for his rebellion is not yet fulfilled. And that punishment will not come by a blow from you, Thumos. My Son will judge all of creation, when time is fulfilled. Only I know when that will be, as not even My Son possesses that knowledge."

Thumos, becoming obviously irritated, replied. "But My Father, why must the disgusting Satan be allowed to continue roaming Your creation freely? He continually wreaks havoc, that disgusting Old Red Dragon, that Father of Lies, that dust-eating, low-life, good-for-nothing..."

Yahweh interrupted Thumos's tirade about Satan. "My dear Thumos," Yahweh answered calmly. "Do you honestly believe Satan is wandering about *freely*, outside of My dominion? All of My creation is under My absolute control. Even Satan does not operate outside of My sovereignty. He can do nothing without My authorization. If there was even one molecule of matter somewhere in My creation that was outside of My control, that could be the very molecule to thwart My plans."

"Do you remember my servant, Job, of long ago?" asked Yahweh.

Thumos nodded that he did. His eyes began to glow a bit, as those memories came back to him. *I have not thought about this story for a very long time.*

"You know the stories about Job very well, Thumos. In fact, I remember very clearly how vehemently you begged Me to go defend Job," Yahweh said. "Little did you know that Satan had to ask permission from Me to even do any of the things he did to Job and his family. *That* was back when you actually awaited My permission to intervene in the lives of My children."

Thumos grimaced, with that subtle indictment from Yahweh.

"Wait," said Thumos, growing more frustrated, as he fidgeted in his seat. "You *let* him do all those things to Job? You are responsible for the pain and suffering that he experienced? The same kinds of pain and suffering that so many others of humankind have endured before and after that?"

"I allow things to be so, in fulfillment of My good purposes," Yahweh replied. "Everything that happens has a purpose. For My elect, I work all things together for their good. No one besides Me is fully capable of deciding what is 'good' or 'bad' from their limited vantage point, from their ability to only see a brief moment in time."

Yahweh rose to His feet, placing His hands on His hips, and He continued. "I am the only one who can see the full picture for all of My creation. My vision is cast across all of time, from beginning to end. No one else can possibly comprehend all things over all of time, as I can, for I created all things, and My ways are unsearchable. No one counsels Me. Nothing created has the right to call My actions into question, Thumos, not even angels."

Thumos noted another accusational look in Yahweh's eyes, of course clearly insinuating that this is precisely what Thumos had been doing. Hanging his head, once again, Thumos felt the pangs of guilt, almost a painful feeling.

Yahweh dropped his hands to his side, and began to pace back and forth. "I tempt no one, nor do I force anyone to sin against his or her will. However, My creation on Earth has fallen, and without My intervention, humans only possess the innate will to sin against Me. Every event that takes place is happening according to My foreordained plan. No part of My creation can thwart Me."

Thumos raised his head. "But I do not understand, My Lord. How can you be both totally in control, yet Your creation still be totally responsible for its own deeds? We angels too, for many in our ranks are fallen."

Thumos saw Yahweh stop pacing, as He looked him squarely in the eyes.

"Thumos," Yahweh said, in a most soothing and comforting tone. "My grace is sufficient for you. Trust Me. Trust whom you know Me to be. This is the way it must be, if I am who I say I am. One day, this will all be made clear to My entire creation, even to those outside of My kingdom."

Yahweh's voice turned more austere once again, as He resumed pacing. "I have a plan that is beyond anyone else's comprehension. No part of My creation may question Me. There is no injustice with Me, no shadow of turning, although many in their minds may think there is. But every part of My creation is a vessel, an instrument in My service. There are vessels of wrath and destruction, while there are vessels of glory and honor. I am the one who determines how each vessel is to be used in either fashion."

Without missing a beat, Yahweh continued. "I will have mercy upon whom I will have mercy, and I will harden whom I will harden. All of My creation deserves justice, which because of sin, that means all of My creation actually deserves My wrath. Mercy is a gift, and I do not grant that gift to everyone. Only My elect will ultimately receive mercy. I could have chosen not to grant that gift of mercy to anyone, and I would fully maintain My justice and righteousness. No one stands before Me on his or her own. Only those covered by My precious Son's shed blood. In My lovingkindness, I have chosen to extend My grace to some."

Thumos now rose to his feet, throwing his palms down to his side, opened toward Yahweh. "But still, My Lord, is it fair to send some of Your creation to heaven and others to hell?," he said in a puzzled and challenging tone.

"Thumos," Yahweh quickly retorted. "Did you not hear what I just said? According to My justice, all of creation deserves punishment. Every sin committed against Me, the Maker of all that is in existence, is a matter of high treason against Me. If 'fairness' is what you or anyone wants, then all of My creation must be condemned. Mercy, by definition, is a gift. It is not deserved, but rather given freely, without regard to merit or what one has done. It is not based on one's birth country, color of skin, their looks, or their intelligence—it is based on the good pleasure of My will."

Thumos relaxed, folding his arms across his chest. He began to nod his head, coming to grips with all of Yahweh's explanations. He started to understand the Father was telling him, yet it was still so overwhelming, and challenging.

Thumos managed to get out "But Lord, there is one other question I must ask…"

He watched Yahweh stop pacing once again, as He raised an open palm toward him. He interrupted before Thumos could finish. "Yes, I already know what your question is, Thumos. Although I did not specifically send you on your 'quest', did I in fact force you to do so, even though your quest was not directly authorized by Me? No, of course I did not *force* you to do this, Thumos."

Thumos watched Yahweh walk toward him, and He placed both of His hands on Thumos's shoulders. With that gesture, Thumos began to feel very calm, very quiet. He closed his eyes, simply listening to Yahweh's voice.

"I created you, and planned that you would be allowed to do this," Yahweh said quietly. "When the flower is watered and given sunlight, is it *forced* to grow? When a human baby is cared for, is she *forced* to grow into an adult? I created these things to do just what they are doing. They are fulfilling the mission I gave them. When the flower, or the baby, grows, it is not resisting that growth, causing Me to in turn 'force' it to grow."

Thumos felt Yahweh's hands leave his shoulders, and he opened his eyes again to see Yahweh begin to walk in a circle around him.

Yahweh continued His discourse. "When you carried out your quest, you were not being forced against your will to do so. I gave you that will, that fire to fight evil, which led you to your quest. All things that happen are done to My honor and glory. I have created all things that I might be glorified. Even the purpose of the eternal salvation of My elect is for My glorification!"

Thumos, still reeling from all of the revelations given to him, tried to put his thoughts into words.

"But My Lord, I thought everyone—even us angels—possessed the power of 'free will'—the ability to make decisions, and choose anything they want, in the face of various circumstances they encounter," he said, as he sat back down in his seat.

"Yes Thumos," answered Yahweh. "Everyone does make decisions. From their perspective, since they do not know the future, they do choose one course of action over another. But from My perspective, from outside the boundaries of time, they are simply fulfilling the plans that I have predetermined for them. If I gave anyone a truly 'free will', as *you* want to define it, I would be rendered incapable of knowing the future with unmitigated certainty, and hence all of My plans would be in constant jeopardy."

Thumos saw Yahweh stop circling around him, and once again He stopped right in front of him.

Yahweh crossed His arms, and continued. "Many want to define 'free will' to mean that I relinquish all My power to people, so they can make their own decisions, completely without my influence or intervention. To give My creation complete and utter 'unfettered free will' would be the equivalent of handing My power over to them. That will not happen again."

Yahweh continued speaking. "If a person truly had a free choice in a particular decision, the best I could ever do in any situation is give a best guess as to the outcome of his or her decision. But until the decision was made, I would not be able to know with one hundred percent certainty what that person was going to do."

Thumos watched Yahweh give a sweeping motion, shaking His head, as He continued to speak. "Can you imagine, Me, playing linebacker on an Earth American football field, trying to read what the offense was getting ready to do, but not knowing for certain until the play is called, then I would have to react to it? 'Chaos' is not a reality in My creation, but in those circumstances, this universe truly would exist in chaos."

At that comment, Thumos looked up at Yahweh, in a shocked reaction. He watched Yahweh walk back over to the other bench, and He sat down once again.

Yahweh leaned forward, resting His elbows on His knees. "Let me give you a very specific example that will help clarify what I am trying to explain to you, Thumos," said Yahweh. "Take Judas, Satan's servant, for example."

Thumos stood up abruptly, as if He was leaping off the ground. "Oh I cannot tolerate him in the least," he interrupted. "Just hearing that name brings back more terrible memories."

Thumos looked back at Yahweh, who was still sitting in the same position. He could tell Yahweh was slightly irritated by his outburst. Without a word, He motioned for Thumos to sit back down again, and he of course acquiesced, sitting back down slowly.

"Now, as I was saying," Yahweh said, raising His eyebrows. "Through My prophets of old, I foretold of his betrayal of My Son. Let us assume he had an 'unfettered free will'. If it came down to the critical moment, where Judas was faced with making the decision 'do I betray Jesus for thirty pieces of silver, or do I remain faithful to him', what might have happened?"

Yahweh paused for a moment. *Should I answer that?* Thumos thought, but he remained silent.

Yahweh resumed. "If he was truly 'free' to make that choice, what if he decided not to betray My Son? I would then have to intervene, forcefully change his mind, basically saying 'No Judas, I have already declared that you will betray Jesus the Christ'. And for that brief moment, where Judas had decided to not betray My Son, I would be a liar. I would be wrong. Until I changed his decision to match My plans. But Thumos, I am incapable of lying."

Thumos felt himself leaning forward in anticipation of Yahweh continuing this lesson. He watched Yahweh lean back in His own seat.

Yahweh, sitting up very straight, speaking with obvious authority, continued. "If My power is not in control of everyone's choices, what power *is* in control? If any decision made, even to the minutest, most inconsequential decision, is not under My power and control, where does that leave My creation? In the end, what I decree is what must happen."

Thumos watched Yahweh rise back to His feet, and begin pacing again. Yahweh spoke again. "My creation can either exist in one of two ways—where I allow everyone to make unfettered free choices (again, in essence, sharing My power with them), then force them to recant when they choose against My plans...which would be a system completely contrary to My very nature and character."

Yahweh paused once again, prompting Thumos this time to speak. "Or?" he asked anxiously.

"Or," Yahweh resumed. "I can predetermine all things, so that nothing ever happens except by My will—whether by My dictated will, or My permissive will. Obviously, I decided on the strategy of predetermination. There is no other way for My creation to exist, and for Me to remain 'God.'"

Thumos remained silent once again, while slipping forward off the bench seat, onto his knees. He placed his hands down on the ground to brace himself, as though he felt very heavy. After an extended silence, he managed to finally speak. "My Lord, I am completely and utterly speechless. As I begin to consider what are all the consequences of what you are telling me…," Thumos stopped again. He was beginning to feel incredibly overwhelmed by his smallness in comparison to Yahweh.

After another long pause, Thumos pushed himself back onto his thighs, sitting in a crouched position. "Lord, I have always of course felt so far beneath You. Now, with all of this, I even more so realize how far beyond me You are. I am unable to put into words what I am truly thinking. To say you are an awesome God, that You are mighty, that You are beyond comprehension, it is the understatement of all of creation. I am completely and utterly unworthy to be in Your presence. How can You stand to allow me to continue in Your presence?"

With that, Thumos fell forward, becoming completely prostrate before Yahweh. He covered his head with his arms.

Yahweh replied. "Thumos, although you are correct—for My ways are not your ways, nor are My thoughts your thoughts, and as My ways are higher than your ways, so are My thoughts higher than your thoughts—yet you are still My creation."

Thumos, still lying face down, heard Yahweh's footsteps coming toward him. Then he felt the gentle hand of Yahweh resting upon his back.

"I still love you, as I do all of My creation. I have a specific purpose for each part of My creation—nothing more, nothing less. I demand complete accountability and responsibility from My creation, and yet I maintain complete sovereignty over My creation."

There was now complete silence. Thumos no longer felt Yahweh's hand resting on his back. He pushed himself back onto his knees, and looked up. Yahweh now sat on the bench seat once again. His hands were resting comfortably on His knees. He was silent, but was flashing a broad, reassuring smile at Thumos.

Thumos stayed on his knees, and hung his head, with his arms dangling limply at his sides. "My Lord, I beg for Your forgiveness. You have removed the insolence and arrogance from my being. Thank you for this unspeakable revelation." Thumos's voice began to break, as he found it difficult to continue to speak. "I just hope You can find it in Your heart to forgive me," he said, in a quivering voice. He could feel waves of remorse pouring over him.

With compassion in His voice, Yahweh replied "Go, and sin no more."

Thumos slowly rose to his feet, and he finally looked up. He was all alone again.

After a few silent moments, Thumos could hear footsteps coming from behind him. He turned around to see the three archangels walking toward him.

Gabriel spoke first. "Well, how do you feel, Thumos?" he questioned, with a smirky grin on his face.

"Feel?" Thumos answered with an overwhelmed sense of exhaustion in his voice. "I am tired," he said.

Raphael spoke. "Do you understand what you have heard?"

Thumos flashed a surprised look at Raphael. "Uh, let's see, let me think about that…NO," he shouted emphatically. "I think I have a lot to let soak in.

I heard everything the Father said, and I am trying to grasp it all. Yet I must admit, there is so much to comprehend. I wonder if I ever will."

Thumos turned and looked at Michael. "Do you understand it all, Michael?" he asked.

Michael responded in his usual, very somber reverent way. "Long ago, we heard everything the Father told you just now. It is truly astounding, and as you realize now—and will further understand later—Yahweh is beyond comprehension. He is exceedingly, abundantly, beyond all that we could ever imagine or think. And any one of us can imagine quite a lot."

Michael paused, glancing toward the other two archangels.

"Could not have said it better, ourselves," Gabriel and Raphael chimed in unison.

Gabriel spoke again. "Even we continually learn and mature, Thumos. And so will you."

As mysteriously as they had appeared, the archangels disappeared, once again leaving Thumos alone.

As the three archangels bolted away together, Raphael spoke. "Did you two see the wound marks on both arms of Thumos?"

Michael stopped abruptly, hovering above the Neutral Realm. The other two archangels followed his lead, and stopped as well.

Michael answered quickly. "Yes, I did Raphael," he said very somberly. "Those were from blade cuts, not wounds from rhabdos strikes."

Gabriel then spoke. "I guess I did not notice, I never looked at him that carefully, but an angel with blade cut wounds? How could that possibly be? We have not seen that in many millennia, not since long before Yahweh's creation of this present age."

Michael spoke again. "No we have not. There is no blade from Yahweh's corporeal creation which can cut an angel's flesh. This can only mean one thing. We must report this to the Father immediately. I pray He already knows what we are about to tell Him, and that as usual, He already has a plan to share with us."

"Wait," exclaimed Raphael, "what do you mean you 'pray He already knows'? Of course the Father already knows about this, right?"

He and Gabriel both looked at Michael, awaiting his acknowledgement of Raphael's statement. They fully expected Michael to rephrase his statement. Michael said nothing, and did not make eye contact with either of them.

Raphael and Gabriel looked at each other, puzzled. They both looked back at Michael once again, with dismay over his lack of response.

"Wait, sur-surely you do not speak of Apollyon, do you Michael?" Gabriel questioned with a stutter, clearly nervous.

Raphael's mouth dropped open. Swallowing hard, he spoke. "Apollyon…loose…that is impossible, isn't he?" he stammered.

Michael, unflinching, answered. "Maybe not Apollyon himself, maybe one the Eleutheros, I just do not have an answer."

"The Eleutheros?" both Gabriel and Raphael said simultaneously, both shooting looks of shock at Michael.

"I had thought we would never see them again…ever," scoffed Gabriel.

"We must go," said Michael matter-of-factly.

All three of them jetted away, in the sound of sizzling lightning bolts.

Thumos sat silent and motionless. He tried to ponder everything the Father had just revealed to him, but this was just too much for his mind to comprehend at the moment. For the first time in his existence, he was uncertain of what to do next. This was a new feeling for him, and it made him uneasy, yet at the same time, a feeling of confidence welled up inside him.

Thumos, the most honored angelic soldier...was becoming *more* than just another angelic soldier.

†HE EΠD

ABOUT THE AUTHOR

JOHN DOUGHERTY has spent his professional career working in information technology by day and dabbling in a variety of other diversions by night, including a few decades of serving in lay ministry. While serving in this capacity he preached hundreds of sermons, taught countless Bible study classes, and wrote dozens of articles.

He enjoys golf, guitars, grandchildren, and all things Kansas City—the Chiefs, the Royals, Sporting KC, KC Symphony, and KC Broadway, to name a few. He thinks (if not for his long-lost metabolism of youth) he could eat the famous Kansas City barbecue every day…maybe not breakfast, but lunch and dinner for sure!

Now he is enjoying bringing to life his angelic hero, Thumos, and a host of other characters that he hopes you will find both entertaining as well as either inspiring or repulsive (after all, there are both good guys *and* bad guys in this story). This is the first book of a series, featuring detectives Lane Madigan and Ian Jelani, whose experience with Thumos will yield life changing results. Happy biblical Easter Egg hunting while you read.

Visit https://www.JRDougherty.com to sign up on his email distribution list to stay in touch with his past, present, and future writing projects… you might even find a few barbecue recommendations there for the next time you're visiting Kansas City!